Praise for

DAMAS, DRAMAS, AND ANA RUIZ

"A heartfelt and often humorous look at the relationship between mothers and teen daughters, love, loyalty, friendship, and the ritual of quinceañera."

—*Austin American-Statesman*

"It takes a lot of hard work and a pile of talent to write such an engaging, touching book. A wonderful quinceañera of a novel!"

—Julia Alvarez, author of *Once Upon a Quinceañera* and *Return to Sender*

"[Acosta] has created a deeper appreciation as to what a coming of age Latino celebration truly is, and then some."

—*Sententiavera.com*

"A well-written family drama."   —*Midwest Book Review*

"A terrific read, illuminating a specific cultural landmark as well as the universal ups and downs of family life."

—*Austin Chronicle*

"One of those really delightful books that you want to read slowly, to savor the flair and the people in it."

—*RealVail.com*

"Here lies the true meaning of the novel, and quinces themselves: learning how to be a woman. Even though the relationships themselves are not easy, there is enough love to fill an entire quince hall."   —*MyLatinitas.com*

ALSO BY BELINDA ACOSTA

Damas, Dramas, and Ana Ruiz:
A Quinceañera Club Novel

Sisters,
Strangers,
and
Starting Over

A Quinceañera Club Novel

Belinda Acosta

GRAND CENTRAL
PUBLISHING

NEW YORK   BOSTON

Grand Central Publishing
Hachette Book Group
237 Park Avenue
New York, NY 10017

www.HachetteBookGroup.com

Printed in the United States of America

First Edition: July 2010
10 9 8 7 6 5 4 3 2 1

Grand Central Publishing is a division of
Hachette Book Group, Inc.
The Grand Central Publishing name and logo is a
trademark of Hachette Book Group, Inc.

Library of Congress Cataloging-in-Publication Data

Acosta, Belinda.
Sisters, strangers, and starting over / Belinda Acosta.—1st ed.
p. cm.
Summary: "While planning a Quinceañera for her estranged niece, Beatriz learns about life and motherhood"—Provided by publisher.
ISBN 978-0-446-54052-0
1. Mexican Americans—Fiction. 2. Mexican American teenage girls—Fiction. 3. Mothers and daughters—Fiction. 4. Quinceañera (Social custom)—Fiction.
5. Domestic fiction. I. Title.
PS3551.C57S57 2010
813'.54—dc22
2009041378

For the missing, the murdered, the disappeared, and the exploited, here and the world over.

ACKNOWLEDGMENTS

My deepest appreciation to all my colleagues at the *Austin Chronicle* in Austin, Texas, but especially Publisher Nick Barbaro and Editor Louis Black, who demonstrated that I was a member of the *Chronicle* family when a portion of my first novel in the Quinceañera Club series was excerpted in the newspaper. Such royal treatment! Special thanks as well to Screens and Books Editor Kimberley Jones, who was patient and supportive during my crazy-writing times, as she was maneuvering through her own crazy-writing-editing times.

I remain deeply astonished and touched by the outpouring of support from mi gente in Austin, Texas, and beyond who, upon learning I was writing this book and *Damas, Dramas, and Ana Ruiz* before it, asked: "What do you need? How can I help you?"

I *still* thank my lucky stars that Stuart Bernstein agreed to be my agent. My continuing shock and awe at Grand Central Publishing editor Selina McLemore's work with an editing pencil. Props to Ellen Jacob for conceiving the Quinceañera Club series and bringing the necessary players to the table.

And finally, un abrazote to my tribe of writers, especially

Vince Lozano and Liliana Valenzuela, with whom I've shared many long talks, encouraging words, shocking horror stories, and an overall understanding that a glass of wine shared with friends is the best medicine for all the slings and arrows survived beyond the writing table.

Belinda Acosta
Austin, Texas
August 5, 2009

Sisters,
Strangers,
and
Starting Over

∾ ONE ∾

Beatriz was floating at the edge of sleep, where memory, dreams, and secrets flirt with the visible world. She was still tired from the day before and wasn't ready to wake up, drifting in the haze of a dream: the sun on her naked back, bare feet in cool water, the smell of a newborn, a first kiss, and laughter. It was the laughter that stirred her—frothy and wild, the way children laugh. At first, she thought she was dreaming of her boys when they were little, wrestling like puppies let loose in the yard. But the laughter wasn't from her boys; it was from one child—a girl. The laughter made Beatriz smile until she realized who it was. When it came to her, she tried to push it away. It was an old memory, a sad memory, and this was supposed to be a happy day. But there it was, like that box stuffed deep in the back of the closet. You can put it out of sight, but it never goes away. Beatriz closed her eyes tight when she felt a slump, as if someone had sat on the bed near her feet. The sensation kicked her from her dream, and she snapped her head up to see who was there, but there was no one.

Beatriz's heart skittered in her chest as she looked around. The only other person she could see was Larry, sleeping like a stone on his side of the bed. Taking in the familiar jut of her husband's jaw and the arc of his cheekbones calmed her, brought her back to the visible world. It wasn't light enough to see, but she knew a moss of reddish-brown hair was sprouting around his mouth, over his jaw, and down his long neck. Longer locks of the same-colored hair fell over his forehead and into the corner of one eye. Beatriz leaned over and swept the hair away with her fingertip, then laid her head on top of her hands to watch him sleep. One deep breath cleared the unease she felt earlier and set her heart back to its regular rhythm. *It was just a weird dream*, she thought. It didn't mean anything. It didn't even make sense.

She steered her thoughts toward the anniversary party later in the day and the long list of things to do. But what she really wanted was to enjoy the stillness, when it was just her and Larry, alone. She wanted to sway in the waves of his breath, sink into the luscious comfort of their bed, and enjoy the tantalizing closeness of him. When Beatriz saw Larry sleeping, she saw the boy she fell in love with twenty-five years ago. Twenty-five years! It amazed her. She'd seen what her comadre Ana went through when her marriage ended—a painfully grinding breakup that almost crushed her. Since watching that, Beatriz began to wonder if long-term marriages were a thing of the past. But here she was, in bed with her husband, the man she loved more than she thought possible.

Larry Milligan was the father of her children, two boys growing up faster than she wanted to admit. At nineteen, Carlos was more than ready to start his life. Especially since he met Marisol. The wide-eyed girl turned his head so quickly it made him dizzy. She was to blame (Larry thought) for Carlos delaying college after he graduated high school. Beatriz didn't mind. She was happy to have their oldest knocking around the house a little longer, working the kitchen at one of the high-end restaurants on the Riverwalk. This didn't thrill Larry. He was counting the days till it was time to proudly ship his firstborn off to his alma mater, where he would study to be an engineer, just like him, or an educator, like his mother, or maybe a lawyer. Although Beatriz and Larry both came from people who worked with their hands and backs, he wanted better for his children. He didn't want them to work hard and die young like his and Beatriz's parents did. *Isn't that the way it should be?* Larry had always thought. And for that, it meant going to college. A good college. Carlos didn't want to disappoint his father, but he had other plans.

As for Raúl, Beatriz wasn't always so sure about him. He was thirteen going on ten, easily lost in his old horror movies and happily goofing off with his younger cousins. The thing Beatriz loved the most about Raúl was that his boyish imagination kept his heart open and his curiosity alive. He wasn't surly like his older cousin Seamus, and she hoped some of Raúl's ability to find the fun in anything would rub off on her moody nephew. And maybe Seamus could show her son how to let his feet touch the ground once in a while. He *was* the one who finally got Raúl to stop wearing a cape to school. Yes, their boys had given Beatriz and Larry many days of joy and aggravation, sometimes at once, and Beatriz couldn't think of a better companion to have shared those days with. Larry was there for all of it, from the simple moments flooded with joy, to the let-me-crawl-under-the-bed blues. Beatriz felt a sudden twinge of affection for her husband and wanted to kiss him, but she didn't want to wake him. It was going to be a long day, and they needed all the rest they could get. But when she rolled away from him and closed her eyes, it was too late. The long list of things to do began running through her mind, one thing after the next, until she was staring wide-eyed at the ceiling. Beatriz sighed. She decided to get up and make sure everything they set up the night before was as they left it.

She wrapped herself in the silky emerald robe Larry had given her last Christmas. He loved how the hue gleamed against her caramel-colored skin, how her crazy curls danced on the quiet sheen of the cloth. He could barely contain himself when she opened the ankle-length robe to reveal the matching slip of a gown, exposing the voluptuous thighs he adored. When she crawled into bed last night, Larry pulled Beatriz toward him ravenously. Unfortunately, they had been working on the house all day and into the evening, getting ready for their big pachanga. Both of them were hungry for some intimacy, but the comfort of their bed was more seductive, and they began to doze off.

"I'm sorry, love," Larry barely uttered before falling asleep. A moment later, Beatriz was also asleep, her head nestled under his chin, Larry's hand cupping the fullest part of her rump, another favorite part of his wife's curvy body.

Beatriz cinched the robe around her waist and padded out of their room. As she made her way through the hall, she touched the closed doors of her boys' rooms, as if she could impart some kind of mother's blessing or intuit their safety. *All is well in Casa Sánchez-Milligan*, Beatriz thought as she continued down to the kitchen.

She surveyed the backyard as she waited for the tea-kettle to whistle. Yes, the extra tables and chairs they'd rented for the party were there, glowing bright white against the adobe fence that separated their yard from the neighbors'. She and the boys had painted it a bright pumpkin last summer, and the color was even richer in the early May light. The small canopy set up next to the house for the bar area was as they had left it, as was the one near the grill in the far corner of the yard. The long tables that would be covered with yards of fresh Mexican oilcloth in bright reds and yellows and cobalt blue were still there, too, standing, end to end, ready for food prepared the day before, and more to come with friends and loved ones. Beatriz and Larry could have catered their anniversary party, or reserved a party room in a nice restaurant, but Beatriz was tired of formal events. She had enough of that at the university. She wanted a party where parents would feel comfortable bringing their kids, where guests could kick off their shoes, and los viejitos could sit in peace but not be ignored.

Beatriz stirred a drop of milk into her tea and then walked out onto the patio. The sun was just grazing the horizon as the wrens cheerfully welcomed the new day. Everything was in place from the night before. So why did she feel like something was not quite right? She walked off the patio into the yard and was startled when she kicked a loquat with her bare toes. Heavy with juice, the fruit fell deep into the grass, invisible until you felt that sick squish underfoot or kicked it, like she'd just done. The tree was especially fruitful this year, littering her yard with bright orange droppings. Those that weren't collected by Beatriz or the squirrels were mashed underfoot or became a feast for the grackles, the big black birds that binged on them. Beatriz picked up as many as she could hold, reminding herself to ask one of the boys to finish what she had started. As she worked, she thought how the aroma was strangely familiar. She'd never smelled the fruit—never even heard of them—before she and Larry moved into their house ten years ago, but something about the loquats had always been as intimately familiar to her as the fragrance of her newborn babies, the scent of her husband at the end of the day, or her own skin.

As she walked through the yard, this time more careful of where she stepped, she admired the thick, shiny leaves of the loquat tree, following its trunk down toward the greenery Ana and her daughter, Carmen, had helped Beatriz plant last weekend. Her gaze hopscotched across the small openings in the adobe fence—she was happy to see bright new foliage curled around the trellises—and then over to where the boys had neatly piled firewood next to the brick grill. The grill racks and utensils sat nearby, freshly scrubbed and ready. She turned back toward the house and looked at the new jade awning Larry and the boys had installed, ready to unfurl from the edge of the roof to cover the patio if it began to rain or the sun got too mean. May in San Antonio could bring one or the other. She turned back to the yard and walked to the far end onto a low riser especially built for the party. The riser was a gift from Beatriz's brother Tony, who assembled it with a few men from his contracting business. Smaller tables would be set on it for eating, cleared for dancing, then set back up when people were hungry again. Eating, talking, dancing, resting. Eating, talking, dancing, resting. Mexican parties seemed to follow the same rhythm, no matter where you found them. Beatriz saw that the jacaranda tree from the yard directly behind hers had showered the riser with mauve florets, and she made another note to herself to sweep them away. Other than that, every corner of the yard was ready to go.

She placed the loquats she'd been carrying on a table, then took one of the wooden chairs stacked against the fence and carried it to the riser, where she opened it with a snap and sat. *What else?* she thought, resting her cup on one knee. Ana was running last-minute errands. Her brother Erasmo and his wife, Norma, were bringing brisket. Carlos was in charge of keeping the bar stocked and manning the grill. Her nephew Seamus demanded that he and his little brother Wally be in charge of hanging the papel picado that would swing from the trees. Beatriz agreed, even though she knew someone else would end up doing it. Wally was only seven, and Beatriz was sure Seamus's fourteen-year-old tough-boy act would not trump his fear of heights. But he was insistent, and she was happy they wanted to be involved. Her nephews were spending as much time at her house as their own, since their mother, Lucy, had started community college. If Larry had his way, he would have had his sister do nothing else but go to work, school, then home with her boys. But Lucy wanted more.

"Looking for love in all the wrong places," Larry said about his sister.

"Ya, let her have her fun," Beatriz said, but she worried about Lucy, too. She was always unmoored, always on the lookout for something better, for something big to change in her life. Maybe returning to school would finally put her on the right path. Beatriz had decided she would do all she could to help Lucy, caring for Seamus and Wally like they were her own, and letting them stay over whenever Lucy asked. But even Beatriz didn't know just how desperate Lucy was to change her life.

After everyone had eaten, Beatriz would make sure her nephews helped Raúl keep the smallest children entertained with a piñata and other games on the side of the house. *All the bases are covered*, she thought. *So what's the problem?* Where did that nagging sense that something was just not right come from? It was a party, a big party, with friends and family coming from every corner of the city and beyond. If something were missing, all she would have to do is ask. *Calma, mujer,* Beatriz told herself. She closed her eyes. The cool morning breeze ruffled her hair and tickled the tree branches high above her. The sound reminded her of the ocean and she began to doze. So, when she felt a hand on her shoulder she lurched forward, tipping her cup and sloshing tea over her knee and down her leg.

"Dios!"

She turned to see who had snuck up on her, but there was no one.

The sun was now high above the horizon, winking through the branches of the trees, and the birds were chirping like crazy. The grackles, kept from their breakfast by the strange creature in the emerald green robe, were perched in the branches high above her, hacking in their strange, asthmatic way, their wings arched and shuddering angrily.

"Quién es?" Beatriz called out. "Who's there?" She turned, wiping the tea from her knee and flicking the liquid from her hand. She could see she was alone, but she still couldn't stop herself from asking, "Hello?"

This was not the first time this had happened to her. In bed, she could say it was just a dream, but the weirdness began a month ago when she was awake. One time she felt as if someone were standing next to her when she was alone in her office. Another time, she was reading e-mail at a coffee shop and was convinced the woman next to her was playing tricks on her. When the woman moved to another table to get away from her mal ojos, Beatriz decided she was probably innocent. The sensation unnerved Beatriz and reminded her of when she was a girl. Her baby sister, Perla, loved to sneak up on Beatriz when she was reading, studying, watching TV, or just lost in her thoughts, and scare the living molé out of her. Beatriz didn't know how she did it, but every time, no matter how on guard she thought she was, somehow her little sister always got her, making Beatriz so mad, she chased the girl with balled fists and blazing eyes.

"Mocosa! You gave me un susto!" Beatriz would scream. "Déjame sola!" Beatriz was furious at the devilish little girl whose only value seemed to be to make Beatriz's teenage years miserable. Perla was the baby of the family—a surprise addition and the only other girl after Beatriz and their four brothers. Perla took delight in tormenting Beatriz, getting under her skin, needling her, annoying her, being the sand in her wet bathing suit, the broken nail, the lone pimple before an important day. But for as much as Perla liked making her big sister miserable, she adored her even more. Beatriz's last memories of Perla were not of her as a young woman but as that devious little girl with the gummy smile, the long, knobby-kneed legs, and skin dark as molasses from playing in the sun.

Ay, Perla, Beatriz lamented. *You should be here.*

When Beatriz returned to the house, the boys were in the kitchen. Carlos was waiting for the coffee to finish brewing, speaking into his cell phone. Wally and Seamus, who had stayed overnight, were rooting through the refrigerator. Seamus found a batch of tamales and unwrapped them.

"Which ones are those?" Raúl asked, peeling a banana. Seamus shrugged.

"I made some beans last night," Carlos said to Seamus, holding the phone away from his mouth. "Pull them out for me, will you?"

"Buenas, muchachos," Beatriz said, walking over to the sink to deposit her cup. She tried not to be too nosy about who Carlos was talking to on his phone.

"Aunt B, do you know where the Tres Leches cake is?" Seamus asked, ignoring Carlos's earlier request.

"No, and even if I did, you're not eating cake for breakfast," Beatriz said. "How about some eggs?"

"No, no, no!" Carlos said, as he ended his call. "We thought we should make you and Dad breakfast."

"We did?" Wally and Raúl said in unison. They looked at each other with surprise, then repeated in unison again.

"We did?" The boys broke into laughter, very amused with themselves.

"Ugh! You're like those creepy girls in that old Godzilla movie you made us watch last night," Seamus said to Raúl.

"I like those movies," Wally chirped, always happy to be included with whatever the big boys were doing. He bobbled over to Raúl, who offered the little boy a piece of the banana he'd just peeled. Seamus threw a tamal at his brother, but Beatriz intercepted it before it hit its intended target.

"Ay, no! This better not be a sign of things to come," Beatriz said, remembering the weird sensation she had experienced in bed, in the backyard, and all the other times before. "Don't even start. And don't think I'll think twice about throwing any of you over my knee if you start acting up. I don't care who's here, entiendes?" Carlos rustling through the pots and pans made Beatriz turn away from the boys, and Seamus took the opportunity to throw another tamal, smacking Wally on the forehead. Raúl caught it before it hit the floor and the three of them doubled over in silent laughter.

"Carlito! I can make breakfast."

Over his mother's shoulder, Carlos could see the boys shaking their heads no behind her back. Seamus put his hands around his neck and stuck out his tongue. Wally covered his mouth with both hands and shook his head violently. Even Beatriz's own son Raúl extended his hands to make the sign of the cross with his index fingers.

"Um, no you can't," Carlos said.

"Ha, ha, ha."

"'Amá, I know how to cook, remember? Besides, this is your special day and I want to." Carlos could more than cook; he was a wizard in the kitchen. He joked that he developed his skills in order to defend himself. Beatriz was a terrible cook. Everyone else in the Sánchez family were excellent cooks, but somehow she'd been overlooked.

"Ay, mi'jo, it's okay."

"I'm cooking, jefecita! And you, you're helping," Carlos said to the boys.

"Yes, master," Raúl said in a raspy voice. Everyone turned to look at him.

"You've got to stop watching those old horror movies," Seamus said.

Raúl stared back at him before hunching his shoulders and letting out a breathy "Hehehe."

"Dude," Seamus said. Wally giggled wildly and imitated his older cousin.

"Ya! We've got work to do," Carlos barked as he poured coffee into an insulated mug with "Go Blue!" printed on it in large block letters. "You, go get me some potatoes and onion," he ordered the boys. "Y 'Amá—take this coffee to your husband and tell him there will be something to eat in about thirty minutes. You want some tea, mi reyna?"

"I'm good, mi'jo," Beatriz said, watching her son prepare the coffee just the way his father liked it. She leaned against the counter. "So, what time is Marisol coming?"

"Later this afternoon."

"How come she's not coming sooner?"

"She always works mornings at the bakery."

Beatriz smiled. She liked Marisol. She liked her a lot.

"Well, you tell her to come earlier, if she can. She's welcome anytime."

Carlos was getting embarrassed. "'Amá, the coffee is getting cold."

"Okay, okay!"

Beatriz went around the room and kissed each of the boys on their foreheads, saving Seamus for last.

"Did you sleep okay, mi'jo?" she asked.

"Yeah. I always sleep good here."

Before Beatriz could ask what Seamus meant by that, Carlos was standing behind his mother holding the cup of coffee, gently pushing her out of the kitchen. "Take this and go already. I got this."

"Okay, okay, pero, oye: After you help Carlos, I need you boys to go pick up the yard. I started a pile of those loquats on the table out there. Bring them inside, por fa'," Beatriz said. "And if you keep throwing food at each other like you were doing before, that's how I'm going to feed you later," she said over her shoulder as she left the kitchen.

Larry was in the shower when Beatriz entered their bedroom. She shut the door behind her and walked over to the window that looked into the backyard. Seamus and Wally were already out, collecting the loquats by throwing them at each other and catching them in plastic grocery sacks. She giggled when she saw how much fun Wally was having but was concerned when she saw that Seamus was throwing the fruit too hard at his younger, smaller brother. She was about to open the window to issue a stern warning when Seamus hit Wally in the cheek with an especially large piece of fruit. She knew it must have stung good, and sure enough, the little boy began to cry. But before she could open the window and scold him, she was heartened to see Seamus take his brother in his arms and comfort him, setting the boy on his knee and tending to him in a gentle way that he ordinarily kept hidden. Beatriz sighed with relief. She'd noticed that Seamus had been more surly than usual lately. Larry blamed it on puberty.

"He'll grow out of it," he said. She thought there was more to it than that, but she went along with her husband, for now.

No blood, nothing broken. Wally was better in a wink. The boys began their work again, this time ignoring each other, picking up the fruit and putting it in their own sacks. Beatriz tapped on the window, and when Wally looked up and saw her, he smiled, holding up his sack with pride. Beatriz pointed to her eyes with her fingers formed into a V and pointed them at Wally, who returned the gesture and went back to work.

Larry was humming to himself, drying his hair with a towel as he walked into the bedroom and saw Beatriz at the window.

"Why, hello, señorita," he said in an exaggerated Texas drawl. He posed in the door frame of the bathroom, then ambled toward his wife with his thumbs stuck in the top of the towel wrapped around his hips. "May I say, you shore are the purdiest woman to walk into this room." He bent down and kissed his wife on the cheek.

"Here. From Carlos," Beatriz said, handing the coffee to her husband. Larry took a quick sip.

"Oh, man! I'm sure going to miss this when Carlos

goes away to college." He carefully placed the cup on a table near them and took Beatriz in his arms.

"Happy anniversary, mi corazón." He pulled Beatriz up toward him and gave her a long, lingering kiss, fueled with all the pent-up passion he wasn't able to muster the night before. "And thank you for being the prettiest woman to walk into my life."

"Oh my!" Beatriz said, suddenly feeling the quickening mound of her husband against her belly.

"I think we have some unfinished business," he murmured into her ear.

"I think we do, too," Beatriz giggled. "Except the boys are downstairs making us breakfast."

"Oh, I don't think they can make what I want for breakfast," Larry said. He hoisted his wife up off the floor and she wrapped her legs around his thighs. He carried Beatriz over to their unmade bed and they fell onto it, laughing. He caressed her face and neck with his mouth, pulling her up so he could cover her breasts with kisses. The dream, the odd sensation in the backyard, the worry about her nephews—all of it vanished. Larry circled his tongue around Beatriz's nipple, and she gasped just as there was a knock on the door.

"Don't come in!" they yelled in unison. Beatriz quickly covered herself with her robe.

"What do you want?" Larry barked. When there was no answer, Beatriz climbed off her husband and tiptoed to the door.

"What is it, sweetie?" she asked through the door.

"Tía Ana is here. And there's some guy here for Dad," Raúl said.

"What 'guy'?" Larry asked irritably.

"He said to tell you he brought the ice."

Larry bolted up and searched for his clothes. Beatriz was puzzled.

"You ordered ice?" she asked.

"He said you have to sign," Raúl said.

"Okay, mi'jo," Beatriz said through the door. "Don't worry, love," she said to Larry. "I can sign for it, can't I?" She pulled her robe closed and checked herself in the mirror.

"No, no, no," Larry said, frantically pulling on a pair of jeans then a T-shirt. "I'll take care of it." Beatriz knew when to pick her battles with Larry, and it was clear this was not one of them. When Larry set his mind on something, it was best to go with the flow. As he was leaving, he took his wife's face in his hands again and gave her a long, moist kiss. "Don't forget where we left off."

By the time Ana came upstairs, Beatriz was already showered, standing in front of the closet deciding what to wear—the eggplant-colored dress that was comfortable, or the white, form-fitting dress that she knew would drive Larry wild.

"Hola!" Ana said, as she tapped on the door and poked her head inside the room. "Can I come in?"

"Sure. How are you?" Beatriz asked, greeting Ana with a kiss on the cheek.

"How am I? How are *you*?" Ana said. "Do you need help with anything?"

Beatriz held up both dresses for Ana to see. "What do you think?"

"I like the purple one," Ana said. Beatriz frowned.

"Okay, I like the white one. Wear whatever you'll be most comfortable in," Ana said. "It's going to be a long day."

Beatriz laid both dresses on the bed and began to shape her hair with her fingers.

"I picked up the new guayabera for Larry you wanted, and I found some more papel picado. Larry's letting the boys watch him hang it." Beatriz and Ana exchanged a knowing snicker over Larry's particular way of doing things. "Oh, Carmen and I made up some party favors last night. Nothing fancy, but they're cute. I think you'll like them."

"Uh-huh," Beatriz said, looking at her face in the mirror, trying to decide how much makeup to put on.

"Bueno, pues—maybe I should let you get dressed," Ana said, noticing that Beatriz was distracted. When Ana reached the door, she turned back. "Are you okay?"

"What? Sure!" Beatriz said. "I'm just—I don't know."

"Did you and Larry have a fight or something?"

"Oh no," Beatriz smiled, imagining what their morning could have been like had they not had the party to deal with. "It's just..." Beatriz felt that wince in her heart, that wound she carried, that never quite healed no matter how much time has passed.

"I just wish everybody could be here."

Ana closed the door and leaned against it. "Tus padres?"

"Yeah," Beatriz said. She hadn't been thinking of her parents, but yes—she missed them, too.

"They would have loved this," Ana said, feeling the absence of her own parents. "When I walked in the house, it smelled so good, I thought your mother was in there cooking. Carlos is amazing. It's like he inherited the cocinera gene from your mom, verdad?"

"Well, I know he didn't get it from me," Beatriz said. She began to brush mascara on her lashes.

"Your brothers and their families are all coming, right?"

"Yeah," Beatriz said. "It'll be nice to have us all together again."

But that wasn't true. Sure, all the Sánchez brothers were coming in with their wives and their children, but there was one sibling who would not be there: Perla. Beatriz wondered if any of them would dare mention her name.

Beatriz decided on the white dress because it matched Larry's guayabera—and because she knew it would make him crazy. When she finished dressing, she went downstairs to enjoy the breakfast Carlos had made for them—a mountain of fluffy eggs; potatoes with colorful strips of red and green bell peppers, onions, and mushrooms, all seasoned with garlic and cumin; agua frescas (made especially for the party); fresh pico de gallo; and even a fresh batch of tortillas the boys made under Carlos's strict direction. Corn tortillas, not flour. It irked Carlos that he had yet to discover the secret to the perfect flour tortilla. How could three simple ingredients cause him so much consternation? It was a skill he was determined to master. Beatriz didn't eat much, but she took pleasure watching the boys wolf down their food with few words, only for mild grunts and happy expressions of appreciation. She and Larry looked at each other and without words knew that this would be a good day.

TWO

The guests began to arrive around eleven o'clock. The first wave were colleagues from the university and Larry's office who intended to make only a brief appearance—until Carlos presented a large platter of ceviche. Some of those guests were still lingering by the time the relatives began to show up around noon. Beatriz was delighted when her sisters-in-law, Connie and Sara, brought sprays of spring flowers for the tables and a lovely corsage for her, made fresh that morning in their flower shop. It made Beatriz happy to hear the voices and laughter bubbling in the house and trailing out into the yard. She had completely forgotten the weirdness from the morning, too busy greeting guests, accepting dishes of food, giving directions, distracted by all the activity. It wasn't until her oldest brother, Erasmo, showed up that Beatriz was reminded of who was missing. Erasmo was the one who looked most like their father, and as he got older, the resemblance was stronger. She welcomed his family into her house, her eyes tightly shut as she hugged him close.

"Qué pasó?" Erasmo asked when he could feel she was holding on to him longer than normal.

"Nothing, it's just that you look so much like 'Apá."

"Yeah," he said. "Norma says that, too. But we're

here, so they're here, too." He patted his sister's shoulder as he edged his way past her to get a look at their youngest brother, Tony, and his wife, Elaine, pregnant for the third time in four years. Beatriz knew her brother was right. She gazed at the swelling crowd with a bittersweet smile, but as she was closing the door she saw something that made her pause: a little girl standing on the curb. She blinked against the sun to try and see her face. When the girl smiled a gummy smile, a jolt of adrenalin nearly dropped her to her knees.

"Erasmo! Erasmo!" Beatriz yelled.

But her brother was lost in the bellows of greetings and laughter that comes from too much time passing between friends and relatives.

"Erasmo!"

"Mande!" her brother finally answered.

"Come here!" Her heart was galloping now. If she was seeing what she thought she was seeing, she wanted Erasmo as a witness. He was the one they would believe.

"Erasmo!" she said.

"Sí, sí, sí. Qué pasó?" he said, coming to the door as soon as he saw his sister's stunned expression.

"Do you see that girl?"

"Who?"

"Over there, the little girl standing by that truck over there."

When Erasmo looked out the door he reared back.

"Little girl? What little girl? That's *my* girl, Angie, and her friend," he said. But the girl he was referring to wasn't the girl Beatriz saw, but a young woman, a couple years older than her Carlos.

"Hola, Tía," Angie said, kissing her aunt on the cheek. "This is my friend Lidia." Beatriz looked past the girls where she thought she had seen the little girl, but there was no one. The two young women continued standing before her expectantly, and then Lidia glanced at Angie self-consciously.

"I hope it's okay I came," she said. "You know me—never one to pass up a good Mexican party." She laughed nervously.

The girl's embarrassment brought Beatriz back to the present.

"Descúlpeme! Of course! Of course, you're welcome! Please forgive me. I have a million things on my mind. Any friend of Angie's is a friend of mine. Pásale, mi'ja, pásale." The girls slipped past Beatriz into the house and sought out the other young adults in the crowd. Beatriz frantically scanned the street again.

I saw her, Beatriz said to herself. *I saw her.*

But, of course, that wouldn't be possible. Perla wouldn't be a little girl any longer; she would be a full-grown woman. *But it was her!* Beatriz thought. She knew it.

When Larry came behind his wife and slipped his arm around her waist, Beatriz shrieked.

"Larry!"

"I'm sorry, love," he said, almost as startled as his wife. "Uncle James is asking for you." When he noticed the stricken look on his wife's face, he pulled her close to him. "What's wrong?"

"Nothing—I mean, I thought—it's nothing. It's okay."

"Maybe you should eat something," Larry said,

remembering that he hadn't seen his wife eat much at breakfast.

"Maybe I should."

"Well then, you're in the right place," Larry said, sweeping his wife back into the house."

By sundown, the party was in full swing. Appetites were fed, drinks were flowing, children who'd eaten too many cookies were having their bellies rubbed by their mothers, and only a few guests were stupidly tipsy. Beatriz still hadn't eaten much and only drank water throughout the day. She wanted to stay clearheaded. Larry, on the other hand, was having a ball. The man couldn't stop grinning, happily glassy-eyed, his hair tousled, his face shiny with sweat from dancing with every able-bodied woman who could keep up with him. He talked and joked with everyone, happy to see each and every person who crossed their threshold, and when the opportunity presented itself, he massaged his wife's ample backside. Yes, Larry Milligan was having a good time.

"Are you having fun, my love?" he asked, as they danced a slow cha-cha, to Rubén Ramos's velvety voice imploring, "No, no, no, no—no soy feliz, sin un amor...." Beatriz looped her arms around her husband's neck.

"Yes, mi amor. It turned out great, didn't it?"

"Well, it will be great when I get you upstairs later."

"Oh really?"

"Oh yeah. I'm going to make you a very, very, very happy woman. Wait till you see what I have in store for you."

Beatriz grinned. She knew that by the time it was all over, they would both fall into bed fully clothed, Larry keeping one foot on the floor to keep the room from spinning.

Erasmo was the first to make a toast.

"You know, when I first met this cabrón, I didn't know what to think," Erasmo said, working hard to keep his train of thought and not slur his words. He motioned to Larry. "Look at him! I would have never guessed such a straight arrow—and I mean straight, as in, won't bend, no way, no how—could make it work with my slightly crazy sister."

"Slightly?" someone cracked.

"Careful," Beatriz shot back.

"Ándale," Norma urged her husband. "Some of us have to go to church in the morning." Norma's feet hurt, and she was ready to call it a night. She had already taken off her metallic-silver sandals and was seated nearby, twirling her thick ankles one way and then the other, her arms crossed over her ample belly.

"What was I was saying? Oh yeah," Erasmo continued. "A skinny Irish kid with my Mexican sister? Who woulda guessed? Pero, it was our sweet 'amá, may God rest her soul, who said it first: 'El Larry is un güero quemado.'"

Question marks popped up among the furrowed brows on the Milligan side of the family.

"It means he's an honorary Mexican, güey!" Erasmo roared. "So, look at us," he continued. "Now, we're family—even if el hombre can't hold his tequila...."

An "ah" soared over the crowd. Everyone knew a challenge when they heard one. The Sánchez men and the Milligan men sized up each other as wives and girlfriends rolled their eyes or tugged at their men's sleeves. Norma shot her husband a venomous look, and Erasmo knew to steer the toast back to good cheer, y nada mas.

"Okay, okay—este—I know we all wish you good health, happiness, and twenty-five more years!" Erasmo said, as he raised his beer into the air. "Salud!"

"Salud!" the crowd repeated with their drinks held high.

"Viva Beatriz y Larry!" Erasmo roared.

"Viva!" the crowd roared back.

"Viva amor!"

"Viva!"

"Viva la familia!"

"Viva!"

"And now," Erasmo said with a mild belch, "el güero quemado says he has something he would like to present to his wife."

Beatriz looked at her husband, who took her by the hand.

"What's going on?" she asked. "I thought we said no gifts?"

"*You* said no gifts," Larry said, as he led his wife onto the riser. The guests clapped as they drew close to hear what Larry had to say.

"Thank you for coming, everyone. Some of you have come from far away, and I know I speak for Beatriz when I say we're touched to have you all here. Mi amor," Larry said, suddenly sober. "You have brought me so much happiness. Now, believe it or not, when Beatriz first met me, she didn't want anything to do with me. It's true! But I told her then and I'm telling you now: Where you go, I go. Where you live, I will live. Your people are my people."

Beatriz got glassy-eyed, recognizing the wedding vows Larry had said to her twenty-five years earlier. "So now, I know we said no gifts this year, but I think you'll be happy I didn't listen to you this time."

"This time?" Beatriz joked, wiping happy tears from her eyes.

Larry motioned to Raúl, who stepped forward to present his father an envelope.

"For you," Larry said. "This is the 'ice' delivery from earlier." Larry was very pleased with himself. Beatriz didn't have a clue. She took the envelope and turned it over in her hand.

"Open it!" the children in the crowd squealed. Beatriz carefully peeled the flap open, and her eyes grew wide when she saw what was inside.

"Are you kidding me?"

"What? What? What?" the crowd yelled. "What is it?" But Beatriz couldn't speak.

"What is it, mujer?" a woman asked. "Tell us!"

"Maybe it's the bill for this party," a man joked.

"No, no, no," Larry crowed. "We were still in college when we got married, and we didn't have any money, so we didn't have a honeymoon. Beatriz has always said she wanted to go to Paris. So, it took me twenty-five years, but I'm taking my bride to Paris!"

The crowd cheered.

"When are you leaving?" Raúl asked. Laughter exploded over them as parents exchanged comments about teenage boys left on their own.

"July!" Larry announced. "But until then, let's keep

dancing and eating cake!" At that moment, Carlos and his girlfriend, Marisol, appeared carrying a spectacular cake shaped like the Eiffel Tower, which they placed on a table before the couple. Everyone clapped wildly when they saw the cake and were impressed when word spread quickly that Marisol had designed and made it herself. Someone turned on the music and everyone began to dance again, as the children in the crowd surged toward the cake.

"Can we eat it?" one of them shrieked.

"Of course!" Marisol said. "But let me get some pictures first."

At that moment, all the fear, all the trepidation, all the weirdness of the day was pushed completely out of Beatriz's mind. She took a big gulp of the champagne that was handed to her and drank more when it was offered. She couldn't remember the last time she danced so much. She danced with her husband, of course, and her sons, then all of her brothers, then the women when the men got lazy, and when he got his second wind, back into the arms of her husband. It was a night full of hearty laughter, aching feet, too much food, lots of drink, sweetness, memories, the clicking of cameras, the gentle sway of skirts, men remembering how much they loved their women, and women seeing the softness of their men.

By ten o'clock, parents with small children began to leave, hauling them like sandbags over their shoulders, as the adults who didn't have to worry about children scattered about for nightcaps and quiet conversation before heading home. Sometime after midnight, the party was coming to its natural conclusion. Ana and a few others began to clean up, folding chairs and clearing tables, while Beatriz and Larry lounged on the couch, talking to Larry's sister, Lucy, who, as always, had arrived late.

"So, tell me about this wonderful trip I've heard about," Lucy said. "Are you really going in July?"

"That's what the ticket says," Larry said. He was mildly drunk, his eyes half closed, enjoying the lull of the evening coming to an end, and the soft warmth of his wife resting against him. Beatriz was lazily eating the fruit in the bottom of her sangria cup.

"Well, maybe not *exactly* July," Beatriz said.

"No," Larry insisted. "We're going in July. It says so on the ticket."

"For how long?" Lucy asked.

"Why?" Larry was suspicious. He had no idea what his sister needed or wanted, but he knew it was something. There was always something with Lucy.

"Well, gee," Lucy said, sensing her brother's irritation. "Seems to me you need someone to housesit, keep an eye on the boys. You're going to need a responsible adult around, and my boys practically live here anyway."

"Carlos will be at orientation in Michigan," Larry said tersely, refusing to open his eyes. "And Raúl has some sci-fi, comic-book geek fest to go to around the same time. No one will be here."

"Well, that stinks. What am I going to do with my boys?" Lucy said. Larry sighed and opened his eyes to look his sister square in the face. This was his and Beatriz's special night. It was their anniversary. Lucy turning their celebration into something about her set him on edge.

"No one is going anywhere until I make arrangements at work," Beatriz said.

"Oh! Work, smerk!" Larry sighed. He had been planning this trip for months, and no matter what, nothing was going to ruin it, he decided.

"So, can I see this magic ticket?" Lucy asked. "It's been forever since I've taken a nice vacation. Maybe if I get to hold it, some of your good luck will rub off on me."

Larry decided to ignore his sister's sarcasm.

"Sure," he said. When Beatriz didn't move, he nudged her.

"You have it, don't you?" she said.

"I gave it to you, love, remember? Outside? After your brother's toast? The Eiffel Tower cake?"

"Yeah, but then I gave it—" Beatriz sat up. "Oh crap!"

"You're kidding me, aren't you?"

"It's okay—I got to run anyway," Lucy said, oblivious to the worry ignited in Larry and Beatriz. "Hey, you don't mind if the boys stay here tonight, do you? They're already racked out upstairs. I can get some studying in before I go to work tomorrow. Is that good?"

Beatriz barely acknowledged Lucy's request, concerned that she had lost the most amazing gift her husband had ever given her.

"Wait! I know exactly where it is!" Beatriz gave her husband a quick kiss as she went to retrieve the envelope from where she had stashed it: under the riser near the loquat tree, when someone pulled her onto the dance floor for a blood-pumping cumbia.

"Good night!" Lucy called to Beatriz's back as she stood up to leave.

"What's your hurry? I thought you wanted to see the 'magic ticket,'" Larry said.

"I'll see it," Lucy said. She slammed the door harder than she meant to but didn't bother stepping back in to apologize.

Ana was folding up the last of the papel picado when Beatriz stepped outside and weaved her way back to the riser.

"Ay, no, mujer. Go back inside. We're almost done," Ana said.

"I just need to get something," Beatriz said. She reached under the riser where she'd stashed the envelope, now damp from lying in the humid space between it and the grass. She stood and turned to leave when she felt the sick squish of one of the loquats between her bare toes.

"Qué coraje!" she said, pulling her foot through the grass to wipe it clean.

"Are you okay?" Ana called.

"Yeah." Beatriz found a stray napkin on the riser and sat down. The smell of the squashed fruit was sickly sweet, and as she wiped her foot, she suddenly remembered why the fragrance had always been so familiar. It reminded her of the time Perla had spilled some of her kiddie perfume into her underwear drawer. She said it was an accident, but what she was doing in Beatriz's things was a mystery that was never solved. And the florid scent never came out, no matter how many times she washed her underwear. Beatriz was suddenly, overwhelmingly sad and angry. Angry that she'd stepped in the muck, sad that the memory of her sister was captured in this annoying moment. She was wadding the napkin in her hand, realizing she needed another one, when she felt someone standing over her. She thought it was Ana.

"Oye, 'manita, could you bring me some more napkins? I stepped on one of those damned fruits. And after that, sit down already. Wrap up some food to take home, have another drink, but whatever you do, stop working," Beatriz said. She looked up, but it wasn't Ana who was standing there. It was a girl. The girl with a gummy smile. As she smiled, the powerful smell of that cheap perfume Beatriz remembered filled her nostrils like a blast of vinegar. The girl's smile faded to a grin, as she waved demurely with her hand near her mouth before running off into the dark corner of the yard. Beatriz couldn't breathe; she couldn't move, she couldn't stand. She wanted to scream, but nothing came out. She could hear Ana talking to someone near the house. She tried to look toward them, but she felt as if she had turned to stone. She tried to inhale, but the breath was jagged and sparse, and her panic turned to alarm when she felt as if her lungs had filled with sand.

"'Amá?" Raúl called from across the yard. His voice was that of a frightened child, not the horror movie geek who set everyone on edge with his lame imitations. "Dad!" he screamed.

"Qué, qué, qué?" another adult responded.

"Oh, my God!" Beatriz heard Ana say. Then, the sound of feet running toward her, and voices, as Ana and several other guests rushed over to Beatriz, who was now sprawled facedown in the grass.

"Did she hit her head?"

"Should I call 911?"

"There's no blood."

"Is she all right?"

"Pues, look at her!"

"Híjole! Is she breathing? She's not breathing!"

"Slap her!"

"You slap her, pendeja!"

When Larry reached his wife he saw her tipped cup and spilled fruit. He picked up his wife and squeezed her as hard as he could around her waist, again and again, until she took in a deep breath and then another and another and collapsed into her husband's arms.

"She was choking," he said to the assembled group and especially to his sons, who were staring at them wide-eyed. "It's okay now. It's okay. Are you okay, baby?"

Beatriz nodded her head, and let Larry lead her into the house as the onlookers murmured among themselves. A couple of the women huddled close to each other and crossed themselves as the men shook their heads in relief.

The few remaining guests left once the excitement was over. Ana, Larry, and Beatriz were alone in the living room. Carlos and Raúl, finally convinced that their mother was all right, had gone to bed.

"I can stay overnight, if you want," Ana whispered to Larry. "It's no problem. Whatever you need."

Larry looked down at Beatriz, whose head was nestled in the crook of his arm, resting peacefully.

"I don't know what happened," Ana said. "She was speaking to me and then I was distracted by whoever was talking near me, and I didn't notice she..." Ana bit her lip. "I'm so sorry, Larry."

"There's nothing to be sorry about," Beatriz said. Larry looked down at his wife and kissed her on the forehead.

"I wish you'd let me take you to the hospital, just to check you out," he said.

"I'm fine," Beatriz said, opening her eyes. "I just choked on a piece of fruit. I'm okay now. I have a headache, is all."

"You're sure you didn't hit your head?" Larry asked, gently raking his wife's hair with his fingers.

"I'm sure."

"Where's the aspirin?" Ana asked. She rose from the chair in which she was sitting, across from Beatriz and Larry.

"I'll get it," Larry offered.

When he left the room, Ana sat next to Beatriz and took her hand.

"I can stay, really. I don't mind."

Beatriz pulled Ana closer to her.

"I didn't choke," she whispered. "Don't tell Larry, but I didn't choke."

"What?"

"Shh! Don't let him hear."

"What happened then?"

Beatriz sat up and looked over the back of the couch to make sure Larry hadn't returned from the kitchen.

"I...I saw her."

"Who?"

"Perla."

"Perla? Perla who?" Ana said. It had been so long since she'd heard that name spoken, she'd forgotten.

"My Perla."

Ana had to think a long time before she finally remembered.

"She was here?"

"Not the way you think." Beatriz's eyes bloomed with tears. "I think something has happened. And I think—I think she was here to say good-bye."

Ana made sure to choose her words carefully.

"I don't think I know what you mean."

"Yes, you do." Beatriz stopped talking when Larry

returned from the kitchen. He handed a glass of water and the aspirin to his wife and sat next to her as Ana stood up, unsure of what to say or do. When the doorbell rang, the three of them jumped, looking at each other stupidly.

"What the hell?" Larry said, as he crossed to the window to peek between the curtains. "You've got to be kidding."

"Quién es?" Beatriz asked him.

"It's the police."

"Don't!" she yelped, as Larry moved to the door.

"What? Why?" Larry said, confused by his wife's fear. "It's okay," he said gently. "Maybe someone complained about the music earlier and they finally got around to coming over. It's nothing, love. Wait here."

Ana sat next to Beatriz on the couch and the two of them listened to the indistinct voices in the foyer and then silence before Larry returned to the living room.

"Ana, can you come help me?" Larry asked.

"Buenas noches, ma'am," one of the police officers said to Ana when she joined Larry in the foyer.

"Buenas. How can I help?"

"This young lady says she belongs here. Can you vouch for her?" the other officer said. They stepped aside to reveal a slip of a girl, who stood nervously on the doorstep. The girl handed Ana a note and began to speak frantically in Spanish.

"Please don't let them take me! Ayúdame! Help me, por favor. I was told to come!"

Ana could scarcely understand the girl, she was speaking so fast. She opened the envelope the girl gave her and read the note before she stopped and looked at Larry, the policemen, and the girl, who had run out of words and stood there panting, waiting. Ana began to improvise.

"Híjole! Someone should have picked her up hours ago! Why didn't you call us, mi'ja?" Ana took the girl by the hand and pulled her inside the house.

Larry didn't know what was going on but knew to follow Ana's lead.

"We thought someone was going to pick her up. We had a big pachanga, and you know how it goes. We didn't hear the phone. I'm very sorry for the trouble, officers. Very sorry," Ana said.

The officers gave Larry, Ana, and the house a quick look, decided they liked what they saw, and let the girl stay. When Larry closed the door, he turned to look at the girl and then Ana, and back at the girl, who carried a small backpack, and a larger, overstuffed envelope clutched against her chest.

"I am not your aunt," Ana said to the girl in Spanish. "She's in here." Ana guided the girl into the living room and Larry followed dumbly. When the three of them entered the living room, Beatriz was already standing.

"Beatriz, there's someone here for you."

But the girl didn't need an introduction. Beatriz knew who she was from the shape of her face, the curve of her eyes, the curl of her hair, the deep amber of her skin, and the gummy smile she suspected was beneath her tightly pursed lips.

"I am Celeste," the girl finally said when she saw Beatriz.

"I know who you are," Beatriz said. "You're Perla's girl, aren't you?"

"Sí," the girl said, somewhat relieved. "I'm from Perla."

Who else could she be? Until this moment, Celeste's existence was unknown, but now here she was, standing in her foyer, wearing her sister's face, looking like a wind-blown waif. As suddenly and fiercely protective of the girl as she felt, she dreaded asking the question she knew had to come next.

"Y tu madre? Where is she?"

"She's gone," the girl said, in a small but steady voice. "Se murió."

Ana gasped, her hand flying up to her mouth. Beatriz felt as if a stone had fallen into her chest. Larry couldn't believe he heard what he thought he heard, and studied his wife's every move. His Spanish wasn't perfect, but if he had understood ...

"Cuando?" Beatriz asked calmly.

"Last month."

"I'm so sorry for your loss," Ana said, lowering her eyes.

Beatriz summoned all her strength to suppress her grief over the ultimate news about her sister, to deal with what she knew she could control. She tenderly extended her hand to Celeste.

"Welcome, mi'ja." Beatriz turned to Larry. "This is my niece, Celeste. Perla's daughter. We need to make her a place to sleep."

"Of course, of course," Larry said. "And Perla?" he asked tentatively. But when he saw the tears sliding down his wife's face, he realized that he already knew exactly what had happened to her.

*   *   *

Larry couldn't sleep. The house was finally cleared of visitors and in the late-night quiet, he began to worry. He worried about Beatriz and her choking incident. He worried about whether the fog around his brain would turn into a full-press hangover. But most of all, he worried about the appearance of Celeste. A meteor hitting the house would have been less astonishing. Larry Milligan loved giving surprises. He didn't like getting them. He prided himself on being well prepared, always ready, never taken aback, never thrown for a loop. If the rug was pulled out from under him, it didn't matter. He'd already anticipated it and bounced back so fast, whoever had tried to disarm him was the one left bewildered. No, the last time he felt taken off guard was when he fell in love with Beatriz.

Larry sat in the armchair near the window while Beatriz slept in their bed. The large envelope Celeste had arrived with was on his lap. He and Beatriz had taken a quick look at what was inside but stopped when Beatriz became distraught at the sight of Perla's death certificate.

"Okay, okay, let's stop. We don't have to do this now," Larry suggested. "Tomorrow. Let's get some rest." Larry held Beatriz until she cried herself to sleep, a thick knot in his throat, wishing he could take away all her pain, all her confusion, all her grief. When he was sure Beatriz was sleeping, he gently pulled himself away from her, got out of bed, and sat in the chair to sort through the rest of the envelope. He turned the reading lamp near the chair toward him so the light would not disturb her.

The first things he saw were some of the official documents he and Beatriz had already looked at. That wasn't surprising. It was the other contents of the envelope that perplexed him: newspaper clippings, articles torn from magazines, and a newsletter about the Women of Juarez— the long trail of young Mexican women, mostly poor factory workers, who had been brutally killed since 1993.

"Las Estamos Buscando," the headline on the newsletter read. Larry puzzled over the headline. *We're kissing them?* No, that can't be right. He ran the words through his internal translator again. *We're looking for them.* He was pleased to make the translation without consulting Beatriz or digging into his dog-eared English-Spanish dictionary.

We're looking for them. He stared at the rows of women's faces on the newsletter, all of whom looked like familiar strangers to him. He reared back when his eyes got to the smaller text beneath the photos: "Juarez Femicide..."

Jesus! Why the hell would Celeste have this stuff? he wondered. *She's just a kid!* Larry didn't know much about girls, but he was shocked that this deeply serious subject was of interest to Celeste. It was disturbing and ugly and tragic. Shouldn't she have pictures of rock stars and shoes, or notes from boys? Something inside him began to growl, like a dog whose senses are on high alert, ready to protect what is his.

Larry took pride in sheltering his family from the harshness of life. The hard things he'd witnessed as a boy were not even remotely visible in the periphery of his sons' lives. Before the police officers arrived on his doorstep a few hours earlier, the last time he had seen a cop at his door was when he was a boy. They were always looking for an uncle, or a friend, or a friend of a friend, maybe Lucy for a short period in her wilder teenage years, or one of Lucy's boyfriends—but they never came for Larry. He was the good kid. The favored son who kept his head low and stayed out of trouble. Although he was never the one they were looking for, he always felt ashamed when the cops came to their door. Worst of all, he hated watching his mother explain to their nosy neighbors what the fuss was all about. Instead of brushing off their shameless prying, she answered them with nervous laughter and sad jokes: "Oh, they're selling tickets to the Policeman's Ball door-to-door now. They didn't come to your house?" or, "The Mr. Donut ran out of donuts and they wanted some of mine!"

His poor mother. She even went so far as to learn how to make donuts so she could give them to her neighbors to sway them to believe her. No one ever did. Larry always helped her deliver the small, plastic-wrapped bundles, listening to his mother tell the recipients that they were doing her a favor, taking the extras off her hands. Larry remembered how his mother winked at him as she explained that the donuts were made from an "old family recipe," instead of the recipe she'd torn from an old *Ladies' Home Journal* and stuck on a kitchen cabinet with a piece of masking tape. Larry hated the neighbors' smirking smiles and the inflated small talk, all meant to get his mother to tell them more about her wonderful donuts. He didn't know if his mother was oblivious to their sarcastic interest or if she was ignoring them. All he knew was that it was enormously important for her to enact this ritual, over and over again, and because he loved her, he would not let her make her donut deliveries—or, as his sister Lucy liked to joke, their mother's "walk of shame"—alone.

Beatriz turned in her sleep to face him. Her face was peaceful and serene, her ripe lips barely pressed together. Larry remembered how they met at a party when they were students at the University of Michigan. He winced when he remembered what a fool he'd made of himself when she told him she was from San Antonio, just like him.

"Well, what are y'all doing all the way up here, little lady?" His Texas drawl had been made thicker from one too many beers, and besides, it had usually worked on the Yankee girls. Beatriz had not been as easily impressed.

"Well, what are *you* doing all the way up here?"

"I'm a student," he said.

"Congratulations. So am I."

"You are? Well, how about that," he said. "So, how come you're not going to school down there?"

"How come *you're* not going to school down there?"

"I got a scholarship," Larry said proudly.

"Me, too."

"Yeah, of course you did."

"What's that supposed to mean?"

"Nothing, I just meant I got an academic scholarship."

"So did I," Beatriz had said, deciding it was time to move on. Larry realized he needed to try a different approach.

"No, wait! Don't run off like that." He tried to think

fast. "So, um—how 'bout them Spurs?" He was relieved when Beatriz decided to give him a second chance. As it turned out, she knew more about the Spurs than he did, and in spite of his drunken missteps, Beatriz decided Larry wasn't half bad.

Later, when he'd finally convinced her to spend some time with him, they had been shocked to discover that although she graduated from a private Catholic high school, her first two years of high school were at Harlandale High, where Larry went for a couple of years until his parents transferred him to Jefferson High. They made this discovery over an early-morning breakfast of coffee and bagels before their classes began. When they put their information together, they had decided that they must have been at Harlandale at the same time, at least one of those years.

"I don't know how I could have missed you," Beatriz had laughed. "A tall bolillo walking down the hall would have stood out among a sea of Mexicans!"

"And I know I wouldn't have missed you," Larry said. He bit his tongue as soon as the words came out. At the time, Larry didn't want to believe he was falling in love with Beatriz, but he was. He told himself that Beatriz was fascinating, unusual, and that it was good to know someone from back home, and nothing more. He was wrong, of course, but he stubbornly fought against the obvious.

"Oh, I bet you had your pick of all the pretty little señoritas," he remembered Beatriz teasing. To Larry, the girls at Harlandale High were all the same to him. He didn't see anything special in any of them, and since most of them spoke a combination of English and Spanish (heavy on the Spanish), he wasn't even sure what he would say, even if he had found a girl that interested him.

"Maybe we were destined to meet here, where you couldn't help but notice me, like la mosca in la leche," Beatriz joked.

"Like a fly in the milk?" Larry asked, eager to add to his stockpile of amusing Spanish phrases.

"Muy bueno! Very good," Beatriz cooed. Larry remembered how his heart had flip-flopped when she complimented him. He quickly took another bite of his bagel and looked away, so she wouldn't see him blush.

"Oh, look!" Beatriz said. Larry looked around them to see what she was talking about.

"No, turn toward me," she explained. When he faced her, her deep eyes caught his and he felt as if she'd captured him in an invisible tractor beam. She reached over and delicately wiped some cream cheese stuck on his face with her forefinger, then slowly pulled her finger back to her mouth and licked it with the tip of her tongue.

That was it. He was a goner.

In Larry's version of the story, Beatriz batted her eyes at him suggestively. In Beatriz's version of the story, she says they didn't have any napkins and the cream cheese on his face was so honking huge, she couldn't understand how he couldn't feel it.

"And you ate it!" he would counter.

"So?"

"It was *how* you ate it! You were—you know how you were!"

"Oh, please," she would parry back. "You could have smeared a dozen bagels with the glob of cream cheese I wiped from your face. And in my family, we never waste food. It only made sense to eat it!"

That was what eventually fused them. Besides the very real attraction, they both understood what it was like to watch their parents skip a meal so that their children could eat. Larry had sad memories of his mother giving him food from her already-sparse plate and vowed that his children would never, ever, have that experience.

Larry would never forget the one time, after he'd helped his mother on another one of her donut runs, when he had gone out to ride his bike and happened upon one of their neighbors depositing the donuts his mother had just delivered into the trash.

"Oh, hello, darlin'," the neighbor woman had said when she saw Larry straddling his bike, watching her from a short distance. The woman waved him over.

"You know I love your mother to death," the woman had said in a low voice. "But honest to goodness, if I keep these in the house I'm going to blow up like a balloon, and my husband, he has the diabetes. So we can't keep these in the house. Here, darlin'," she said, pulling the wrapped donuts from the trash and handing them to Larry. "Why don't y'all go have a nice treat? It'll be our secret, okay?"

Larry remembered holding the package as the woman quickly strutted back to her house. He remembered riding off to one of his favorite places in a nearby park, confused and hurt by what had just happened. He hadn't had much of a sweet tooth, and his mother had threatened him with something worse than death if he even thought about taking one of the donuts for himself, and the picture of the donuts in the recipe she used looked delectable. But when he finally took a bite into one of his mother's donuts, he was embarrassed all over again. His mouth flooded with a greasy wad of sugar. He spit the glob from his mouth and broke the rest of the donuts into small bits and threw them onto the ground. A few birds flocked over the crumbs, picked at them and dropped them, cocking their heads as if reconsidering, then finally flew off with the huge crumbs—to use as building material for a nest somewhere, Larry decided.

Beatriz stirred in her sleep and Larry looked up at her, brought back to the present, remembering his original task. He stuffed the newsletter and the other papers Celeste brought back inside the envelope. *She's just a kid*, he repeated to himself. *She's just a girl*. But there was something about all the information, this mess from the outside world that Celeste brought into his house, that gnawed at him. When Beatriz began to murmur in her sleep, he went over and sat on the edge of the bed next to her. He was relieved when he could hear her steadily breathing but worried when he saw she was frowning. Beatriz whined and her mouth began to tremble. Larry leaned down and whispered in her ear.

"Shh, shh. It's okay. You're safe. I'm here, baby. I'm here. It's just a dream." He kissed her lightly on the cheek, gently stroked her hair, and whispered to her some more until she calmed down. After a moment, Beatriz lazily opened her eyes.

"Hey," she sighed.

"Hey, yourself," Larry said, pleased he had rescued her from a bad dream.

"You're still up?" she asked

"I couldn't sleep."

"Why can't you sleep?" Her voice was sticky with sleep, her eyes too heavy to keep open.

"All the excitement, I guess," Larry said.

"What time is it?"

"It's early. Go back to sleep, baby."

"I can't sleep if you're not here with me. Come to bed," Beatriz murmured.

Larry returned to the lamp and turned it off, then crawled into bed with his wife. They lay facing each other, their heads sharing the same pillow, their foreheads grazing. Larry was finally drifting off to sleep when Beatriz spoke again.

"It's going to be a lot different with a girl in the house."

"Hm-hmm."

"All these years, surrounded by my boys. I'm going to like having a girl around. Sweet."

"It's nice she came to visit you," Larry said.

"I'd like to paint the guest room for her. Get new sheets, pillows, and matching curtains...make it bien pretty..." She fell asleep before she could finish her thought. It was just as well. Larry had fallen asleep moments earlier. Neither of them was coherent long enough to realize that they were sailing on two diverging wavelengths. Neither of them heard the faint, distant thunder, warning them that they were going to be surprised by a furious storm.

✆ FOUR ✆

It was the pain skulking in Celeste's abdomen that woke her up and filled her with dread. She sat up in the couch her aunt had made into a bed for her, quickly made sense of her surroundings, then bolted from the room, anxious to find a bathroom. She had no idea where she was going, but she knew she had to move fast. She padded barefoot down the hall, recognizing the foyer where she was delivered the night before and the living room next to that. Through the dining room there must be a kitchen, and in there, she hoped, maybe a bathroom. Her instincts were good. Across from the patio door was a narrow door to a half bath. Celeste rushed in, closed the door, and hurriedly prepared to empty her bladder. As she sat on the commode, she realized the source of the pain in her abdomen. Her underwear was stained a garish crimson. She groaned and quickly inspected the jeans she'd slept in. The blood hadn't seeped through yet, which brought her some relief, but now she was annoyed on top of everything else. Maybe that's why the policemen didn't hurt her last night. Maybe they could tell she was not clean down there—or worse, they could smell her. That idea made Celeste shrivel with embarrassment. She pulled off her jeans and her underwear. She thought about trying to wash them, but it was no use. They were ruined. She stuffed her underwear into the bottom of the small wastebasket and unfurled a long length of toilet paper that she folded, and folded again, placing it between her and her jeans. That would hold her for a while, she hoped.

As she washed her hands, she began to cry silently, feeling stupid and grimy and achy and so breathtakingly alone. She wanted to go home.

I'm here, like you wanted, 'Amá. Now what? Celeste thought. She waited for some sign from her mother. A sound, a voice, something, anything. But there was nothing. She splashed her face with water and ran her hands through her now-flattened curls. She was wearing the same clothes she'd been wearing for two days—a bright white hoodie over a T-shirt and jeans. She was dying for a shower. But it was probably upstairs and she didn't want to go up there. Besides, she didn't want to get undressed in this new place, surrounded by strangers.

When Celeste left the small half bath, her belly was growling, her hunger wrestling with the other pain in her abdomen. A large platter of wedding cookies sat on the kitchen counter, and she immediately went to the tray, pulled back the plastic and took one of the cookies. But then she changed her mind. She wiped the ghost of powdered sugar on her jeans and re-covered the platter. The wood floor was cool beneath her bare feet and she suddenly felt chilled. She shoved her fists into the pockets of her hoodie and wrapped herself tight as she began to retrace her steps back to the room where she had slept. She paused in the living room, a room much softer and more inviting than the office space she slept in, which had been full of sharp edges and cold, mismatched fixtures. The living room was large and airy, painted in greens and browns, with matching curtains. *Bien fancy*, she thought, like a hotel. A huge fern sat where logs should have been in the faux fireplace, and above that, a parade of photographs and cards. She tiptoed over to get a better look. The picture she noticed first was of Beatriz and Larry, looking much younger than they did the night before, and then another one of them closer to the present day. Curly lettered cards singing "Felicidades!" and "Happy Anniversary!" were propped up between photos of boys, all the same, but at different ages—smiling, pouting, or making faces at the camera.

Celeste didn't know who was whom, but she could see that the boys favored Larry, lanky and lean. Only two of the boys had Beatriz's dark, espresso-color eyes. The oldest had the curly hair, like her aunt Beatriz, while the rest of the boys had straight hair like Larry. The boy with the round nose like Beatriz's and the older boy with the curly hair were the perfect café con leche blend that could come from the ruddy Larry and la morena beauty of Beatriz. The other two boys were different. Their skin was pale, flecked like vanilla ice cream, which looked even paler against their black hair. Although the light-skinned, raven-haired boys were in many of the photos with the other boys at the same birthday parties, the same baseball games, the same picnics, Celeste could see there was something wild about them, something damaged, something that only another damaged kid could recognize, even if she didn't have the words to express it. She knew them better than she, or they, might expect. She continued studying the photos intently, trying to get as much information from them as possible. She could see her aunt Beatriz's world was filled with things Celeste had seen only on TV: Little League, Boy Scout uniforms, lunchboxes, braces, holidays filled with large, brightly colored boxes, and mountains of toys and food. The one thing she didn't see was something she couldn't name but that she hoped would make itself obvious to her—something that would tell her without hesitation that she belonged there.

Lost amid the photographs, Celeste was surprised when the boys came tumbling down the stairs like wild monkeys. She wanted to go back to the room she slept in, but if she did that they would see her. She silently dashed back into the kitchen and into the half bath, hoping they were leaving the house. But as soon as she closed the door to the small room, she heard the boys in the kitchen hunting for food.

"She was totally into me!" Seamus declared, heading directly for the refrigerator.

"She didn't talk to *you* for a half hour," Raúl said, tearing the plastic off the wedding cookies and grabbing several.

"That was only because she felt sorry for you when all those little kids started to chase you."

"We were playing tag! Besides, what would a girl like that want with a runty leprechaun like you?" Raúl asked.

"Tell him, Wally. She was totally into *me*!" Seamus crowed.

"I don't even know what you're talking about," the little boy said.

"You know, Carmen! She came to the party and was totally into me," Seamus said.

Wally didn't understand why his brother was so excited, and he was more concerned with his empty stomach. "I'm hungry," he whined.

"Hold on." Seamus rummaged inside the refrigerator for something to feed his brother.

Celeste didn't know what to do. Maybe they wouldn't take long. Maybe she could slip out unnoticed. Maybe if she stopped breathing and closed her eyes, they wouldn't see her. She anxiously sat on the commode and waited for them to go away.

Raúl was the one who found her when he opened the bathroom door.

"It's a dame!" he said in an elastic, cartoonish voice, mimicking a line from an old movie musical he once saw. He'd been dying to use the line ever since but had never had the chance.

Wally and Seamus ignored him. They were used to their cousin saying goofy stuff all the time.

"It's a dame!" Raúl said again, louder and more insistent, taking in the dark, willowy girl with the lopsided curls, barefoot and shivering in the half bath.

"What the hell are you talking about?" Seamus finally said, gnawing on a leftover chicken wing. Wally finally went over to see what his cousin was talking about.

"Oh! Who's that?" he asked.

"What did I say?"

Seamus walked over to where the boys were and the three of them stood, looking at Celeste, who was anxiously biting her lower lip, staring back at them suspiciously.

"Who's that?" Seamus asked.

"I dunno," Wally said. They both looked at Raúl, who only shrugged.

"I am Celeste," she said loudly.

"Who?" Seamus demanded.

Before Celeste could speak again, Carlos walked into the kitchen, his hair frizzy and his open robe revealing his bare chest.

"Jesus! Could you guys be any louder?" Carlos yawned. "What's wrong with you tontos?" But the boys were quiet now. Carlos walked over to where they were, wondering what held their attention.

"What the hell is wrong with you all?" Carlos pushed the boys out of the way, and when he saw Celeste in the bathroom, standing there like a rabbit cornered by a pack of dogs, he shooed the boys away as he pulled his robe closed and quickly cinched the tie around his waist. "Descúlpeme! I didn't know you were here."

"Yeah, but *who* is it?" Raúl said to his big brother's back.

"Who sent you?" Carlos asked Celeste, but he didn't wait for her to answer. "Did la señora from next door send you? Ella le envío?" He turned to the boys. "Move, you dorks! She's here to help clean up, I guess." Carlos didn't think Celeste looked old enough to be their neighbor's cleaning woman, but like most of the women who took jobs cleaning other women's kitchens in the neighborhood, Celeste could be described as having "el nopal en el frente." It literally meant "a cactus on the forehead." He knew the term because Marisol used it to describe herself, meaning she was a Mexicana, through and through;

not only proud of her heritage but of her dark skin, large black eyes, and her small stature. And though Carlos was sure the girl didn't live in their neighborhood, he could see there was something familiar about her, something that he recognized but could not name.

"Mira! You all act like you never seen a girl," he scolded the boys.

"What's going on?"

Beatriz's voice couldn't break the younger boys' trance, who all still stood staring slack-jawed at Celeste from behind Carlos's back, like she was a road map they were trying to read upside down. When Beatriz got to the huddle, the boys splintered into other parts of the kitchen as Beatriz gently whispered to Celeste.

"Come on, mi'ja. They act like a bunch of payasos, but they're not that bad." She motioned for Celeste to follow her. "Boys, I would like you to meet Celeste. She's your cousin from El Paso. She got here last night."

The boys all looked at each other, each thinking what Seamus said out loud.

"She is?"

"Yes. She's going to be staying with us, verdad?" Beatriz said, looking at Celeste for confirmation, but the girl kept her eyes on the boys.

"Where?" Seamus demanded. He did not like where this was going.

"Where, what?" Beatriz said. "With us, silly! Oye, your uncle is going to drive you and Wally back home, and why don't you two"—she motioned to Raúl and Carlos—"go with him?"

"C'mon, boys," Larry said from the kitchen door,

already dressed and ready to go. "We'll go by way of the Waffle House." He jangled his keys, making Raúl and Wally leap like trained dogs, tearing out of the kitchen and running upstairs two steps at a time to change. Seamus and Carlos stayed behind.

"Shay, make sure you and your brother pick up all your things," Beatriz said.

"And make sure you get *all* your books for school," Larry added. "I know you have a test tomorrow, right? So, no forgotten math books, or notebooks, or anything, you hear?"

Seamus brushed by his uncle as he left the kitchen, his jaw clenched and his brow furrowed.

"C'mon, son. The bus leaves in five minutes," Larry said to Carlos, as he left the kitchen.

"I don't mind cooking for us," Carlos offered.

"No, no, mi amor—just go with your father, okay? We're going to stay here," Beatriz said to her son. "Your dad will explain," she added in a low voice.

"'Amá, I called her the maid!" he whispered to his mother.

"Carlos!"

"I know!" Carlos turned back to Celeste. "I'm real sorry for being un tonto," he said.

"No importa," she said. "If you didn't come, those boys would still be staring at me."

Carlos extended his hand to Celeste. "Con much gusto. It's nice to meet you. Welcome." Celeste nodded politely and took her cousin's hand. He was surprised at the girl's firm grip. As he shuffled out of the kitchen Beatriz put her hand on his shoulder and held him back. She had to stand on her tiptoes to kiss him on his cheek, and Carlos, feeling like he'd received his mother's blessing, continued up to his room to change.

Ana was coming into the house as Larry and the boys were leaving. She had a small basket filled with clothes under her arm, with a crisp brown paper sack perched on top. From the living room window where Larry had announced the arrival of the police the night before, she watched the boys pile into Larry's SUV and then pull out and away.

Beatriz came into the living room, guiding Celeste with her hands on her shoulders.

"Ah, buenas días," Ana said cheerfully. "I found some things mi hija Carmen wasn't wearing anymore, and I thought…I couldn't tell if you brought much in that little backpack of yours. I thought you might like to look through here. You might find a couple of things you'd like."

"That's nice," Beatriz said. "Gracias. Isn't that nice, Celeste?"

Celeste nodded and stepped forward to shake Ana's hand.

"You are such a tiny thing!" Ana said. "But I bet there's something in there that will fit. If you want."

"I bet you're starving!" Beatriz said, watching Celeste's face again for some clue as to what she was thinking. "Why don't I make us something to eat and you can take a shower. Let me show you where it is, and when you're finished, we'll have a nice breakfast. 'Stá bien?"

"Sí," Celeste said meekly. "Thank you."

Beatriz took Celeste upstairs to the bedroom where Seamus and Wally had been sleeping, and Ana followed with the basket.

"Why don't you set your things in here while you shower," Beatriz suggested. "And when you're done, you can finish changing in here."

"Is this where the boys sleep?" Celeste asked, noticing a pair of boxer shorts on the floor.

"Ay! Los cochinos!" Beatriz said, swiping up the shorts and throwing them out into the hallway. "My sons, your cousins, Carlos and Raúl, have their own rooms. This is the room that Seamus and Wally sleep in when they stay here. They're your cousins, too. Once removed—or is it second cousins? Seamus and Wally belong to Larry's sister, Lucy. Larry, mi marido, es tu tío. So, they're your cousins, too."

Celeste was confused, and Beatriz began to run through the family tree again when Ana gently broke in.

"You know what? I think we should let her take a shower," Ana said. "There's time to get the who's who later. Verdad?"

Beatriz took a long, calming breath.

"Yes, yes. Of course! That makes sense. Here," she said, handing Celeste two thick towels. The girl thought there must be a mistake.

"You want me to use these?"

"Of course," Beatriz said.

Celeste pressed her hand into the soft pile. "I will be careful."

"I'll leave the basket here," Ana said.

"We'll be downstairs. Come down when you're ready," Beatriz said.

"Oh! And in here," Ana said, handing the brown bag to Celeste, "are some things you might need. If not now, save it for later."

When the two women left, Celeste carefully peeled open the sack and was relieved to find it filled with a deodorant, a small bottle of shampoo, a powdery soft bar of soap, a brand new box of sanitary pads, and a smaller box of tampons. She had forgotten those items when she gathered her things for her long trip. Those were the kind of things her mother would have taken care of. Celeste knew that she would know better next time. Pulling out all the new things and bringing the box of soap to her face to breathe in its scent brought Celeste a momentary happiness that she hadn't experienced in weeks.

Downstairs, Ana put water in the teakettle while Beatriz pulled out eggs, a bowl of chopped pineapple, and whatever else she could find in the refrigerator to make breakfast. The two of them mindlessly ate cookies as they waited for the water to boil.

"So?" Ana began. She didn't know where to go from there.

"So," Beatriz added. "I'm—stunned! I just can't believe it. I mean, I believe it, but it's not real to me yet."

"I hate to ask this," Ana said carefully, as she brought down two mugs and a box of tea from the cupboard, "but, well—are you sure she's who she says she is?"

"Oh, I'm sure," Beatriz said. "She looks exactly like Perla, don't you think?"

Ana couldn't remember. Too much time had passed

without Perla's name even being mentioned. There were no photos that she remembered seeing, no indication that Perla had ever existed.

"And besides, Celeste's birth certificate was in the packet of papers she brought," Beatriz said. "It's her. She's for real."

"What else was in the packet?" Ana asked, spooning some pineapple into small bowls.

"I don't know. I haven't looked though it yet. Larry has, a little. It was so late, and with all the excitement…"

Ana nodded. "So, what happens now?"

"I guess—I guess I'll enroll her in school. I need to call my brothers and tell them. I should take her to the doctor for a checkup. I really haven't had a chance to talk to her and find out what happened," Beatriz said as she dropped tea bags into mugs. "But it's just—even with her standing there in living color—I keep thinking I'm going to wake up and it's all going to be a dream."

Ana could see that Beatriz was as distracted as she was excited. She had never told Ana much about her sister, and now Ana wasn't sure where to begin asking questions.

"My brothers are going to freak out," Beatriz said after a long moment.

"What does Larry say?"

"We were both so stunned and exhausted from yesterday, we thought we should get some sleep and deal with it all in the morning. He's fine with her staying here," Beatriz said, not imagining that her husband would have it any other way. She began to crack some eggs into a bowl.

"So—Perla," Ana asked carefully. "You never heard from her after, you know, she left?"

"Nope." Beatriz began to whisk the eggs, thinking of the last time she talked to her sister. If she could do it all over again, things would be different. Not only would Celeste *not* be a stranger to the family, but that knot Beatriz carried—the one that untied from time to time and wove itself over her like a lead blanket, heavy with guilt—would not exist. She contrasted her last image of Perla, tired and desperate, with the vision of Perla as a child that she saw in the backyard, in the street, and in her dreams. Was it a ghost? A phantom created from the memories the day had stirred? Whatever it was, it was the image of Perla that Beatriz wanted to believe was how Perla lived the rest of her days: happy and carefree.

"She was something," Beatriz said after a long silence. "A little wild. Not bad, really, but so hardheaded, that one! She was only a little girl when I was a teenager, and híjole, she knew how to get under my skin! But she really looked up to me." The regret rose to the surface like bubbles in soda water. "When I moved away to go to school, things weren't the same. She started messing up, and my parents were pretty old by the time she was a teenager. So—" Beatriz's throat began to tighten. She had stopped beating the egg but still gripped the whisk, struggling to maintain her composure by focusing on the frothy yolk.

Ana remembered the story from a distant conversation. "They sent her to live with Erasmo and Norma for a while, didn't they?"

"Yeah. But they were still newlyweds then, and they couldn't be bothered. I mean, Norma was having problems. She was pregnant with Angie, and it was hard on her. They spent a lot of time in the hospital—Angie was a preemie. And then 'Apá got sick, and 'Amá in the middle of all that, and the other boys were all working and getting on with their lives, and Perla—Perla just got lost." Beatriz dropped the whisk. There was more to the story, but that was as much as she could say for now.

"But where was she?" Ana asked.

"They sent her to Corpus. She liked it there, living with our tía. She liked being near the water. But then some boy broke her heart and she wanted to come back. She came back home the same year I left for college. But she wasn't the same. She was very headstrong, and my parents just couldn't deal with her. So…"

Beatriz began to chop the onion, pepper, a jalapeño, and a few potatoes so clumsily, Ana thought she might cut herself.

"Here, let me do that," Ana offered. She took the knife and finished chopping. "What did you mean last night?" she asked lightly. "In the living room, before Celeste came. Something about Perla?"

Beatriz was hoping Ana had forgotten. She turned for a plate to place some of the wedding cookies on and stared at the teakettle, willing it to boil.

"You're not going to tell me?" Ana said. "It seemed pretty important last night."

"It's nothing," Beatriz said. "I had a dream. I had been dreaming about her, about Perla. When I passed out, I thought—I don't know. How much did I drink last night?" she joked, but Ana was not convinced. Beatriz scooped up a handful of chopped potatoes and dropped them into a heated skillet.

"You didn't drink that much," Ana said. "And you're

not a very good liar." She would have pressed Beatriz more, but Celeste came back into the kitchen.

"There you are!" Beatriz said grandly.

The girl's hair was wet and limp. She had on a new top, thanks to Ana, but still wore her jeans and her white hoodie. She felt so much better after a hot shower.

"Celeste, I have a hair dryer you can use. Why don't I show you. You don't mind, do you?" Beatriz said to Ana.

"No, I got this. Go on," Ana said, stirring the potatoes.

Beatriz took Celeste through the house and up to the bedroom she shared with Larry. The girl shyly followed her aunt, shocked at how large the room was, how it had its own bathroom and a huge closet. The bedroom was bigger than the entire casita she had shared with her mother. But what really shocked Celeste was how Beatriz would not stop talking—about the house; the color and type of paint to redo the guest room, just for her; window treatments, pillows, shams, and duvets—whatever came into her mind. Beatriz spoke so quickly, Celeste didn't think she took a breath. Her excitement began to unnerve Celeste.

"Why don't you sit here and we'll scrunch your hair dry," Beatriz instructed. She sat Celeste in a small chair in front of her dresser and used a fresh towel to squeeze the excess water from the girl's hair, shaping portions of damp curls with her hands. All the fuss over her hair was kind of nice, Celeste thought, but she was just as happy to pull it back into a ponytail, like always, like her mother did.

"There are so many people for you to meet," Beatriz said, as she worked. "Everyone will be so..." She couldn't continue. Thinking about the reality of her sister's death, and with it, all hope that she would ever see her again, made that stone fall into her chest again. When she realized Celeste was waiting for her to finish her thought, Beatriz careened away from the painful topic so quickly the screech was nearly audible.

"Everyone will be so happy to meet you!" Beatriz said brightly. Celeste was working hard to believe that her aunt Beatriz meant well, but the more Beatriz spoke, the tinnier her voice sounded.

"We hadn't heard from your mother in so long. We, I..." Beatriz's voice began to crack, but she was determined to be cheerful. She thought that that was what Celeste needed from her. Beatriz wondered what Perla had told Celeste about the family and what, if anything, Perla had told Celeste about her. She shifted gears again, making Celeste's head spin a little.

"You know what? We're going to make this day as fun as possible! We're going to have a little party for you. We'll have a welcome-home party! And we'll go shopping and get you some new clothes. We'll have cake! And we'll put you in school..." Beatriz was saying things as they came to her. "It will all work out. This is your home now."

Celeste looked at Beatriz in the mirror through the curls tumbling over her eyes. Beatriz caught her looking and smiled, and Celeste turned her glance to the floor. She could tell Beatriz was trying very, very hard, but all this talk about parties and shopping and pillows struck her as a feeble substitute for the wound she was carrying inside. Celeste's anxiety about her aunt was growing with each word Beatriz spoke, but she knew she wanted to honor her mother's last wish: that Celeste return to the family in San Antonio and live with her aunt Beatriz. It didn't make sense to Celeste that her mother wanted this, after all the years of not talking to the family and barely mentioning Beatriz until the year before she died. But Celeste would honor her promesa to her mother. Except now that she was in this strange house, in a strange city, with this woman nervously fluttering over her, the absence of her mother suddenly felt as raw as the day she died.

One of the few documents Beatriz and Larry examined before they went to bed was Celeste's birth certificate. Beatriz remembered that her father was listed as "unknown." She didn't want to know if there was a man who was now gone or a man who just wasn't mentioned. That would be like Perla, Beatriz thought, to cut out what was unnecessary or, in the case of Beatriz and the family, had gravely disappointed her.

"Oh, this looks great!" Beatriz said, as she fluffed the girl's hair.

Celeste bit her tongue, watching her curly hair grow into a frothy cloud instead of the simple, sleek ponytail she was used to.

Beatriz suddenly remembered good times with Perla—helping her with her hair, painting each other's nails. Occasionally, when Beatriz was in a playful mood, she'd let Perla "fix" her hair with ribbons and bobby pins and half a can of Aqua Net. Her wistful memory was suddenly interrupted by a terrifying thought:

What if there is someone Celeste had left behind?

Someone who might want to claim her? Now that she had Celeste—and, in a sense, her sister—back, she didn't want to lose her. Not again.

"So," Beatriz began carefully. "Did you…do you…it was just you and your mother? No brothers, no sisters?"

"No. Just us," Celeste said.

"Y tú padre? Was he around?"

Celeste knew she must have a father, but whoever he was, wherever he was, she didn't know. For other children, this might have been the cause of late-night pining, the start of a long journey to discover who he was. For Celeste, it was just the way it was: her and her mother, until she was taken from her in the worst way possible.

"No. She never talked about him," Celeste said plainly.

"Do you ever wonder?"

"No."

"So, how did you know to come here?"

"She told me to. Mi 'amá."

This information heartened Beatriz. "I wish someone would have called us. We would have come for you instead of you coming out here all by yourself," she said. She wasn't meaning to, but her voice was taking on a singsong quality, like she was talking to a young child or an adorable puppy. "Who decided it was okay for you to come all the way out here by yourself?" She did not wait for a response. "Well, you can't live where no one can take care of you."

Celeste watched her aunt part her hair one way and then the other, neither of which Celeste particularly liked.

"Yes, yes! To the left I think," Beatriz decided, looking at Celeste in the mirror but completely oblivious to the dismayed look on the girl's face.

Celeste could feel her frustration and her loneliness and the still-raging grief for her mother all rolling together. So when a slip of Celeste's hair got caught in Beatriz's ring, she shrieked much louder than was necessary. But that wasn't what startled Beatriz. It was that fierce spark that flashed through Celeste's eyes. She knew where she'd seen that look before.

"Lo siento!" Beatriz said. "Perdón!" Celeste began to cry, allowing Beatriz to believe it was because of having her hair yanked. Beatriz quickly separated the twisted hair from her ring.

"Oh, my God! I'm so sorry! Are you okay? Should I get you some ice?" Beatriz swooped in to hug Celeste and could instantly tell that the girl did not want to be touched. She withdrew from the girl immediately. She thought she'd imagined it, but no. There in the girl's watery eyes, the message was clear: Don't touch me.

Beatriz stepped away from Celeste and stood there a moment before slowly turning away, her heart sinking as she hung the towel to dry. Celeste cried silently, rubbing her scalp.

Why am I here, 'Amá! Celeste screamed inside her head. *I don't need anyone! I can take care of myself. I hate being here!*

Beatriz was no mind reader, but even she could tell that Celeste's silence was not because she was extraordinarily polite, compliant, or shy. She was overwhelmed. Of course she was overwhelmed! Beatriz knew, with that fleeting flicker of fire she saw in Celeste's eye, that there was more to this quiet wisp of a girl than what was visible on the surface. She felt as if she were separated from her niece by a thick piece of glass that she desperately wanted to pass through. If only Celeste would let her in! She would make things better! She would make up for everything, all the lost time, all the misunderstanding between her and her sister. She knew she could! Her desire to connect with this girl was thick with want and fueled with good intentions. But the one thing Beatriz failed to realize was that while Celeste was her mother's daughter, she was not Perla. Perla was gone. Celeste was a different person entirely, one whom she would have to learn to know, just as much as Celeste would have to learn that Beatriz was just as human and vulnerable as anyone else, no matter what her mother told her.

FIVE

The waitress was clearing plates from the table where Larry and the boys were seated, piling them like clattering leaves on her tray. She was amazed. Except for leftover swirls of syrup and melting globs of butter, the plates were picked clean. Larry was wedged in the corner of the booth where he sat with the boys, all of them leaning back, their bellies full of eggs, waffles, juice, and sausage. Larry and Carlos ordered coffee, while Raúl mindlessly rolled the corner of his paper place mat with his fingers. Seamus gulped the last of his milk and let out a big, contented belch, wondering if his uncle Larry would let him order coffee, too. Wally scanned the restaurant for his mother, who was finishing her shift.

"So," Larry began. "I guess you're wondering why I called this meeting." He was trying to sound playful and cool, but underneath he was anxious. He didn't know how he was supposed to tell the boys what he had to tell them, or if he wanted to. It was big news, and even he hadn't come to understand all that it meant and who it would affect.

When Carlos saw that the younger boys were not turning their attention to his father, he nudged his brother,

Raúl, under the table. Raúl lightly elbowed his cousin Seamus, who did the same to his brother, Wally.

"So, about who you saw this morning, Celeste. She got here last night. She's your cousin. She belongs to your mother's sister," Larry began.

"Aunt Norma?" Raúl asked, knowing that couldn't be right.

"No, your mom's sister," Larry said to Raúl and Carlos, then to his nephews, "Your aunt Beatriz's sister, Perla."

"Perla? Who's Perla?" Wally asked.

"Well, she—okay, look. This is kind of weird. I don't want you to ask your mom," Larry said to Raúl, and then, turning to Seamus and Wally, "or your aunt Beatriz a lot of questions about this, so pay attention now." Larry yawned. He hadn't slept most of the night, keeping an eye on Beatriz, leafing through the papers Celeste had brought, wondering if there were some answers to be found there about Celeste, about Perla, and what should happen next.

"Perla was the youngest girl after your mother," Larry said. "She was kind of a last-minute addition to the family."

"You mean an accident?" Wally said, rubbing his swollen belly.

"Yeah, like you!" Seamus cracked. No one else thought the joke was funny. Larry looked at Seamus the way he did so the boy knew he'd better be quiet and listen.

"Perla was a kid, like you guys," Larry began, nodding at Raúl and Seamus, "when Beatriz went off to college. Her brothers, Erasmo and the rest, they were already grown up and gone. And Perla—" He stopped talking when the waitress brought their coffee to the table and didn't begin again until she was long out of earshot. "So, anyway, Perla, well, there was some trouble. I don't know all the details and I don't know that I need to, but I know *you* don't need to know. Anyway, she ran away from home. I don't know why. Something happened between her and the family and she left."

"She was knocked up," Seamus said plainly. Wally's eyes widened. Carlos and Raúl looked at each other and then looked at their cousin, thinking he'd better watch himself.

"Like I said," Larry said. "It's not anything you need to know about."

"Why didn't they go look for her?" Raúl asked.

"They did. They tried. It was like she fell off the grid," Larry said. "It's one of those things that families don't like to talk about."

The boys sat silently staring in every direction, letting the information sink in until Seamus spoke again.

"So, what's she doing here?"

"Well," Larry sighed. "It looks like her mother died."

"Perla? The one who ran away?" Raúl asked.

"Yes, according to some of the documents she brought with her, that's what it looks like."

"You don't believe her?" Seamus asked.

Larry didn't know what he believed.

"So now what?" Carlos said, making all heads turn toward him, since it was the first time he'd spoken since they sat down.

"Well, she'll stay with us for a while, and then she'll go back to El Paso."

"Why can't she stay forever?" Raúl asked, suddenly feeling tenderhearted toward the frail girl he startled in the bathroom earlier. "Can't we keep her?"

"She's not a pet," Larry barked. He didn't mean to be so brusque, but the arrival of Celeste and all it might mean was beginning to dawn on him.

"I'm sure someone is waiting for her," Larry said, as he reached for his coffee. At least, that was what he was hoping.

"Yeah, and what do you want with a wetback in the house anyway?" Seamus said. All heads snapped toward him.

"I beg your pardon?" Larry said with an arched brow.

"Well, I mean, you know…she looks like she just crossed over, right?" When no one answered him, Seamus sat up in his seat defiantly. "Well, she does!" The boys pulled away from Seamus like he'd just let out a loud pedo.

"What the hell, dude?" Carlos said. "In case you hadn't noticed, you're sitting with a bunch of Mexicans!"

"Nuh-uh! You're half-breeds, 'cause you married into our family," Seamus proclaimed, like he was making all the sense in the world.

"You all married into *our* family," Raúl countered.

"All right, all right, all right!" Larry said. He wanted to get back to the original subject. "Look, we don't have all the details, but I can tell you this: her mother just died, so be nice to her."

"Okay," Wally said. "So, that means don't hog the

bathroom so long." He shoved his brother, and Seamus pushed him back harder than he needed to.

"I don't hog the bathroom as much as you, you perve."

"Well, that's not going to be a problem," Larry broke in, "because you're going to be spending more time at your house." He looked around for his sister, Lucy. When he finally saw her, he pointed at his watch. Lucy held up a finger and ran off in the other direction.

"You mean we can't come over anymore?" Seamus picked up the metal rack that held small jelly packets with the hook of his index finger, twirling it back and forth. Larry put his large palm over the boy's hand, pushing the rack back on the table.

"Of course you can come over, but probably not stay overnight as much." This unnerved Larry almost as much as it did Seamus and Wally. Lucy had been having a hard time keeping her boys under control. Larry knew he was the closest thing to a stable male presence they had. Not like the long line of losers Lucy had been bringing around.

"So, we have to watch her when you and 'Amá go on your trip?" Carlos asked. "I mean, I have to watch her?" Carlos was worried. He and Marisol had saved their money to go apartment hunting near the culinary school soon—something he hadn't gotten around to telling his parents.

"She's not going to be here that long. Don't worry. You are not going to miss that orientation," Larry said.

Carlos's heart slumped. He still had to break the news to his dad that he had no intention of going to orientation or going away to college. The words were fluttering inside his mouth.

"Thanks, Dad" was the only thing he could sputter, sinking into his seat like a ground-in stain.

Lucy came to the table and fell into the booth with the boys. No one said anything, and she looked around the table.

"Well, it's nice to see you, too!" she teased, tickling Wally in the ribs with two of her press-on nails.

"You smell like sausage," Seamus said.

"Thanks for noticing. I've been working all morning. What have you been up to?"

"Nothing."

"Did you get enough to eat?"

"Are you kidding?" Larry snorted. The boys looked like overstuffed empanadas. "Are you done?"

"Yeah, well, I need to ask you about that. I got asked to take another shift," Lucy said. Larry sighed deeply. "I could use the money. Would you mind keeping the boys till three-thirty?"

"Lucy..."

"I know, I know!" she said, taking a quick sip of her brother's coffee. "It's just, if I take this shift, I don't have to work tomorrow night, and I can, well, I have plans," she said.

"With who?" Seamus asked.

"None of your business," Lucy snapped. Seamus and his brother looked at each other and then down at the table. The muscle in Seamus's jaw began to ripple under his skin.

"What?" She bit the end off a paper-covered straw and playfully blew the remaining wrapper at her boys. The tube hit Seamus in the chest and he batted it away.

"Jesus! Just because I'm your mother doesn't mean I'm not allowed to have some fun once in a while." No one spoke for a long time, and Lucy didn't like the cool silence. "Besides, you *like* staying with your uncle Larry and aunt Beatriz. You tell me that all the time! If I didn't know better, I would think you liked being with them more than me." Lucy was smiling, but her cheery voice was as fake as her nails. "And you boys like hanging out, doing all your guy things, right?" She was looking at Raúl, who looked back at his aunt and smiled politely.

"Not anymore. We can't," Seamus said. He pushed his brother out of the way so he could get out of the booth, nearly knocking him onto the floor.

"Ow! You dork!"

"Seamus!" Larry barked. "Where are you going?" If Lucy had asked the question, he would have ignored her. If Larry weren't there, he would have pushed Wally all the way to the floor and stepped on him on his way out of the booth. But Larry was there. Seamus worked harder to stuff down the anger that was working its way through him.

"I have to pee."

"Me, too," Raúl said.

"I wanna go!" Wally said. The boys tumbled out of the booth and waddled to the restroom.

"Go with them," Larry ordered Carlos. "Make sure they don't destroy the place. I need to talk to your aunt."

The waitress delivered a plate of fries and set it before Lucy, who quickly covered them in ketchup. She used the nails of her thumb and forefinger as pincers to eat them, her remaining fingers splayed like a fan.

"What's up?" she asked.

"You tell me what's up." Larry said.

"With what?"

"Well, first of all, what happened to you last night?"

"I had a date. I told you."

"No, you told me you had to study."

"I did! I don't have to study twenty-four hours a day, do I? I came and made my appearance. And the boys were having fun."

"Okay, okay—so has this new guy met the boys yet?"

"No."

"Is he going to?"

"I don't know," Lucy said, wiping her fingers on her apron. "You were the one that said it wasn't such a good idea to introduce the boys to every new guy right away. Just the ones that seem serious."

"Yeah," Larry began slowly. "Except none of them are serious."

"Ha, ha, ha," Lucy mocked. "This one might be."

Larry snorted.

"Smart-ass."

"What's up with Seamus?" Larry asked to change the subject.

"Shay? He's fine," Lucy said.

"So why is he acting out? Are things okay at home?"

"Things are crazy, like they always are," she said. "It's not easy being a working mother, trying to go to school. And boys are hard. That's why I have you. You said you would help me, remember?"

"I remember," Larry said. He more than remembered. Lucy was older than Larry, but Larry was always the one who took care of things. The problem with Lucy was that the things she wanted and the things she needed never seemed to rhyme. And like a child who didn't get what she wanted for Christmas, she was unhappy. Lucy always wanted a do-over. She was the one most likely to give up, drop out, get discouraged, and feel that the world was against her. Larry didn't understand how she managed to work herself into all the tangents she found herself in, but he was the one who helped her back out of them, especially when she got pregnant with her boys, each by a different man. Lucy's choice in men was as bad as her common sense. Seamus's father was around for a while, showing up on birthdays and holidays, until he finally, silently, and without fanfare, just stopped appearing. Wally's father was some guy she fell into bed with one night after a party. She never bothered to tell him she was pregnant, and when Larry or anyone else in the family suggested it, she flew into a rage, telling them it was none of their business. One by one, the family fell away. No one could put up with Lucy's inability to keep both feet on the ground for an extended period of time. Larry was the first one—the only one in the family—who would take her back and help her out. She was always grateful, always full of thanks, but somehow, when she arrived at a new fork in the road, she never remembered the wrong turns of her past and seemed to make the same mistakes from the time before, and the time before that.

Larry was patient with Lucy, but now that she was pushing middle age, even *his* patience was wearing thin. He knew he had to be there for her boys, but he didn't know how much longer he could hold out for his sister.

"Look, Beatriz's niece came in last night, and I don't know how long she's going to stay. So you need to keep your boys."

"What niece?"

"Her sister's kid."

"Beatriz has a sister?" Lucy said, licking her fingers.

"She did. She died—"

"What? Jesus..."

"—and we're going to keep her niece for a while, until we can find out why she's here and who she left behind. That's as much as I know," Larry said, finishing off the last of his coffee.

"So, what's the problem?" Lucy asked after a moment. "Why can't my boys stay over?"

"Lucy, we don't have the room, and it's a touchy situation. And Beatriz—she's stressed out. We need the space."

Lucy knew that nothing stressed out her sister-in-law. If anyone was stressed, it was her brother. He never did well with a change in plans, and spontaneity made him queasy. Lucy never understood why Beatriz put up with him all these years, but she assumed it was more of that unearned luck that always seemed to be in short supply when it came to Lucy's life.

"Well," Lucy said, wiping her fingers with a stray napkin on the table, "I wouldn't want my boys to be in your way. Why don't you just throw them out back with a bowl of water?"

"Lucy!"

"They're just my kids," she said sarcastically.

"That's right. They're *your* kids."

"What's that supposed to mean?" Lucy asked. When Larry didn't answer, she pushed the plate of half-eaten fries away from her. "You just don't get it, do you?"

"Oh, please..."

"Everything is easy for you. The world twirls just so for you, huh? Well, guess what? Some of us live in the real world with real problems."

Larry refused to let his sister get to him. Not again. Not this time. When the boys came back to the table they didn't notice the icy silence between the adults.

"Fries!" Wally dug into the plate with Seamus leaning over his shoulder to pick at what his brother left behind. Larry stood up and motioned to Raúl and Carlos to remain standing.

"Come on, we're leaving," he said to his sons.

"Can we get a to-go box?" Wally asked.

"No, you're staying here with me," Lucy snapped.

"I thought you were working longer," Seamus said uneasily.

"I am," Lucy pouted. "Don't worry, the regular manager isn't here today. You can sit at the break table in the back. You have homework or something to do, don't you?"

Seamus and Wally whined and flopped into the booth.

"Get up!" Lucy demanded. "C'mon! They're waiting to turn over the table."

"What the fuck, Mom!"

As soon as the words fell from Seamus's mouth, Larry had him by the arm and pulled him into the air and onto his feet.

"Get up!" Larry demanded. Seamus swallowed his tongue. Wally didn't need anyone to tell him to straighten up. "If I hear you talk to your mother like that again, I'm going to knock you into next week!"

"See? See how they are?" Lucy said. Larry couldn't stand it.

The waitress whose shift Lucy agreed to take came up behind them.

"Hey, Luce—can you stay for me, or what?" Lucy looked at her brother, who had released his nephew and was staring at him hard.

"I'm not through with you," he said to Seamus. Then he turned to all of the boys: "Go get in the car before I change my mind!" The boys charged past Larry with Raúl and Carlos following them.

"When do you get off?"

"Three, three-thirty."

"Be sure to come and get them at three-forty-five, on the dot," he said to his sister between his teeth.

"I will! I will!"

"I mean it, Lucy!"

"Damn, you act like I'm a crack mom or something!" Lucy laughed and looked at the waitress, standing there unsure of what she had walked into.

"Chill out!" Lucy said to them both.

Larry and the waitress left the restaurant at the same time.

"Hey, I'm sorry. I hope I didn't wreck your plans by asking her to take my shift," the woman said meekly. "I just really, *really* needed the time off."

"I know the feeling," Larry said before he climbed into his SUV, where the boys were obediently buckled in, their hands in their laps, waiting patiently for what was next.

Celeste couldn't remember the last time she ate so much and was thankful for every piece of food she put in her mouth. Beatriz was on the phone most of the time, talking to her brothers, telling them they needed to come back to the house because they wouldn't believe who was there, while Ana sat with Celeste, wishing Beatriz would let her make the phone calls so she could spend time with her niece.

"Quieres más, mi'ja?"

"No, gracias. No more. Everything was good, señora." Celeste looked around the large kitchen, taking in how full it was—no shelf was empty, no cupboard was bare. Every seat had a cushion, the windows had nice curtains, and the floor was smooth and flat, without cracks or soft spaces that bowed underfoot. The house was well worn and lived in, but everything looked brand new to Celeste.

"So let me guess," Ana said. "I'm going to say you are twelve. Is that right?"

"No! Fourteen. Almost quince. Fifteen."

"Verdad?" Ana was shocked. The girl was so small! Ana wondered if she had been malnourished in her early life.

"Ay, perdón!" Ana teased.

Celeste neatly folded the thick paper napkin Ana had given her and daintily placed it next to her plate. "Are they rich?"

"Quién?"

"La señora," Celeste said, looking toward Beatriz, who had wandered off as she babbled on her cell phone. Ana wanted to laugh but realized that to Celeste—whose entire life was apparently stuffed into the small bag she was clutching when she had arrived—Beatriz's life must look large to her.

"They aren't rich like you see on TV, but they have a good life. Son buena gente. Very good people. You'll see," Ana said.

"Okay! We're all set!" Beatriz said, breezing back into the kitchen from the dining area, where she'd wandered off to finish her calls. "Everyone is coming back late this afternoon! Even Tony! They were on their way to see Elaine's parents in San Angelo, but they decided to come back for our little welcome party. Isn't that nice?" Beatriz didn't wait for Celeste to answer. "You'll get to meet all your uncles, my brothers, and their wives, your aunts," she explained. "They were all gone by the time you got here. Oh!" Beatriz suddenly remembered something else. "I need to make one more call, and then we can go."

Celeste looked at Ana nervously. "Go where?" she whispered.

"Go where, mujer?" Ana shouted after Beatriz, but it was too late. She was already immersed in another phone call. Celeste's head sank into her shoulders, and Ana could see something was wrong. She ducked down to catch the girl's eyes.

"Qué paso, mi'ja? What's wrong?"

"She talks a lot."

Ana laughed. "Yes, she does. She's kind of a wheeler-dealer, entiendes? At her job, she works with many important people to make things happen, and then here at home, she's like the traffic cop with all the boys. She knows how to get things done. But don't worry, once she settles down, you'll see—she's one of the best people you could know. She's excited to have you here."

"She is?"

Ana was startled by Celeste's remark. "Well, of course she is!" She started to laugh at Celeste's surprise, but one look at the girl's troubled face and she knew something was wrong, wrong, wrong.

"Thank you for bringing me las cosas," Celeste said quietly.

"The clothes?"

"No, las otras cosas. En la bolsa. Can you tell? Can people tell?" The idea made Celeste cringe.

"Ay, no mi'ja," Ana said, trying to sound as casual as possible. "Well, I thought maybe. You do something mi hija does when she has her period. She hunches forward, así. Pero, no, I didn't know. But I was right?"

Celeste's head sank down as she nodded.

"The first time was last month!" the girl whispered urgently. "I knew it would come someday, even though 'Amá..."

Talking about her mother made Celeste cry, and she was tired of crying. What she would have said if the words could have come without tears was that her mother used to tease that she wished Celeste could stay a little girl forever.

Celeste remembered how her mother would take Celeste in her arms and hold her tight, saying, "I'm going to keep you small forever!" She liked the idea when she was a little girl, but as she got older, she began to worry that her mother had wished it so hard, she somehow made it come true. So when Celeste finally began menstruating, it caught her off guard, and on top of her mother getting killed, and all the strange, new changes coming her way, Celeste had no sense of what was normal and ordinary. Bleeding, she thought, was the way it was going to be, every day, for the rest of her life.

Ana patted her hand. "Did you figure out what to do?" she asked gently. "With the cosas in the bag?"

"Yes," Celeste said. "I followed the pictures on the paper in the box, and 'Amá told me about it."

"Well, if you have any questions, be sure to ask your tía Beatriz."

"Oh," Celeste said, twisting her mouth.

"What, mi'ja?"

"Can't I—I wish I could go with you to your house."

What had happened in the short time Celeste and Beatriz were alone together? Ana thought. She knew she had to find out, and fast.

Beatriz made Celeste and Ana jump when she burst back into the kitchen.

"Okay! I'm done! No more calls! So you know what we need to do? We need to go shopping! What do you say? Ana, can you come?"

"For food?" Ana asked, as she stood up and offered her chair to Beatriz. "Why don't I take care of that and you two stay here and visit." A look of unease shot across Beatriz's and Celeste's faces.

"Sit down," Ana said to Beatriz gently.

"No, no, no—if we leave now, we can get to the mall right when it opens," Beatriz said.

"The mall isn't going anywhere," Ana said, knowing full well that Beatriz not only hated shopping but she hated malls. Ana sat down across from Celeste, leaving the chair closest to her for Beatriz.

"I was just going to tell Celeste that I wish she and her mother could have come to visit. I would have loved it if she were around to play with my kids. And she has cousins, lots of them, verdad?" Ana was nodding at Beatriz, wondering what was taking her so long to pick up the cue to sit down, calm down, and have a conversation that didn't include having a cell phone pressed against her face. Beatriz looked at her watch and began to search for her keys when Celeste began to speak.

"I asked her. I asked her all the time, when I was little, who we belonged to," Celeste said. Beatriz froze. Celeste was opening up the way she wanted, the way she was hoping for. "She wouldn't say," Celeste continued. "But she began to talk about her more and more before—before she died." Celeste was talking to Ana as if Beatriz wasn't in the room. She spoke quietly, and deliberately, but without emotion. Not like she was trying to hide her feelings, but as if she were exhausted from whatever she'd experienced before arriving, as if the life she'd lived in her fourteen years were filled with more experiences than anyone could imagine.

Beatriz was so startled at what she'd just heard that she finally sat down. Ana's eyes darted back and forth between Beatriz and Celeste, trying to will Beatriz to ask a question. Any question. But Beatriz sat there dumbly. Ana was perplexed. She had never seen Beatriz so tongue-tied and ill at ease. This was a woman who had negotiated with state senators and congressmen and a house full of boys, but when it came to this one, small girl, she acted as if speaking were a brand-new experience to her.

"I think I'd like to hear a little about when you two were girls," Ana finally offered.

"What?" Beatriz said.

"Tell us a story about Perla, when she was Celeste's age."

Ana could see that this brightened Celeste's mood, but Beatriz was suddenly filled with terror.

"Oh! She doesn't want to hear about the past!" Beatriz exclaimed. Ana wondered if her friend had lost her mind. Beatriz suddenly jumped up. "Vamos, y'all. I've got a charge card in my purse, and I'm not afraid to use it!"

Ana sighed. "Let me call my kids and let them know."

She barely had time to finish her call before Beatriz hustled everyone into her car. They traveled the long, curvaceous street of the neighborhood and then suddenly they were on the highway. Celeste had no idea of where they were going but was excited by the cars zooming by. Beatriz drove faster than Celeste thought possible, careening in and out of traffic until they entered the parking lot in a huge shopping center. Celeste had been to shopping centers before, but the ones she was used to had stores like the Dollar General, a heavily gated Radio Shack, a Cash-Now pawn shop, a nail salon that reeked of acetone, and a family-owned drycleaner with the doors flung open to let the heat escape. Walking by that open door, Celeste remembered how snatches of Spanish could be heard among the women working inside, all of them small and dark, resembling Celeste and her mother, their T-shirts and jeans covered by thin cotton smocks that tied at the waist. They tended to fluffy gowns or were engulfed in clouds of steam as they busily pressed suits and other clothes that looked like they belonged to very important people, maybe movie stars or rich businessmen—no one who had to wear a smock to make a living.

The shopping mall Beatriz took them to was huge, with giant, shiny department stores at the end of each broad passageway. The floors were buffed as slick as ice. Everywhere Celeste looked, there was highly polished glass and chrome, signs lit from behind, and piles and piles of merchandise. It excited her, but at the same time it made her feel exceptionally small, even in the company of these two women who she knew were trying to make her feel welcome. To them, all of this was ordinary and expected.

Beatriz wanted to go everywhere at once. She rushed into a store that sold hair clips, headbands, ribbons, combs, picks, and other trinkets. Before Celeste or Ana had even walked past the first display, Beatriz bought forty-five dollars' worth of hair jewelry and handed the bright violet bag full of goodies to an astonished Celeste. Across the mall she noticed a candy store and insisted they go there, where she bought a huge sack of jelly beans, bubble gum, and fat pralines. On the way to another shop, Beatriz tried to figure out Celeste's size—Celeste could have told her if Beatriz had stopped long enough to ask and listen to the response—but got distracted when she saw a shoe store on the other side of the mall. She instantly wanted to go there.

They scuttled to the shoe store as Celeste wondered what was wrong with the shoes she had on now: sporty pink and brown Mary Janes she'd chosen herself. She remembered squealing with delight when she saw them and felt good buying them because she thought the rubber soles would last a long time. Cute *and* practical? It was too good to dream for. The shoes were the first purchase Celeste had made for herself, by herself, without any adult supervision. She thought she had done a good thing.

"Whoa, whoa, whoa!" Ana finally called out, forcing Beatriz to pause and face her. "You're flying from place to place como la loca. What are you looking for?"

"I don't know!" Beatriz said breathlessly. "Everything! She needs everything! Something nice that she can meet everyone in. I don't know. Jeans? New shoes for sure."

Celeste looked down at her shoes and suddenly felt as if they were old and shabby instead of "qué cute"! She looked at Beatriz's feet. Her sandals were elegant and strappy, her feet smooth, with perfectly shaped and polished toenails that looked like bright red jelly beans.

"Her shoes are fine!" Ana said, pulling Beatriz away from the store. "When is everybody coming?"

"But there is so much she needs," Beatriz said frantically.

"Ay, mujer!" Ana whispered to her friend. "We have to do it all today?" She turned to look at Celeste. "Mi'ja, is there anything that we have to get today? Something that can't wait?"

"Anything! Anything, mi'ja!" Beatriz said to her niece, the urgency in her voice causing Ana to shake her head.

"I—I just need to go to the bathroom," Celeste finally eked out.

"Okay, mira. Here's the food court, and over there is the bathroom," Beatriz spoke as if talking to a kindergarten class. "Let's all go! Vamos."

"No, no, I don't have to go—and neither do you," Ana said pointedly to Beatriz. "You can go alone, right, mi'ja?"

Celeste nodded her head anxiously.

"Do you need money for the machine?" Ana asked.

"I have some change, thank you," Celeste said, rapidly walking to the restroom.

"We'll be right here!" Beatriz called after her. She meant to be reassuring, but to Celeste it sounded more like a warning.

As soon as the girl was gone, Ana abruptly turned to face Beatriz. "What the hell is wrong with you?"

"Nothing!" Beatriz said in a voice a full octave higher than usual. "I'm just excited is all! There's so much to do, so much to—I don't know where to start."

"Well, you don't have to do it all in one day," Ana said. "Cálmate! You're making her a nervous wreck. You're making *me* a nervous wreck! What happened when the two of you went upstairs? Things were going fine before you were alone with her, and now they seem—"

"I, I…I don't know," Beatriz said. "All I know is that she hates me."

"She said that?"

"She didn't have to. She hates me, and I don't know if there's anything I can do to change her mind. And the worst thing is, I probably deserve it."

Ana was not used to seeing Beatriz unmoored. She was the one who was always pulled together. Nothing ever rattled her. She was always the calm one in the middle of a storm.

"Ay, mujer, ven' acá." Ana made Beatriz sit at a table in the food court where they could see Celeste when she returned from the ladies' room. "What happened back at the house when the two of you went upstairs?"

Beatriz took a deep breath. "I pulled her hair."

"What?!"

"Look, all I know is she hates me!"

"Okay, okay, you said that before," Ana said calmly. "Tell me exactly what happened. What did you say to each other?"

Beatriz rubbed her temples and tried to recall what had happened.

"I asked her if she knew her father, and she said no. Then I told her we could have come and got her, and I told her—I don't know! I told her all sorts of things, and then I pulled her hair!"

Though she was trying to make a joke, Beatriz was clearly upset. Ana thought she understood what had happened.

"Oh..."

"Oh, *what*? Tell me!" Beatriz's voice took on a hysterical edge.

"Well," Ana said very slowly, trying to model the behavior she wanted Beatriz to follow. "It sounds like there was a lot of telling and not a whole lot of listening."

Beatriz allowed the words to sink in and then finally understood what her friend meant. She sat back in her chair and groaned. "I should be good at this!" she said. "What's wrong with me?"

"Okay, so look," Ana said. "Let's do this another way. Right now, you don't really know what she's thinking or feeling. Why don't you start by telling me what *you're* thinking and feeling?"

Beatriz hung her head back and stared up at the fluorescent lights, closing her eyes against the glare. "I want to make it all better. I want Celeste to want to be with me. I want her to need me. I want her to trust me. I want—I want my sister back, but since I can't have that, I want Celeste to, I don't know, help me start over."

"Wow," Ana said after a long pause. "That's an awful lot of stuff to expect from one girl who just lost her mother and God knows what else."

Beatriz pulled her head up to look at a passing swarm of teenage girls, all chomping on wads of gum and laughing at something only they understood.

"You can't buy her affection," Ana said. "What you need and want from her will only come with time. And I hate to tell you this, but you can't *make* her feel anything."

"But what about what she needs and wants from me?" Beatriz asked.

"I think you need to be quiet so you can hear her and find out," Ana said. "It might not all come in words. You know that, right?"

Ana's advice began to make sense, but Beatriz was still driven by her anxieties.

"I just feel like—all these years have gone by and I have so much to make up to her, and to my sister. I want to do it right this time." Beatriz thought about the last time she saw Perla. She thought about telling Ana about it, how she would have done things differently, but reliving that moment filled her with shame.

Ana knew her friend like her own reflection in a mirror and sensed that something was still unspoken. Whatever happened had injured Beatriz deeply, leaving her uncharacteristically frantic. Ana affectionately stroked Beatriz's hand. "Mira, you need to go slow. Go. Slow," Ana said. "Have you even found out what happened over there? How Perla died?"

Beatriz shook her head no, her eyes welling with tears at the thought of her baby sister being gone, really gone. "I...I can't. I'm sure it's in the packet of papers she brought. I just can't deal with it," she said, wiping her eyes.

"Okay, okay," Ana said, patting her friend's hand. "Take it slow. You want Celeste to meet the family? Let her meet the family, but don't make it a circus. Make it as casual and easy as possible. You don't know what she's been through and what she has to say about it. Give her some time."

"Okay," Beatriz said, getting her bearings back. "Okay. But I feel like there is so much I should do, so much I should know. Like why were you asking her about needing money? What was that all about?"

"She started her period."

"What? How did you know? How come I didn't know?" Beatriz exclaimed.

"Ay, mujer!" Ana said. "Listen! You need to listen! Take a breath, step back. Stop treating her like a novelty. Just let her be."

Celeste came out of the restroom and walked toward the women, her hands shoved deep in the pockets of her hoodie, the hem of it pulled down over her backside.

"'Sta bien?" Beatriz asked. Celeste nodded. Beatriz took a deep breath. "Okay. We have a new plan," she announced, working hard to speak calmly and clearly. "We're going to get a few things and go back to the house. Qué necessitas the most?"

Celeste looked at Ana anxiously.

"Tell her, mi'ja."

"Di'me. Anything, anything," Beatriz interjected. Ana shot her a "calm the hell down" look. After a long moment, Celeste finally spoke.

"Chones, por favor. Nada mas," Celeste said. She was worried that the request would catapult them to a new store where Beatriz would buy her a pair of underwear for every hour of the day, for every day of the week. Instead, Beatriz remembered Ana's advice and calmly said, "I know just where to go."

∽❧ SEVEN ❧∾

Although it seemed as if she should be able to sleep standing up, Josie Mendoza couldn't summon sleep—peaceful, restful, uninterrupted sleep—any more than she could will the sun to go down. Ten, twenty minutes, sometimes up to an hour, was the most she could hope for. Her body would go limp, but her mind was still alive, like the wick of a candle just blown out—the fire extinguished, but the scarlet bud on the tip lingering. It was not that Josie didn't want to sleep. She was dying to sleep. But she hadn't slept—really slept—since Perla died.

It had taken Josie only a few years to build her writing credentials with some targeted assignments in a few small publications that led to bigger, more prestigious magazines. So she was ready when she was asked to write the book *Women of Juarez: Then and Now.* She was more than prepared to pull all her resources, all her skills, all her energy, into this one project. Like a long-distance runner, she felt like she'd been training to write this book all her life. So she was taken aback in a big way when the project turned out to be more demanding than she imagined. It wasn't just the obscene violence, the wounded families, and the astonishing facts behind the long and tragic story; it was that she had broken the cardinal rule all good journalists knew not to break: She became emotionally involved.

In the beginning, she had to work hard to earn Perla's trust. She knew interviewing Perla was a huge "get," because no one else had written about her. She thought it was because no one else knew about her, when in reality, Perla was desperate to guard her privacy. Josie had researched Perla's labor-organizing efforts in the electronics factory where she worked in Juarez and the relief work she was doing in El Paso for the families whose mothers, daughters, and sisters had become some of the murdered. Everyone called Perla "fierce" and "brave." A few even called her "la chingona," which Josie translated to something like "the ass-kicker" (but with the utmost respect). They meant she was a fighter, a survivor, and, more important, she knew how to get things done. Josie was determined to interview her. After weeks of painstaking cajoling, coaxing, and pleading her case through an intermediary, Perla finally agreed to talk to Josie. They met at a taco cart Perla suggested. Josie came fully prepared with her notebook and her recorder and her list of carefully prepared questions. She sat under a sun-bleached umbrella, lazily perched over a rickety folding table the vendor had erected near the cart, keeping an eye out for Perla as the lunch rush peaked and then subsided. After an hour past their agreed meeting time, Josie started to wonder what her plan B should be, when someone approached her from behind.

"You can put all that away. We're not ready for that yet," Perla said. When Josie turned around, she was shocked.

Based on the way Perla Sánchez had been described to her, Josie was expecting an Amazon woman, not the petite figure that stood before her. Perla was dressed simply in blue jeans, her T-shirt neatly tucked in at her small waist. Her long, black hair was slicked back from her dark, round face in a ponytail that hung behind her head, exploding into a frothy bouquet of curls.

"Okay. I'm here," Perla said, as she moved to stand across the table from Josie. "What do you want?"

Josie reared back. "I want to talk to you." She could see Perla was completely no-nonsense, ready for work, with no tolerance for chitchat. She could also see that she was the one being interviewed.

"Why? What do you get out of it?" Perla asked.

"Me?"

"How do I know you're not going to, you know, sensentualize what's going on here?"

Perla misspoke, and Josie knew she needed to correct her without making her feel foolish. "I have no intention of *sensationalizing* anything."

"All I know is people come here all the time to pick the meat off our bones and write stories for their shiny magazines. Then they go back to their nice lives while things for las mujeres here stay the same. How do I know you're not going to do that?" Perla demanded.

Now Josie understood why people called Perla "la chingona." But she could feel her own inner chingona coming to life, too.

"You don't," Josie said flatly. "But I can tell you this: I've known what's been happening here for a long time. I want justice to be served just as much as you do. You do it your way. I do it mine. The more people know what's happening here, the more chance there is that things can change."

Perla stared past Josie for a long time before the taco vendor struck up a conversation with her. She obviously knew Perla and wanted to treat her well. Perla politely waved off the offer of free food to the vendor's heartfelt objections, then graciously accepted, making the vendor beam with pleasure. The women were so immersed in their small talk Josie thought the interrogation was over. She began to pack her things, when Perla suddenly returned, seating herself across from Josie.

"Ándale, then. I don't have a lot of time. I hope you're prepared."

After that afternoon at the taco cart, she and Perla began to meet regularly. As much as Josie tried, Perla never wanted to talk about herself. She always stayed focused on the women—the murdered, the missing, their families, and the justice that they were still owed. She changed the subject when Josie innocently asked, "Where are you from?" Perla dropped a few clues here and there but would never answer Josie directly. It wasn't until Perla discovered that Josie also had a daughter that the distance she kept between them began to shrink.

"Qué milagro!" Perla said, as she looked at the small photo Josie had carefully trimmed and pressed into a locket she always wore under her blouse. "What do you call her?"

"Paciencia. Paz for short."

"Qué chula!" Perla declared. When she let her guard down, she was as delightful as a babbling stream. "Where is she?"

"With mi madre, en Austin."

"Ay, qué bueno," Perla said with a sigh. "Then she's safe." She thought a moment before she asked the next question. "And her daddy?"

"He's dead."

"Ay, perdón."

"No importa," Josie said. "He was never part of our lives, if you know what I mean."

Perla did know what Josie meant and left it at that.

"I miss her terribly," Josie added. "I haven't seen her in weeks, but I have to work, and my work takes me away for a long time, and I—"

"You don't have to explain yourself to me," Perla said. "We all do what we have to do."

Josie was grateful that Perla didn't offer any verdicts about Josie being separated from her child, or any unsolicited advice about how it was a shame her career overrode her role as a mother, or any other critical commentary that Josie had already tortured herself with. Although they were very different from one another—Perla in her T-shirt and jeans, Josie in her regulation black slacks, white blouse, and always close-cropped hair—they understood each other in that small moment. And maybe that was the reason Perla shared with Josie the book she kept with notes for her daughter Celeste's quinceañera.

"I started it when she was a baby," Perla explained. "When she got old enough, Celeste started making her own notes." She brushed her fingers over a thick piece of paper that looked like it came from a cereal box, a word-hunt game where Celeste had found her name, another word for the color of the sky, and carefully scrawled a circle around it in blue ink. The two women chuckled, wondering how the little girl thought a word game could be worked into a quinceañera. Josie was slowly flipping through the pages of the quince book, the two of them sitting at Perla's kitchen table in the big room that served as the dining room, living room, and bedroom for Perla and her daughter. Birthday parties were fun, and a quinceañera was a birthday party like no other, Josie thought. And looking around at Perla's modest home, she couldn't help but wonder.

"So tell me something," Josie began carefully. "Quince-añeras can be expensive. Why is it so important to you to have one?"

"They can be whatever you want them to be," Perla said. "They don't have to be fancy, with limos and choco-late fountains and all that."

"Okay, but why?"

"Why?" Perla sat back in her chair. "Este…when I was young, I didn't think I was going to live past the age of fifteen. I couldn't imagine the future. Gracias a la Vir-gencita, I found what I was meant to do in this life. This might look silly to you, but it makes a difference, I think, for a young girl to see that her life matters."

"That's not silly," Josie said. "Not when you explain it that way."

"I just want her to know her life makes a difference," Perla said. "If she thinks so, maybe she will make more of her life than I did with mine. Like you're doing with yours."

"Ay, no. I just tell other people's stories," Josie scoffed.

"Sí, but not everyone gets their story told. If you don't tell it, who will?"

As their interviews continued over the next few months, and Josie was getting deeper and deeper into her project, she knew she was working on the story of her career. It consumed every waking hour, and it demanded all of her attention and all of her skills. What she didn't know was that this would be the story to haunt her for the rest of her life.

After leaving El Paso once and for all, Josie was making good time on the I-10. She was heading toward San Antonio, even though she'd told her mother—promised her—that she was on her way home to Austin. She was long overdue to see her mother, her crazy aunt Chata, and especially Paz. She'd told her mother she'd be home Sunday afternoon, and that was Josie's plan, until she helped clear Perla's house. When she found the quinceañera book left behind, she knew what she had to do. Josie wasn't sure how her mother was going to take the news. She lit a cigarette and used her thumb to punch her mother's number on her cell phone as she steered with her free hand. The phone rang and rang and rang. Very unusual. Josie hung up and called her mom at her beauty shop.

"I only have two girls left," Rita said instead of her usual "Bueno! La Rita's Casa de Belleza!" Josie wondered for a moment if she'd dialed the wrong number.

"Hello?"

"Hello?"

"Hello?"

"Those pins over there, mi'ja. Over there. *Over there!*" Rita ordered. "Sí, who is it?"

Josie could tell Rita was distracted. "It's me, Josefina."

"Oh, hi, mi'ja...Not that dryer! El otro! That one's broken," she said to someone in the shop and then, in a lower, frostier tone into the receiver, "Mi angelita—my fat ass."

"You're working on Sunday?" Josie asked.

"Yes, my friend Gloria's niece is having a quinceañera in Elgin or Lockhart or wherever the hell she lives, and this was the only day she could get all the girls over here. Hey!" she yelled to someone else in the shop. "Watch the little one over there! She's going to—No, mi'ja! Leave the dog alone! Sí, that's *my* dog, but no—the curlers are not for the dog. Oh, my gato! Come 'ere, Tom Selleck. Come 'ere, boy."

Josie could hear the clatter of a tray, a radio babbling, giggling, and voices talking over each other in the background. Tom Selleck, Rita's current mascot and usually friendly Maltese, was yipping unhappily. It was unusual for Rita to work on a Sunday, but the soundtrack in Rita's shop was familiar, perpetual, and chaotic. Josie often joked that her mother's shop was the place where the hociconas—the chatty little hens, as Josie liked to picture them—roosted. It was the place where Rita's long-time customers came in to share bits of gossip, whether you wanted to hear it or not. All of that was drenched by music on the radio or a game show on the TV overhead, laughing, whirring dryers, running water, birds chirping, or a dog barking—depending on what poor creature Rita had rescued. Josie learned early on how to endure it, weaving an invisible cocoon around her as she did small chores around the shop when she was a girl, or, more to her liking, sat in an empty side chair with a book in her lap, willing herself to fade into the wallpaper, all the time plotting for, and eventually achieving, what she wanted most of all: silence—surrounded only by her books, her pens, her notebooks, and, later, her laptop with unlimited wireless access. Yes, that was heaven to Josie. A writer's life, but most important, quiet on demand. Rita was as different from her daughter as Josie's short, unpolished nails were to Rita's brightly lacquered ones.

"Fourteen up-dos and then Gloria tells me at the last minute she wants a perm." Rita snorted into the phone.

"Maybe I should call back," Josie said.

"No, I'm ready this time. Go ahead." Josie could hear her mother crank a small kitchen timer so she wouldn't overcook Gloria like she did that one time Gloria never forgot and probably reminded Rita of so she would open up her shop on a Sunday to what sounded like a horde of girls, their mothers, their tías, their abuelas, and anyone else who wanted to go along for the ride to her mother's East Austin shop.

"Over there!" Rita suddenly yelled, making Josie pull her phone away from her ear. "Allá, in that box over there. There! That's where the hairnets are."

Josie already knew what the plan was: Get the hair set today and hold it in place for a day or more by sleeping in hairnets.

"That's really going to work?" Josie asked.

"N'ombre!" Rita scoffed. "Gloria is telling the girls to sleep sitting up until the quinceañera next Saturday. No one asked me. She can tell them whatever she wants."

Josie suddenly felt self-conscious. "Can I say hello to Paz?"

"She's with your aunt Chata."

"When are they coming back?"

"I don't know. She took her to church, and after that she likes to eat with las viejitas—la bat pack—at Luby's. Why?"

Josie didn't like the sudden crimp in her mother's voice.

"You're going to see her in a little while, aren't you? Where are you, anyway?" Rita asked.

Josie took a long drag from her cigarette and waited for her mother to fill in the silence.

"Josefina—you *are* still coming, aren't you?"

"Yes," Josie said. "But I have to make a stop first. In San Antonio."

"San Antonio!" Rita cried. "Oh, my gato! That's more than a stop!" Josie could hear the sound of the radio being changed from one station to the next, but Rita was oblivious. "What's in San Antonio?" she demanded.

"I have to make a delivery," Josie said. She could feel the grief over Perla's death welling up and wrestling with her guilt over not going home the way she promised. "You remember that woman I told you about?"

"Which woman? You told me about a lot of women."

"The one who got killed," Josie said softly.

"The one who got what?" Rita said loudly over the background noise. Josie couldn't bear saying it again.

"The one I told you about, 'Amá."

"Quién? Speak up! I can hardly hear you."

"Perla Sánchez!" Josie finally yelled into the phone. She could feel her heart pounding and her emotions raging. On the other end of the phone, she could tell her mother was leaving the main room of the shop, walking into the kitchen, and out to the yard that linked the shop to the house. There, it was quiet and away from nosy eyes and ears.

"What about her?" Rita asked. Josie was relieved that her mother's voice had softened and was filled with concern.

"Well, I helped some of the mujeres in El Paso clear out her house, and I found this book that her daughter should have. It's a scrapbook for the quinceañera they were planning—Perla and her daughter, Celeste. The girl was sent to be with her family in San Antonio. I doubt she meant to leave the book behind, but there it was in the house, and I couldn't just leave it there…" Josie took a moment to regain her composure. "I need to deliver it. I need to deliver it myself. I have to. It's the least I can do." Josie took another long drag from her cigarette to calm herself and waited for her mother to speak. "'Amá? Are you still there?"

"I'm here," Rita said forlornly.

"I know you're angry, but—"

"I'm not angry, mi'ja. I'm not angry. It's just—oh, my gato—I wish…You know it's not your fault la pobrecita got killed, verdad?"

The tears began to well in Josie's eyes. She couldn't see and immediately made for the nearest exit.

"It's not your fault, mi'ja. It's not your fault," Rita repeated as Josie maneuvered her car to the off ramp and into a nearby gas station. "You hear me? It's not your fault."

But that was not how Josie felt. She was sure that Perla making herself more public, and Josie digging and poking, asking questions, talking to all the people she talked to while researching her book, had made Perla more

visible and put her in the middle of a bull's-eye. Josie
was sure that Perla's work and everyone she was working
with was making a difference, that the murder mystery
of the Women of Juarez would be solved, and that those
responsible would be brought to justice. She knew it in
her bones. But she was sure that word got back to those
faceless, heartless, soulless bastards, who then murdered
Perla. There's nothing more dangerous than a woman
who's discovered the full range of her power. A powerless
woman is a woman who can be controlled, and Perla had
moved beyond that. That was fine and good. But Josie
making a show of it... *Yes*, Josie thought, *I may as well
have pulled the trigger myself.*

Rita could hear her daughter sniffling on the other end
of the phone, and she was torn. It had been a long time
since Josie had seen Paz, but she could sense the enormous
weight her daughter was carrying around. She wasn't sure
what she could say to make it better.

"Oye, so do me a favor," Rita said, changing the subject. "When you have a quinceañera for Paz, don't have
a big production. Just make it something simple—a mass,
pink cake at home, y nada más." It was an awkward transi-
tion, but Josie knew her mother was trying to comfort her.

"A quinceañera! Paz is only..." Josie's voice trailed off
as she tried to calculate how old her child was.

"She's twelve," Rita said stiffly.

Twelve. That didn't seem possible, but Josie realized
her mother was right. Paz was twelve.

"The years fly by faster than you think. She'll be a teenager soon, and then ya, she's gone," Rita said. Reminding
Josie that she was missing watching her daughter grow up

only made her feel worse. "Maybe it will go out of style by the time she's this age," Rita continued, "pero, I doubt it. I hear the girls say all the time, 'Only one girl gets to be the prom queen, and you might not get married, but everyone turns fifteen.'"

Rita had moved too far from the shop, and reception on her portable phone was beginning to crackle. She began to work her way back inside.

"Go do what you need to do, Josefina, pero remember: You have a girl here who needs her mother. I'm doing what I can to help you, but if she stops asking about you..." Josie felt as if she'd be punched in the stomach.

"She's not asking about me?" Josie asked.

"Of course she's asking about you! You're her mother, pero, I'm just saying—when she stops asking about you, it's already too late, entiendes?"

Josie dropped her head onto the headrest.

"So when is Paz coming back?"

"I don't know. I told Chata to keep her as long as possible because I had all this going on today."

Paz was in good hands with her aunt Chata, even if Chata was as brittle as an old newspaper. Josie thought her daughter should be around kids her age, but as soon as the thought came to her, she bit her tongue. She was in no position to make that suggestion to her mother, given all that she and her aunt were doing for her and Paz.

From the background noise, Josie could hear that her mother was back in her shop again. "Oh, my gato! I told you to keep an eye on the baby!" Rita wailed to someone in the room. "Oye, Josefina, I got to go," she said back into the phone. "These people are gonna tear down my

shop if I let them. I'll give Paz un abrazo for you, but you
come home as soon as you can. Take care of your business
over there, then get yourself home."

"Okay, 'Amá."

"Don't forget, Josefina! I know your work is important, but so is your family!"

"I know, 'Amá, I know!"

"And stop smoking!" Rita blurted. "Why are you
smoking again?"

Damn! How does she do that? Josie wondered as
she stamped out her cigarette in her car's overflowing
ashtray.

"Why do you think I'm smoking?" she stammered.

"It will make wrinkles and give you the cancer. If you
don't believe me, take a good look at your aunt Chata
when you see her. Call me when you get there," Rita
snapped.

A loud clatter, Tom Selleck yelping, and the sound of a
baby screaming on the other end of the phone were the last
things Josie heard before the line went dead. She dumped
her cell phone onto the passenger seat as her annoyance
merged with her guilt. The one thing Josie neglected to tell
her mother was that she had no idea where Celeste was
among the sea of Sánchezes that must live in San Antonio,
but she knew she would do her damnedest to find her.

EIGHT

Beatriz bought enough barbecue to feed a small nation. Buckets of potato salad, beans, coleslaw, pickles, corn on the cob, and anything else that could be served fast and easy. She sent Ana to Marisol's family's bakery to see if she could buy a whole sheet cake. She planned to decorate it with fresh fruit and then write in lime green frosting "Bienvenida, Celeste! Welcome Home."

Celeste never saw anyone move so fast. Beatriz was cleaning and setting up, all while talking on her cell phone.

"Can I help you?" Celeste asked her aunt between calls, feeling awkward and useless as her aunt whirled about.

"No, no—well—no! Why don't you go decide what you want to wear?" Beatriz offered. In spite of Ana's urging to slow down, Beatriz managed to buy Celeste several new outfits on their way out of the mall: a sweet, casual dress with a matching sweater; two pairs of jeans; a swingy, peasant blouse in bright white; and two fitted blouses, one in chambray blue, the other in a tangy coral that looked electric against Celeste's dark skin.

"Where should I go?" Celeste asked.

Beatriz stopped, sweaty and breathless from stooping and stuffing debris from yesterday's party into a trash bag. "Why don't you go in the room you slept in last night?

Unless you want a full-length mirror. Do you need a mirror? Do you want to fix your hair? I can help you put it up. Do you want me to help you?" Beatriz bit her tongue. She could sense she was beginning to speak at warp speed again and took a deep breath.

"I'll go decide what to wear," Celeste finally offered.

"Sure! That's a good idea!" Beatriz said. "I told everyone to come over after three. Where's Larry?" she suddenly said to herself, as she handed shopping bags to Celeste. "Is that everything?" She stood for a moment, staring into Celeste's face, as if writing and rewriting the list of things to do inside her forehead. "Oh! Ice! We need more ice! And soda. I better call Ana. And Larry. What else?" Celeste shrugged, but Beatriz was already punching the numbers on her cell phone with her thumb.

"Go on, mi'ja. I'm taking care of everything," Beatriz said.

Celeste was happy to leave Hurricane Beatriz behind her. When she got to the office, she closed the door with her backside and leaned against it. She slid down to the floor, the shopping bags all around her like giant crumpled wads. Any other girl would be thrilled with all the attention—all the gifts, clothes, and trinkets Beatriz seemed so eager to buy her. And it wasn't that Celeste wasn't thankful, and even a little excited. It was just that she would have traded any of it—all of it—to see her mother's face again. That, and Celeste was used to getting by with much less. She opened the shopping bag to pull out one outfit and looked at the price tags. She almost dropped the blouse when she saw how much it cost—as much as a week's groceries! The jeans were twice as much. Celeste couldn't believe it. She held them up to look at them, studied the seams and the snaps to figure why they cost as much as they did. She could buy three pairs of jeans for the same price at the St. Vincent De Paul store she and her mom used to visit, when they could, on Wednesdays and Saturdays. Those were the days when the new shipment came in. The clothes weren't new, but they were clean, and with a little starch everything looked as good as new. Everything her aunt Beatriz bought her was nice, Celeste thought. Better than nice. But she didn't want to get too used to this life. This life was bright and new and expensive, but it was not hers.

In the kitchen, Beatriz was pulling out all the leftovers from the night before as her brothers Miguel, Rudy, Tony, and their wives arrived all at once, heading in through the backyard, waving at Beatriz through the window. She motioned for them to come through the patio door as she continued working.

"Hey, we rang the doorbell but nobody answered," Miguel said. "I was beginning to think you were playing us."

"Pásale, pásale," Beatriz said, making way for them in the door. The men immediately gravitated to the barbecue Beatriz placed on the stove, while the women looked around for ways to pitch in. Tony helped his very pregnant wife, Elaine, take a seat at the kitchen table. Erasmo and Norma arrived at the same time as Larry and the boys.

"You're back!" Larry said, eyeing the twelve-pack of Shiner Erasmo carried under his arm.

"Well, yeah," Erasmo said, confused that Larry didn't

know what was going on. "You wanna beer? Looks like you could use one."

Larry and the boys were flushed and their T-shirts were damp. He'd taken them to the park to shoot some hoops and work off their breakfast, and he thought he was bringing Seamus and Wally home to wait for their mother while Raúl settled down to do his homework. He already thought about offering Carlos some cash so he and his brother could go out for fast food and maybe a movie, so that—at long last—Larry could have some private time with his wife. He was bewildered and a little put off when he saw Beatriz's brothers and their wives back at the house. Larry wandered to the kitchen, where everyone was chatting and getting drinks.

"There you are!" Beatriz cried. She crossed over to kiss Larry on the cheek. "Hmm, salty."

"I've been calling you for the last hour. How come you didn't pick up?" Larry felt clueless. He hated being clueless.

"I'm sorry! I left my phone in the car when we were at the mall, and then I was using it most of the afternoon. Are you hungry? Boys, are you hungry?"

Beatriz didn't have to ask twice. The boys had already picked up plates and were ready to dig in.

"Not yet!" Beatriz demanded. "We're waiting for the cake!"

"Whose birthday?" Wally asked.

"It's no one's birthday. This is a welcome party!" Beatriz said. "You guys look like you've been running around all afternoon. Go clean up first."

Seamus and Wally wailed loudly.

"You're not eating a thing until you clean up. Go!"

"Their mom is coming pretty soon," Larry said.

"No, she's not. She just called and said she was running late," Beatriz said. "She asked if you could drop them off, and I said that was fine. Isn't it?"

Beatriz could see the color rise up Larry's neck, over his face, and up into his scalp.

"Or Carlos could take them."

"No, no. I'll take them. C'mon boys," Larry said stiffly, pointing them through the door. "Go do what she says. Beatriz, I need to talk to you. Upstairs."

Beatriz followed Larry into their bedroom and began looking for a clean shirt for him to put on. Larry closed their bedroom door behind them and looked at his wife, his hands on his hips.

"What's going on?" he asked.

"I don't know. Lucy said she was running late, and I left it at that." She could see that Larry was flustered, but she wasn't sure why. Lucy running late was nothing new.

"No, I mean, what's going on downstairs?"

"What do you mean, what's going on? We're having a little party for Celeste is all. Spur of the moment—I know how you hate that, but I didn't see any reason to wait, especially since everyone was in town from yesterday. Don't you have any clean polo shirts?"

Larry pulled off the sweaty T-shirt he was wearing and stripped off his shorts to take a quick shower, while his wife spoke to him over the sound of the running water.

"I was thinking, I'd love to enroll her in that all-girl's school near where the boys go, but maybe just public school for now," Beatriz said, laying out clean clothes for her husband. "That's probably what she's used to. And I think I should take her for a checkup. The school is going to want to have her current health records before they enroll her. I hope her immunization records are in that envelope she brought."

Beatriz didn't notice that Larry hadn't said a word. When he finished showering, Beatriz was waiting for him, holding out a towel for him to step into, babbling nonstop about how she wanted to redo the guest room—buy new furniture, paint the walls, buy new curtains, and on and on and on. She finally took a breath when Larry sat down on the edge of the bed.

"What are you doing?" he asked.

"What do you mean, what am I doing?"

"Come 'ere," Larry said, holding out his hand to his wife and pulling her to sit on his lap. "Just what do you think is going to happen with her?"

Beatriz was confused. "She's back. It's like she's back," she said, looking into her husband's eyes. "I know it's not Perla, but it might as well be. I see her in Celeste's face." Beatriz thought about what Ana had asked her earlier in the day. "Don't tell me you don't believe she's the real thing?"

"No, she's the real thing all right. I looked at some of the documents she brought. I think she's telling the truth. It's just…"

Beatriz pulled back to get a better look at her husband. "It's just what?"

"Well, Carlos is going away to school this year, and Raúl will be out of the house soon enough. And then, I don't—"

"You don't what?" Beatriz said.

"My nephews...Lucy needs help with her boys. And I want to do my part, but we're supposed to be enjoying our time together."

Beatriz stood up and crossed to the opposite side of the room to lean on the dresser. "You don't want her here?"

Larry didn't answer.

"Larry!"

"I don't know what I want!" he bellowed. "I mean, this is so unexpected! And then today, I see my nephews are out of whack...and Lucy's being Lucy...and how come we didn't talk about this?"

"What is there to talk about? My sister is dead, Larry. The sister who I...the sister who I can only hope forgave me before she died. And if not, the least I can do is take in her girl. And by the way, they're not your nephews, they're *our* nephews. If they need us, we can make room. I don't mind—"

"But I do," Larry said.

"Larry!"

"I want to do what's right, but I also want to spend time with my wife! I bought those tickets to Paris for us! But something's up with Lucy's boys, and I can only take one charity case at a time."

"Paris isn't going anywhere," Beatriz said. "And Celeste is family. She's not a charity case. I'm not turning her out. She doesn't have anyone else."

"That's not true. There's a whole house full of other choices downstairs."

Beatriz and Larry were suddenly and painfully speechless. This tear in their relationship was unexpected, like a weak spot in an otherwise flawless weave of cloth. In spite of what everyone said about them, they were the first ones to say their marriage wasn't perfect. There were scratches and nubs, but nothing that had ever threatened the integrity of their life, their marriage, or the way they assumed the other saw the world. But this thing that had come up between them now was not a small snag that could be darned over quickly. If left untended, it could tear into a longer, wider gash.

"I don't believe you," Beatriz said. "I'm going downstairs. You come down whenever, if you want." She turned on her heel to leave.

"Baby!"

"Don't 'baby' me!" she snapped, turning back to face her husband. "I don't believe this! Where have you been? Your nephews have been a mess for a long time. You're just now noticing? I've been telling you that for how long? But I never said, 'Let's not help them out.' I've always said, 'Let's make room. Let them in.' And now—now, someone on *my* side of the family needs a little help, and you can't be bothered? You're a real piece of work, Larry Milligan. A real piece of work."

She was already out the door before Larry could stop her. She pounded on her boys' bedroom doors and on the bathroom door where Seamus and Wally were cleaning up.

"Ándale!" she bellowed. "The food is getting cold!"

By the time Beatriz got to the bottom of the stairs, it was strangely quiet. The boys tumbled down after her but softened their steps when they sensed the change in atmosphere. Larry tiptoed down a few feet behind them. When they all reached the kitchen, the silence began to make sense. Ana had arrived with the sheet cake and Connie and Sara were helping her decorate it with kiwi fruit and berries at the kitchen table. Norma sat with her arms crossed over her belly, making suggestions but not lifting a finger to help.

"There, there—no! Not like that! Oh, that's better! Que linda! Eso! That's just how I'd do it!" Norma said. Connie and Sara exchanged glances and rolled their eyes. Norma had a way of talking that was as soft and gooey as a marshmallow but felt like a chancla upside the head. She always believed it was her power of persuasion that got people to see things her way, when in fact it was her just wearing them down.

The men watched the activity mutely, each holding a beer, staring at Celeste, who was sitting quietly in the corner, facing them all. She was wearing the dress Beatriz had bought her, and although the kitchen was warm with all the gathered people, she kept the matching sweater on so she could better hide the price tags. If she was careful, she thought, maybe her aunt Beatriz could return the clothes later.

The women were all smiles, murmuring like kittens as they worked. Beatriz's brothers, Celeste's uncles, were standing next to each other, shoulder to shoulder, silent as pillars. Beatriz took up a spot at the end of the lineup and smiled at Celeste. She could see the girl was shocked into silence and didn't understand why until she turned to look at her brothers, wondering who had stolen the tongues of the ordinarily talkative men. When she faced them, she saw their eyes were glassy, their faces soft as clay. Erasmo was the first to pull out his kerchief, breathing into the wadded cloth to silence a sob he could no longer hold back. He turned away as the other brothers stared down at their beers. Beatriz put her hand on her big brother's shoulder.

"Goddamn," Erasmo whispered, as he wiped his swollen eyes. "She looks just like her."

"I know," Beatriz said. "But she's home now! She's come home to us!"

From where he stood just outside the kitchen, Seamus couldn't understand what all the fuss was about. Why were the men standing silent as worn horses? Why did his uncle Larry looked so anxious? Why did his aunt Beatriz looked like she was about to burst out laughing or crying—he couldn't decide which—and why didn't his brother, Wally, seem as worried as he was? When Wally began loading his plate with potato salad, Seamus caught the fiery look in his uncle Larry's eye as he crossed over to him, but then his aunt Beatriz was there, too, whispering that it was all right, handing him tongs to dig into the barbecue she'd just unwrapped, releasing the mouthwatering aroma of smoky charred meat. Not one of the men stirred, which Seamus thought was just plain spooky.

"Go on, go on," Beatriz whispered. "There's plenty. Go ahead. There's nothing fancy going on here. It's just family," she said, pushing past Larry in a way that was too polite to be rude, too abrupt to be unintentional. Seamus didn't know what was going on, but he knew it had everything to do with Celeste. Her appearance had changed everything, and he didn't like it.

"Why don't you boys go ahead and get your plates and go outside?" Beatriz suggested.

"I don't want to go out there," Seamus said. He and the boys had been given those instructions many times before, but this time, the idea of being put out of the house made him angry.

"Do as your aunt says," Larry said, backing up his wife.

"It's okay," Beatriz cooed. "You don't want to go outside? Go in the living room then. Don't make a mess. I just cleaned up in there."

The boys went outside anyway. When Seamus saw that Carlos stayed behind with the adults, he hated that he was sent off like one of the little kids. He decided he needed to take charge of something. Anything. When they got outside, he looked around and insisted they pull out one of the folded tables put away from last night and set it up close to the house.

"Why?" Wally asked, as he sat down to eat on the steps near the patio door. He set his drink cup on the step next to him. Seamus knocked it over with his foot.

"That's why."

"Shay!"

"Stop crying, you big baby!" Seamus barked. "I'll get you another one." The three boys pulled a table near the house, and Seamus made his brother and his cousin Raúl sit with their backs to the house so he could keep an eye on what was going on in the kitchen through the sliding glass door.

Wally dropped his plate onto the table. "What's wrong with you?"

"You!" Seamus said. He passed him his drink cup. "Here."

"She seems fine to me," Raúl said.

"Who?" Wally said.

"Celeste. Our cousin."

"*Your* cousin," Seamus said.

"What's your deal?" Raúl asked.

Seamus tore off a hunk of meat from a pork rib and chewed. "Shut up."

"You shut up. You're the one who's freaking out over her."

Seamus stared down at his food. He didn't think how he was feeling was so obvious.

"You're freaking out over her?" Wally asked.

"No one's talking to you," Seamus snapped. Then he turned to Raúl. "All I want to know is, where did she come from? Who sent her here? And why did she come here?"

"What, do you think she's an alien from another planet?" Raúl laughed. "She's just a girl. She doesn't look like she's going to bother anyone."

"What do you care?" Seamus spat. "You live here. They're not going to get rid of you."

"Huh?" Wally said. He stopped gnawing on his corn on the cob to stare wide-eyed at his brother. "Get rid of who?"

"You got corn on your mouth. Wipe your face," Seamus snapped.

Wally wiped his face with the back of his hand, but only managed to move bits of corn from one side of his mouth to the other. "Get rid of who, Shay?"

"Do it right!" Seamus demanded. He took a napkin and began grinding his brother's face in it.

"Ow, you buttface! Get off me!"

"Hold still!"

When Seamus heard the sound of the screen door being slid open, he stopped what he was doing. Larry and the other uncles stepped out onto the patio, each one holding a plate heaped with meat in one hand, a beer in the other.

"What's going on?" Larry asked suspiciously.

"Nothing," Seamus said, shooting a look at his little brother, who decided to hold his complaint for something bigger.

Larry and the other men walked to the far corner of the yard, pulling up chairs to sit in a circle on the riser. The way they were—stony and silent, alternately looking out into the distance as they chewed, as if gathering their thoughts from the sky and digesting them with their meal—made the boys see that something was being worked out. What that was exactly, the boys didn't know, but they knew to keep their distance.

As Carlos stepped out onto the patio, he was typing a text message into his phone with his thumb. Then he snapped it closed and went to join the men.

"Come here," Raúl called to him.

Carlos moved closer to the boys and sighed an annoyed sigh.

"What's going on?" Raúl asked in a low voice. Seamus noticed that Carlos did not sit down. He set his phone on the table and ate from his plate as he stood over them.

"What's going on?" Raúl asked again.

"He doesn't know," Seamus blurted.

"I know more than you," Carlos said.

"Why are they acting so weird?" Raúl asked.

"Because…" Carlos thought for a moment. "I guess it's like someone came back from the dead to them."

"Like a zombie," Seamus said.

They all looked at Seamus.

"That girl, she's like a zombie or a vampire, here to suck your blood or eat your brains," he said in a spooky voice.

"Shut up!" Wally said, trying not to be scared.

"What the hell are you talking about?" Carlos asked.

"He doesn't like Celeste," Raúl said.

"What? Why?" Carlos said. "You haven't even talked to her."

"He thinks she doesn't belong here," Raúl mumbled through a mouthful of barbecue.

"Well, neither do you, but we let you hang around," Carlos joked, looking at Seamus.

Wally finally got an idea of what his brother was worried about. "You mean she's going to stay here? Forever?"

"That's what it looks like," Carlos answered his little cousin. "Except I think everyone has a different idea of what should happen."

"Everyone who?" Raúl said.

"Them and them," Carlos said, nodding first to the aunts and then to the uncles. "I think 'Amá wants her to stay here."

"Where are we going to stay?" Wally asked.

"At your house," Carlos said.

"But—" Before Wally could say any more, Seamus kicked his little brother under the table. "Ow!" Wally screamed but quickly quieted down when his brother gave him a bloodcurdling look.

"But what?" Carlos asked, but he didn't bother waiting for an answer. His cell phone buzzed, rattling so violently it danced across the table and fell off onto the grass. Wally leaned over to pick it up.

"'WELL?'" he recited from the text written on the screen. "Well what?" he asked.

Carlos snatched the phone from the little boy. "None of your business, hombrecito."

Carlos went to join the men when his father called him over, happy to leave the boys behind.

Raúl surveyed the scene around him and tried to make sense of what was going on, what was not being spoken. Seamus and his anxiety toward this new but otherwise harmless-looking girl didn't make sense to him. Neither did the way the adults weren't talking about something—some unknown, unspoken thing that hung over them, thick as tar. When he looked into the house, the women were giggling and smiling, each one taking turns sitting next to Celeste, leaning in to listen or talk to her. Beatriz brought out the camera and took pictures, one after the next, while the men sat outside, exchanging few words, quietly eating, and nursing their beers.

"Raúl, come help me," Carlos said, as he walked back to the house. "They want some more beer." Raúl did what he was told, happy to get away from his angry cousin. When they got to the refrigerator, Carlos didn't see what he was looking for.

"Hey, 'Amá, where's the beer?"

Beatriz and all the women turned toward Carlos, looked at each other, raised their Shiners, and burst out laughing.

"I guess we need some more," Norma said, all red-faced and shiny. She was sitting at the table across from Elaine with Celeste between them. "Who's good enough to drive?" Norma asked, knowing full well she wasn't going to budge.

"Me!" Elaine said. This only made the women laugh harder. The boys didn't understand what was so funny until Elaine suggested they give her a stick to enable her to drive, since it had been weeks since she could reach the pedals, with her enormous belly full of baby jutting out before her. She softly rubbed her tummy and looked at Celeste.

"If it was a girl, we were going to name her Celeste, after your grandmother," Elaine said. "That's such a pretty name. Isn't that a pretty name?" she asked the women. They all nodded in agreement.

"Thank you," Celeste said politely, picking at a slice of cake someone had served her.

"I wanted to name her after my mother..." But before Elaine could puncture the air with the *P* in Perla, everyone, including Beatriz, looked at her with a silent and harsh *Cállate!* that sucked the air out of the room. Elaine swallowed her tongue and backtracked, acting as if she'd forgotten her own mother's name.

"Qué tienes?" Norma shot at Elaine. Celeste was confused. Norma didn't ask like she was concerned something was wrong with Elaine, but as if she was accusing her of a great offense.

"Nothing! I'm sorry. I'm sorry, the baby just kicked," Elaine lied. She shuddered at the unknown penalty she would endure if she'd broken that one, unspoken family rule: Never mention Perla's name. Even Beatriz didn't know how that rule came into being or when it was understood that she would not be included in talk of old times or mentioned in the family tree. She knew it was wrong—to have Perla's name erased from their tongues, even if she was alive in their memories—but she went along. Her silence was her way of hiding her shame. She didn't know what it meant for the others.

"Do you know what you're having?" Ana asked in an attempt to ease the sudden tension in the room.

"What we all have," Norma blurted before Elaine could speak. "Boys! The last time we had a girl born in this family was with my Angie."

"No! Is that right?" Ana asked.

"It's true. We all have boys," Beatriz said.

"And I'm going to have two," Elaine finally broke in. "So you can see why we're so excited to have another girl in the family." She gave Celeste's shoulder an affectionate squeeze.

"We love our boys, but I miss having another girl in the house," Norma said nostalgically. "My Angie is living in the dorms at UT, and oh, our house is so big and empty these days!"

"Well, we could all go over to your house," Elaine joked. "With my little ones and two more coming, I don't know how I'm going to do it."

"Don't you have a sister who's going to help you?" Norma asked.

"Well, yes. But that's just for a little while," Elaine said. "She has her own family."

"What about your mother?" Norma asked.

"She's got her hands full."

"With what?" Norma challenged. But she didn't wait for Elaine to answer, turning her full attention toward Celeste.

"We live on a ranchito, just outside San Antonio. Mi esposo, your uncle, boards a few horses and I raise chickens and sell eggs and have a nice garden. It's bien pretty. I bet you'd really like it out there, mi'ja," Norma said sweetly.

"Well sure, if you like the smell of chicken poop and horse manure," Elaine cracked.

"It's beautiful," Norma snapped. "A minute ago, you wanted to bring your whole family out there."

Elaine tittered nervously and Norma imitated her with a smarmy grin that bared all her teeth. *Who does she think she's dealing with?* Norma thought.

Beatriz looked around the room and saw that Connie and Sara were tight-lipped but watching what was happening very closely.

"Well," Beatriz began. "It is a lovely place to visit and the perfect place to let a pack of wild children blow off steam."

"Whose wild children?" Elaine asked. "Esos?" She pointed with her chin out the window to Seamus and Wally. Celeste looked around at the women, who, except for Beatriz and Ana, were new to her. She was unsure if the ricocheting tension she felt was real or imagined.

"When are you due?" Ana asked, trying to steer the conversation back to something cheery and light.

"July twelfth, but the sooner the better, if you ask me.

You want to feel?" Elaine asked Celeste, motioning to the huge moon in her lap.

"Really?" Beatriz said. "The twelfth?"

"Why would I make that up?"

"Nobody said you were making anything up. It's just that's the same day as Celeste's birthday, isn't it, mi'ja?"

"Sí," the girl said timidly, unsure of what this news would unleash.

"Verdad?" Norma said, as if Celeste's being born in July was the most amazing thing she'd heard. "And how old will you be, mi'jita?"

"Quince."

"Quince! Quince! Oh! Well, you know what this means?" Norma said grandly. "We need to throw you the biggest, brightest quinceañera we can pull together—in what? A couple of months? Híjole! That's not much time, but we can do it! We pulled my Angie's quinceañera together in about that time, once she finally agreed to have one."

"Not that she had much choice," Raúl heard his aunt Connie whisper to his aunt Sara.

"We had it at the ranchito, and Angie rode in on a white horse. Bien hermosa!" Norma continued.

"Well, that's not necessary," Beatriz broke in.

"Why don't you want her to have a quinceañera?"

"That's not what I said," Beatriz said. "I actually think that's a nice idea, but—"

"Pos, sí!" Norma interrupted. "I think we need to do something more than this last-minute picnic to welcome Celeste to the family, verdad?!" Norma looked around the room. "Verdad?"

"That does sound like fun!" Elaine said, struggling to sit up in her chair against the weight of her incubating babies.

"Wouldn't you like that?" Norma asked Celeste. "Well of course you would," she said before Celeste could consider the question. "Oh, we could plan the whole thing, you and I," Norma said to the girl as if no one else were in the room. "There's a beautiful church not far from our ranchito, and we could have the party at our house—"

"Outside?" Elaine scoffed. "An outdoor party in July will be miserable, and your house is too small for a party."

"No, it's not."

"Well, for a *nice* party," Elaine said as sweetly as she could. Norma ignored her.

"Oh, mi'ja! I would be so honored. And everyone can help—well, except for you," she said to Elaine. "You're going to be too busy with your brand-new babies. But we'll help. All of us! Right?" Norma looked around the room at the other women, who all smiled and nodded as if they knew what was good for them, except for Elaine. She was darting mal de ojos at Norma so hard, you could practically see lightning shooting from her eyes. Norma pretended she was oblivious.

Beatriz couldn't believe what she was seeing. She had brokered deals on behalf of the university with arrogant academics, demanding donors, powerful politicians, and snarky staff members all the time. But witnessing the dueling movidas between Norma and Elaine—in her own house? First Larry and now this? She had no idea the mujeres could be this sneaky, but more important, she couldn't believe she had been blindsided on her own turf. Carlos took the icy silence as his chance to break in.

"'Amá? The beer?"

"Go tell whoever wants beer to go get it themselves," Beatriz said steadily. "I'm not finished here."

By the time Larry left for the beer run, Norma had scrawled some preliminary plans for a quinceañera on a pad she found in Beatriz's kitchen.

"You know," Norma said, very pleased with herself, "Celeste could come stay with us tonight—or even the whole week! Then she can get used to the house and see how the quinceañera would happen."

"Well, she *could*, except I should enroll her in school tomorrow," Beatriz said.

"We have schools," Elaine offered.

"You don't have room," Norma said.

"Yes we do. In the nursery."

"And after the baby is born, then what?" Norma demanded. Elaine bit her tongue. Norma was calling her hand, and she was not ready to reveal it. She was not ready to let Norma win and give up on her idea of having Celeste live with her and Tony to help care for her babies. Her needs were more important than Norma's, Elaine thought. She needed some real help. Norma just wanted company.

"Why don't we ask Celeste what she wants?" Beatriz said. But when the women looked around the room, Celeste was gone.

"She went to change. She's okay," Ana said to the

startled faces staring at her. "Just a little too much excitement."

"Yes, well, it's been a long day. Next time, we'll have to show you the plans we have for redecorating the guest room into Celeste's bedroom," Beatriz said, adding with a sharpened point, "but it's getting late, and you have a long drive, don't you, out to the country?"

Connie and Sara decided they had had enough and went to fetch their husbands. They were happy not to be involved in the fray, and their husbands were more than willing to let Erasmo, Beatriz, and Tony work out whatever was going to happen with Celeste.

When the uncles had finished eating they wandered over to Erasmo's truck, each taking up a spot like men at a boardroom table, their forearms resting on the walls of the truck bed, waiting for the beer and a decision. Carlos went with his father for the beer, and Larry ordered Seamus and Wally to join them so they could be dropped off at their house on the way. Raúl managed to stay behind, escaping to his bedroom to do his homework. Beatriz was in the kitchen wrapping up leftover cake. Norma and Elaine sat at the kitchen table, their arms crossed, each refusing to leave before the other.

"Ya, me voy," Ana whispered to Beatriz at the counter.

"Why? It's still early!"

"I need to get home, 'manita. I've been out all day."

"No! No! I need you! See how they are?" Beatriz hissed. "Like vultures. And she's not talking to me. I need you."

"Who? Celeste?" Ana asked. "She's not saying much

to anyone right now. Remember what I said? I think if you can be quiet long enough, you'll hear what she has to say."

"But she likes you. And what if—what if she hates me?"

"Why would she hate you?" Ana asked.

"I don't know what my sister told her about me," Beatriz finally admitted, avoiding Ana's eyes. Ana couldn't imagine what Beatriz could have possibly done to instill this much fear and remorse.

"You know what," Ana began. "I know this is easy to say now, but I bet whatever you think you did, it probably didn't mean anything to Perla. It was probably a speck. Probably nothing she would even remember, if she were alive."

Beatriz snickered. "Yeah, but those specks have a way of taking on a life of their own, like that one piece of lint on a black cloth. You just got to—"

"Stop driving yourself crazy. Just remember this: Perla sent her daughter here to be with you—not to them. Remember that." Ana looked at her watch. "Ay, mujer. Descúlpame, pero I really got to go. It'll be okay, really. Calm down. You're already doing much better now than you were earlier. Really."

But Beatriz could not calm down, wondering what Celeste knew about her, what she must think, and if she could even hope to make right what she did, those many years ago, when she turned Perla away.

NINE

Raúl finished his homework quickly and decided he
would relax with one of his old movies. Since no one
was around to argue with him, he had his choice: *Destroy
All Monsters, The White Zombie*, or *The Wolf Man*. He
plucked them from the stash in his room and went downstairs to watch them in his father's office, where the big
screen and DVD player were hidden in a large cabinet. He
entered the room without knocking, not noticing Celeste's
things, even as he stepped over her small backpack. As he
opened the cabinet, he kneeled in front of the DVD player,
reading the backs of the crystal cases before finally loading in the movie he liked the best: *The Wolf Man*. He'd
seen it dozens of times, but he never got tired of it. He
looked for the remote under and around the DVD player
where it was supposed to be, and when he couldn't find
it, he sat back on his haunches, wondering if Seamus had
played one of his stupid tricks by hiding it.

"Is this what you're looking for?"

Raúl turned around and saw Celeste. She was standing behind the couch, holding out the remote toward
him. She had changed back into her familiar jeans,
T-shirt, and bright white hoodie zipped up to her neck.
Raúl jumped up.

"I forgot you were in here!"

"It's okay," she said. She laid the remote on the couch and returned to the big chair behind the desk where she was curled up, looking out the window, when Raúl came in. The chair was huge. Raúl remembered that even when his father sat in it, if he were turned, facing the window, you couldn't see him, either. Celeste sat in the chair, pulled her knees up to her chin, and wrapped her arms around her legs. Her abdomen wasn't throbbing as much as before, but with all the new people and the excitement, she was happy to nest in the huge chair, away from it all.

"I can go," he said. "I have a portable DVD player in my room, if you want to rest, or whatever."

"I don't care," she said quietly.

"You like scary movies?" Raúl asked after a moment. He was waiting for her to screw up her face and say no.

"I like the old ones," Celeste said.

"Really?"

"Yeah, really," she said. "They're the best."

"You can watch this one with me, if you want."

She left the chair and moved to the couch, sitting at one end while Raúl sat at the other. The blank screen glowed in silent anticipation until Raúl said what had been on his mind ever since he learned about Celeste.

"So, your mom is dead, huh?" If adults were in the room, they would have scolded Raúl for being blunt, but after what she experienced in the kitchen, the warped tension and unspoken words, Celeste welcomed his directness.

"Yeah."

"Was she sick?"

"She was killed."

"Killed! Wow! That sucks."

"Yeah," Celeste said quietly. "It sucks."

"So, was she, like, in a car accident?"

"Someone killed her," Celeste said.

Raúl's eyes widened. "Do you know who did it?"

"I hope not," she said.

Raúl looked around the room and noticed the small backpack he'd stepped over earlier. "Is that yours?"

"Yeah."

"That's all your stuff?"

"Yeah."

"It's not very big."

Celeste shrugged. She stood up to get the pack, opened one of the pockets, and pulled out a framed photo. It was a picture of Celeste and Perla.

"Is that your mom?" he asked.

"Yeah. Just last year."

"She looks nice," he said.

"She was nice." She wiped the glass with the sleeve of her hoodie and held the photo on her lap, facing Raúl.

"You look like her."

"Thank you."

"So, she was my mom's sister, huh," Raúl said. "We didn't know."

"I didn't know about you, either. Not until a few months ago when she started telling me about your mom and growing up here."

"What was she like?" he asked. "Your mom."

Celeste thought a moment.

"She liked pan dulce on Sunday and popcorn at the

movies. She loved to dance, and she worked too much. She liked parties. And cooking. She made the best tortillas, but I could never make them as good as her. Maybe I will, someday." She paused. "What is she like, La Señora Beatriz?"

"My mom? She's cool," Raúl said, nodding his head. "She's good. She works at the university, where she can boss a lot of people around. Her favorite color is green. She likes parties, and dancing, too. She likes to cook, but we like it when she doesn't."

"How do you eat?"

"Oh, we eat. My dad cooks or takes us someplace, but Carlos is the one who cooks the best around here."

"Quién?"

"Carlos, my brother. The tall one. The oldest of all the boys you saw. He's nineteen. He's going to go to cooking school out East, except my mom and dad don't know yet." Raúl said the last part like it was a juicy piece of gossip.

"How come you know?"

"I'm not supposed to know," Raúl said. "I found out by accident. But don't tell anyone. You're not going to tell anyone, are you?"

"Who am I going to tell?" Even though she'd just met a roomful of relatives, she couldn't think of a single person she would tell this secret to, even if she wanted to. "Cooking school," she repeated. "They'll teach him how to run a restaurant?"

"I guess, but mostly how to cook fancy dinners. And his girlfriend, she wants to be a pastry chef. I don't think my dad is going to like it," Raúl said, shaking his head.

Celeste turned the photo so she could look at it.

"So, you're going to live here?" Raúl asked. "Once Carlos leaves there will be an extra room."

"I live in El Paso," Celeste said, slipping the photo back into her backpack.

The neglected DVD player clicked loudly before turning itself off, reminding the kids of what they were originally going to do.

"You still wanna watch the movie?" Raúl asked.

"I'd rather go out there," she said, turning around to look out the window, where she had been gazing at the jacaranda tree. "I need some fresh air."

"Okay." A new idea came to Raúl. "Wait here and I'll be right back."

Raúl was excited as he ran out and up to his room. For once, he didn't have to beg and whine or plead with someone about watching his favorite movies. *What is Seamus worried about?* he thought. *Celeste is pretty cool, for a girl.*

Josie opened her last pack of cigarettes as she passed Comfort, Texas. Although she was exhausted, dying to lie down, and smothered with guilt about not seeing her daughter, she was determined to get to San Antonio. She had to. And besides, if she understood what was said while cleaning Perla's house in El Paso, she had no choice.

She knew it was crazy—driving with no idea where she was going, or any notion of how to find Celeste. That was not how she usually worked, but her desire to make things right was so compelling, she knew she had to follow her hunches and hope that everything else fell into place. If only she could remember where had she put those notes about Perla and her family. She knew she had them somewhere. Perla shared very little about her personal life, and the few things Josie knew, she'd gathered surreptitiously—small clues dropped along the way when they were discussing something else. Josie tucked those tiny bits of information into the margins of her memory, scrawling them down or tapping them wildly into her laptop. When she couldn't locate the notes on her computer, she looked through her handwritten notes but couldn't find them there, either. She was beginning to worry that her exhaustion was affecting her ability to keep things straight, and if she couldn't do that, she couldn't work, and if she couldn't work...

Josie began to panic. *Relax,* she told herself. She concentrated on the whir of her car flying down the highway, hoping the sound would calm her and help clear the clutter from her sleep-deprived mind long enough to help the information that she knew was lurking in the background come into the light.

Instead, she found herself remembering when she helped clear Perla's house. The women who'd gathered to do that sad work only allowed her in reluctantly. She was considered an outsider. Perla apparently hadn't told anyone that she and Josie had become friends, and learning that had hurt Josie more than she would admit. The mujeres—Perla's coworkers, other community organizers, and women who had known Perla much longer than Josie—were polite enough. When Josie showed up, they offered her coffee and pan dulce and let her listen to their memories of Perla, shared as they swept the last of her things into three drab garbage bags: one for the St. Vincent De Paul, one for the trash, and one for the few remaining items to be divided among those assembled at the house. The items of value were things that would mean something only to the person who claimed them: a nearly new broom, a calendar from a local Mexican restaurant, a children's coloring book, a lavender pen. When Josie asked where Celeste had been sent, the women merely shrugged or muttered, "No sé," and carried on with their work. But Josie knew they were lying. Someone must know where Perla's girl was. She tried to press for an answer, asking one of the younger women in the house. The woman consulted the eldest woman in the room, who looked at Josie over her shoulder and shook her head, making a slight wave of her hand in the air that simply but pointedly said, *Ya, mujer. This does not involve you.* The young woman smiled meekly at Josie and stayed near the old woman so Josie would not ask her again.

It was Josie who had found the quinceañera book among Perla's things. No one had argued with her when she refused to put it into the trash bag. No one had fought her for it; no one had even comforted her when she began to weep, her hands lightly grazing the cover. When Josie had collected herself, she announced to the assembled women that she was going to make sure the book was returned to Celeste, whether they helped her or not. The young woman began to say something, but the elder sharply shushed her, making the woman's head collapse into her neck like a turtle as she looked furtively among the others, then turned to go back to work. No one spoke when Josie left the house with the book. But as soon as she passed the threshold, Josie could hear the hissing back and forth in Spanish. They thought she wouldn't understand them:

"Was that a good idea?"

"N'ombre! We should go after her!"

"That book doesn't belong to her! What's she going to do with it?"

"Shh! She's going to hear you! She's right there."

"Ay, qué no! She won't understand. No one understands what's going on here."

"Ya! Let her take it!" the elder barked, making the other voices fall silent. "If she does what she says she's going to do and returns the book to la muchacha, then God bless her. If not, then may all the angels and the saints, and la Virgencita herself hound her until she loses her mind. Bueno, I need a new comal. Anyone mind if I take this one?"

The memory brought the pain back fresh for Josie, and she wiped the tears from her eyes before they had a chance to escape down her cheeks. She had tried not to let the women hurt her feelings—tried not to let *anyone* hurt her—but they had. No one seemed to remember that Josie was at the morgue to witness the grim business of identifying Perla's remains. No one seemed to appreciate how hard she was working to keep it together, to be brave, to do her job, to stay out of the way, observe at a respectful distance. She remembered seeing many of the women in the house hovering over Celeste at the morgue, keeping her away from all unnecessary people, including Josie. She remembered looking at Celeste, sitting there like a flower growing in the fissures of broken concrete, looking small and alone. It was the most heart-wrenching thing she'd witnessed, among many, many, many heart-wrenching things. But Josie steeled herself, walked over to Celeste, and offered her hand and her condolences to the girl. Celeste took Josie's hand numbly. She thanked her politely, but mechanically, not really seeing her. Josie couldn't believe how brave the girl seemed until she remembered whose child she was. Afterward, Josie walked stiffly out of the building and into her car, where the tears overtook her and she sobbed inconsolably.

Josie always told herself that her job was to gather the facts, tell the story. If she did her job well, then the crying would be left to someone else as they drank their morning coffee or took the train to their safe jobs with pensions—or at least health and dental—which was much more than women like Perla could ever hope for. But since Perla's death, maintaining such stoicism had been impossible.

Josie gripped the steering wheel tighter. *Think! Think!* she screamed at herself. What did she know? She knew Perla's last name was Sánchez. But there must be thousands of Sánchezes in San Antonio. Where would she start? She remembered something about King William's Columns—a family stone-making business? She knew there was another name, and it was...Josie tried to summon the name to her lips, but it wouldn't come. Frustrated, she pulled off the highway and into a Dairy Queen, driving to the far end of the parking lot. She jumped out of her car without turning off the ignition and got into the backseat, where she began digging though her boxes, sifting through clippings, maps, notes, all the research material she'd collected for her book. When she came up with nothing, she unpacked her laptop, fired it up, and launched a search. Still nothing. She slapped the laptop shut and returned to the front seat, slamming the door loudly. She turned off the ignition and sat there a moment, frustrated. She needed a cigarette, but only the crumpled remains of the empty packs were left. She began to pick through her ashtray until she found a cigarette extinguished too soon, lit it, and began to think.

King William's Columns...King William's Columns. Nothing else came to her. She leaned her head back and closed her eyes. She tried to relax when the other worry came lurking back to her: *You have a girl here who needs her mother. I'm doing what I can to help you, but if she stops asking about you...*

Her mother's words still stung her. But it wasn't the first time she'd heard them. Paz was five when Josie made a deal with Rita to take her little girl, when she was accepted to an exclusive, yearlong writing fellowship in Boston. Josie knew it was a once-in-a-lifetime opportunity but didn't know how it would be possible with a child to raise. She was resigned to turning down the fellowship when Rita stepped in. Her mother had sat her down at the rinsing station of her beauty shop after closing one night and handed Josie a Shiner from the kitchen. She spoke while standing in the door frame.

"They say women can't have it all, but you're sure as hell going to try," Rita began. "If you were my son, no one would say nothing. They might talk about you leaving your little girl behind, but not to your face, and not to me, so y qué? I don't understand everything about your work, but if they pay and it's honest work, I'll help you. What I *do* know is that children need stability, and if you have to run around to get your life going, I would rather you leave her with me than with strangers." Her mother paused and took a swig of her beer before continuing. "Your aunt Chata said she would help. I'll do it for a year. One year. You hear me?" Rita finished off the rest of her beer in one long gulp before she pointed the bottle toward her daughter's astonished face and said, "But if she stops asking about you, you can't blame me. Entiendes?"

Josie nodded numbly, realizing the gift her mother was offering her and the risk she might be taking.

"Now, let me do something with that hair," Rita had said, dropping the empty beer bottle with a clank into a bin near her. "You can't go out into the world looking like that!"

It had been seven years since they had that talk. Josie was feeling the distressing push-pull of wanting to be a good mother while not wanting to let all the opportunities that had come her way pass her by. If she could get her career going, she and Paz could have a good life. If things went really, really well, she might even be able to take care of her mother and her aunt Chata, too. Rita could end her twelve-hour days in the shop and retire. She was only doing what she had to do, to make a better life for her and her child, wasn't she? Josie wasn't always so sure anymore.

A sudden tapping on the window startled Josie so much, she dropped her cigarette. Frantically she searched for it between the seats as the tapping continued.

"Ma'am? Ma'am!"

When Josie finally found her cigarette and made sure it hadn't set her upholstery on fire, she looked out the window. The manager from the Dairy Queen was standing outside the car looking in at Josie through the windshield.

"Ma'am!" the woman said again, motioning for Josie to roll down her window. The stale cigarette smoke that billowed from Josie's car made the woman wrinkle her nose. "Are you waiting on an order?" she asked.

"No."

"Are you high?"

"What?"

"I'm telling you straight up, I'm fixin' to call the police if you're high."

"No, I just pulled off to look for something," Josie explained.

"Well, we reserve these spots for people who are waitin' on drive-thru orders."

"I'm sorry. I just needed to look—"

"Well, you might-could find a rest stop up the road a piece, and I think there's a couple of hotels east of here. But I can't have y'all sittin' out here. People get the wrong idea when they see someone like you out here, and we run a family business."

"Well, so much for Southern hospitality," Josie sneered under her breath, but the woman heard her.

"Oh, honey. You're not in the South. You're in Texas. Now, how 'bout I bring y'all a cup a coffee for the road?"

Josie turned the key in her ignition, then looked at the manager's name tag. "Oh, that's okay, Miss Miller…"

Josie felt as if she'd been hit with a giant cartoon mallet. "Milligan! Milligan! It's Milligan! Oh, my gato!" Josie screamed then broke into wild laughter. The manager jumped back from the car.

"Oh! I could kiss you, Miss Milligan!"

"Miller!"

"Whatever! I'll be getting along, now! Thank you, thank you, thank you so much!" Josie crowed. She was elated as she pulled back then squealed off and away onto the frontage road.

"Y'all don't come back," the manager said, watching Josie's car merge onto the interstate. She couldn't be sure, but the manager thought the last thing she heard from Josie was a piercing, gleefully sustained "Ajua!"

TEN

The phone was ringing when Larry and his nephews entered Lucy's apartment. Seamus went to answer the phone but his uncle got to it first.

"Hello?" Larry said, and then, in a more exasperated tone, "Where the hell are you?...I've been calling you on your cell phone for the last hour...Didn't I just get you a new charger?...I don't care what Beatriz told you, you told *me* you were picking up the boys at three-thirty. Three-thirty, Lucy!...That's not the point!"

Seamus ushered his brother to their bedroom to unpack their things.

"Don't say anything," Seamus said to his brother.

"But—"

"I mean it!"

The two of them listened to their uncle's side of the conversation from their bedroom.

"Well, where the hell are you?...I said, where the hell *are* you?! We're already here...At your place, where else?...Okay...okay...Okay, Lucy!...Good!" Larry slammed down the receiver. "Jesus!" he said, before he turned around to look for his nephews. They had been slyly watching him from the door frame of their room and scurried back to unpacking when their uncle turned to find them.

"Boys!" he called. He went to their room when they didn't answer. The boys were folding their clothes, neatly placing them in their hamper, when their uncle found them. "What are you doing?"

"Putting stuff away," Seamus said.

"You're folding your dirty clothes?" Larry asked, running his hand through his hair, trying to calm down. "Your mom said she'll be here in ten minutes."

"Okay," Seamus said.

Larry stood in the door watching the boys.

"You don't need to fold your dirty clothes," Larry said, noticing a pair of the boys' briefs that had obviously been washed with something red.

"Told you," Wally said.

"Let me show you how to sort clothes so you don't turn your underwear pink again." Larry began pulling out the clothes and throwing them into piles while the boys watched.

"Look, I don't want you to think we don't want you at the house. It's just that things are different right now. We have to work things out."

"I know," Seamus said. He was focused on the "things are different" comment, thinking about Celeste, and that because of her, things were worse than different. They were turned upside down and inside out like his brother's pants.

"When is she leaving?" Seamus asked.

"I don't know," Larry said, throwing a navy blue T-shirt

onto a pair of jeans. "I don't know. But until we figure out what's going to happen, you're going to be spending more time here, okay?" The boys nodded. "There!" Larry said, satisfied with his work. "Now you know how to do this. Like goes with like. See? Things like this help your mother, so remember, okay?"

"Okay," the boys said in unison. Larry walked back into the living room and looked around. The apartment was neat, the dishes were washed, and he even saw marks on the carpet from a recent vacuuming. Maybe his sister *was* doing her best.

"You don't have to wait," Seamus said. Wally pulled at his brother's arm and Seamus batted his hand away, but Larry didn't notice. He was still looking around the apartment. The house was neat but covered with a thick layer of dust.

Okay. Maybe she's not the best housekeeper, but the place is presentable, he thought.

"Well," Larry began, "you sure you're going to be okay if I take off now?"

"We're not babies," Seamus insisted.

"No roughhousing or acting stupid, okay?" Larry was moving into the kitchen, and Seamus was willing his uncle not to open the refrigerator or cupboards. Unlike the cupboards at his aunt and uncle's house, theirs were filled with random things like minced ham, dry pasta, a bottle of capers, and a small tin of cat food their mother bought when she found a stray cat in the parking lot. Seamus set the cat free when he got tired of it peeing in his shoes. Larry stopped checking out the apartment when his cell phone chirped.

"Yeah, son. I'm coming right out," Larry said as he slapped his phone closed and looked at his nephews. "I can trust you not to set the place on fire?" he asked.

"Yes," Seamus said, retrieving his math book and setting it on the table as if he were going to study.

"Do you need help?" Larry asked.

"No, I'm almost done."

"I need some help," Wally said.

"No, you don't," Seamus snapped, and then to his uncle: "I can help him. His math is easy."

"No, it's not!"

When they heard the sound of keys jangling outside the door, they all turned their attention to it. Lucy came into the apartment with a pizza box and a bottle of soda. She dumped her huge purse on the floor, and Seamus noticed that it was deflated. Not a good sign.

"Pizza!" Wally exclaimed, as he ran to his mother.

"Hi, baby. Put this on the table and get some plates and napkins. Seamus, go get some cups with ice." She and Larry exchanged icy glances.

"And forks!" she called to the boys in the kitchen. She took a deep breath, dropped onto the couch, and put her feet up on the coffee table.

"The boys just ate," Larry reported.

"Well, good. The pizza will keep," Lucy said. She dropped her head over the back of the couch.

"I'll see you guys later," Larry called to the boys. "Bye," he said stiffly to his sister.

"What? No lecture?" she asked.

"You want one?"

"Not really. You can go. I'm here. Happy?"

"Yes, as a matter of fact, I am."

"You know, it takes a village to raise a kid," Lucy said.

"I'm not going to get into this with you right now," Larry said, as he opened the door.

"Fine."

"Fine."

"Mom! You want some Diet Coke?" Seamus called from the kitchen.

"Yes!" she answered.

"Okay, boys, see you. Be good. Don't be bad," Larry warned, as he left the apartment.

As he walked back to his car, Larry felt confident that everything was under control at his sister's house. He felt as if he'd done his part to get Lucy back in line. If only he could be as sure about things back home. He wondered when he and Beatriz would be able to continue their discussion from earlier. He'd already given up hope that there would be any lovemaking. He knew he had said what he had to say, but now wished he'd phrased the part about Celeste differently. He wished he hadn't caused the pained expression on his wife's face. But most of all, he wished he didn't feel the way he felt about Celeste coming into their lives.

Seamus and Wally set the table—three plates, three napkins, three forks—and sat down to eat.

"It's ready!" Wally announced from the table. Lucy stood, picked up her purse, and went into her bedroom. Seamus's stomach lurched.

"Mom!" he called. "What are you doing?"

"Go ahead and eat if you want!"

Seamus got up from the table and went to his mother's room. Larry hadn't bothered to go in there, but if he had, he would have seen it was a disaster area: an unmade bed, clothes drooling out of dresser drawers, and the small desk her brother handed down to her, thick with junk mail—all piled over the textbooks Larry helped her buy when she enrolled at San Antonio Community College. As Seamus suspected, Lucy was stuffing another change of clothes into her huge purse.

"What are you doing?" Seamus asked.

"I'm just getting a few things. I'm going to stay over-night with my friend," she said. Seamus clenched his jaw. Lucy left a drawer empty when she grabbed a wad of clean underwear and threw it in her bag, then went to her clothes hamper and pawed through it. When she found the other uniform she was looking for, she sniffed it and threw it over her shoulder and started to leave the room, but Seamus was blocking her way.

"Excuse me." He didn't move. "Seamus!"

He stood a moment before sluggishly moving out of her way. When she passed through the apartment to the kitchen, she saw Wally sitting at the table, his hands wedged under his knees. He had opened the pizza box and placed one slice on each of the three plates. He was waiting, even though every instinct of his seven-year-old body was straining to dive in.

"I gave you a piece with lots of pepperonis," he said proudly to his mother.

"Oh, honey, I'm not hungry," Lucy said. She opened an

accordion door in the kitchen that hid a stacked washer-and-dryer unit, threw her uniform in the dryer, and set it on fluff.

"You guys go ahead and eat, if you want," she said, looking at her watch. She dug into her purse for her makeup bag and sat down at the table to reapply lipstick, then touched up her mascara, looking in a compact mirror. The boys watched her mutely.

"Sit down, Seamus," she said, as she used her pinkie finger to clean the edges of her lips. When the boy did not move, she snapped her compact shut and threw it back in her makeup bag. "Stop looking at me like that!" she ordered. "Go ahead and eat, baby," she said to Wally. "It's getting cold." She took a sip of her soda. "Pizza is best when it's hot, but I love it for breakfast, too. So, don't eat it all and you can have it for breakfast tomorrow morning," she said.

"Cold pizza sucks," Seamus snarled.

"We have a microwave." Lucy said. "I know you know how to use it."

"Don't you like us anymore?" Wally whimpered. Tears were rolling down his cheeks.

"What? Are you crazy?" Lucy said. "Why would you say such a crazy thing?"

"Because you're never here," Seamus said. She ignored her older son and tried to comfort Wally.

"Come here, baby." Wally got up and flopped into his mother's lap. "Oh! You're such a big boy!" she groaned. "Such a big boy!" She lifted his chin so she could look into his watery eyes. "Why are you asking me such silly questions? I love you like crazy," she said. "I'm going to stay with my friend tonight, and you guys are such big boys now, I know you'll be fine, right? I didn't know your aunt and uncle were going to change their plans on me."

"When are you coming back?" Wally sniffed.

"I'll be back, silly! Don't be so frowny or you'll end up with a sour face like your brother over there," she joked. Wally laughed, only because his mother tickled him behind his ear. "Okay?" she asked, and repeated louder when neither of them answered, "Okay?"

"Okay," Wally whispered, sliding off his mother's lap and sitting back in his chair. Lucy got up to pull her uniform from the dryer then balled it up and stuffed it in her purse.

"It's going to wrinkle," Seamus said.

"It's polyester. It's fine."

Seamus crossed to the table and fell into his chair with his arms tightly folded across his chest.

"Okay, so you've got pizza and plenty of soda. I'll be back," Lucy said.

"When?" Seamus asked.

"Before you know it!" she said. And before Wally could get teary-eyed again, she had her keys in her hand and was at the door. "Remember what I told you?" she warned. They kept their eyes on their pizza, refusing to look at her. "Remember?"

"Yeah," they finally answered.

"I've got my cell phone and I've got my charger this time," she said, holding it up.

The boys' silence sucked the air from the room.

"Jesus! You act like I'm going off to war or something. I'll call you night-night later!"

Maybe she would. Maybe. But Seamus was prepared

to lie to his little brother—to tell him that he was asleep when their mother called, and she told Seamus not to wake him up, or better yet, that he couldn't wake him up. Wally would call him a liar and punch him and Seamus would work hard not to punch him back. Maybe he would or maybe he wouldn't. But he would try.

Lucy was out the door before the boys could ask any more questions. The buzz from the dryer's alarm punched a hole in the silence, and Wally began to whine.

"What if she doesn't come back?" Wally asked his big brother.

"She'll come back. She still has clothes here," Seamus said.

"Why can't we tell Uncle Larry? I bet he'd let us sleep over there."

"Because she said not to," Seamus said, but the words didn't sound right to him.

"I don't like it when she's not here!"

"I know, but we'll be okay. Besides, with that girl over there, they..."

"They what?"

Seamus was flustered. He didn't know what life was going to be like with Celeste around. All he knew was that the attention over her made him feel like a stray dog that no one wanted to take in.

"We don't need them," Seamus said.

"I'm going to tell."

"No, you're not," Seamus warned.

"I don't want to be here alone!"

"You're not alone. I'm here, aren't I? You don't want to be a Wednesday's Child, do you?" Seamus asked.

"No!"

"Well, then, you better not say anything."

"Wednesday's Child" was a segment carried on one of the local news channels where an orphan was showcased in hopes of "finding a family of their very own." Seamus used to make fun of how the kids looked like puppy dogs, always on their best behavior, well scrubbed, and in their best clothes, their tails practically wagging. The backstory on their parents was always explained in shorthand with terms like *substance abuse*, *incarcerated,* or more plainly, *abandoned*. When Wally acted up, Seamus warned him: "You better be good or else you're going to be a Wednesday's Child."

"What about you?" Wally asked.

"I can take care of myself, but you're young enough that they'll take you away and we'll never see you again," Seamus said.

"Shut up!" Wally said. "I'll go live with Aunt Beatriz and Uncle Larry! I'm too little to be a Wednesday's Child." The featured kids were usually Seamus's age, the older, less cuddly kids, but the ones in most desperate need. "And anyway, she hasn't done anything bad," Wally added, convinced that since Lucy hadn't beat them, robbed a bank, or sold drugs, she hadn't broken any laws. But Seamus knew better. He didn't want her to get in trouble—maybe even go to jail. He couldn't live with that. But her leaving them alone and making them keep it a secret, that chipped and chipped and chipped away at him so much it was starting to cut near the bone.

It had been fun the first few times Lucy left her boys alone. Seamus had been twelve. It was only for a day, but he was relieved when his mother finally came home at sundown. The next time, it was overnight, and lately she had been gone for whole weekends. Lucy usually asked Beatriz and Larry to keep her boys, saying she had to work or study, and at first, that was true. But when it didn't work out for one reason or another, instead of changing her plans, Lucy left the boys, stocking them up with pizza and cold cereal, telling them that nobody, and especially their aunt and uncle, needed to know. They were big boys and it was their private business. Seamus was put in charge, and he liked that he could decide if it was okay to have popcorn and soda for dinner or donuts and Halloween candy for breakfast. They liked hanging out with their cousins, but at home, no one was around to make them go to bed at ten, or take a bath, or do chores, wear clean underwear—or any underwear at all! But after a few more times, even if he wouldn't admit it, Seamus liked not always having to be in charge and welcomed the presence of adults. In time, he thought, maybe his aunt and uncle would get so used to having them around so much that it would make all the sense in the world for them to move in, like they'd always been there to begin with. Like they belonged. But that was before Celeste. Seamus didn't know what was going to happen with her around. And the fact that his uncle didn't know either made him decide that the best thing to do—the only thing to do—was to take charge, be the big brother, and try and keep things as normal as possible. It was their secret. He needed to protect his little brother, and even though he was upset with his mother, he needed to protect her, too.

"Look, would you like it if Mom goes to jail?" Seamus asked.

"No!" Wally wailed.

"Then keep your mouth shut!"

"I can sleep in Uncle Larry's garage!" Wally said. "I have a sleeping bag!"

"Shut up! No one is going to sleep in a garage anywhere, and stop asking me questions! If you want to be a Wednesday's Child, go call Uncle Larry, but if you want to stay here and not have Mom go to jail, then you better listen to me," Seamus said. The distress on his little brother's face made him angry and heartbroken at once, and it confused him. There was something inside Seamus that wanted to punch his little brother in the face to stop the roaring emotions inside, but something else that wanted, above everything else, to be held. He fought off his own tears, and his face turned red and rigid.

"What's the matter?" Wally finally asked, blinking through his tears and wiping the snot from his nose with the back of his hand.

"Use your napkin," Seamus said. The little boy picked up the paper napkin he'd carefully folded in half when he set the table and wiped his nose with it.

"Blow," Seamus said. Wally blew his nose, shooting a wad of mucus into the napkin. He took a deep breath to blow again, this time making a honking noise. He giggled and did it again. This time the honking noise was deeper and louder, like flatulence.

"Now you know why I call you fart-face," Seamus said with a smirk. Wally blew his nose again, this time making a high squeaking noise that surprised them both. The two boys laughed until their bellies ached.

"Okay, okay. That's enough," Seamus said. His brother acting like a dork eased his anger and confusion for the moment. "If you don't eat your pizza, I'm going to put it away. We can eat it tomorrow, like she said." Seamus could feel his anger subsiding as he began to be a big brother to Wally, not in a bossy way but in the caring way he was capable of when no one was looking. "Later, you're going to take a shower. I'll wash some clothes after you finish so you'll have something to wear to school."

"Can you wash my Spurs T-shirt?" Wally asked, picking an onion off his pizza and putting it on the table. Why their mother couldn't remember that they didn't like onions, Seamus didn't know. What he did know was that it was up to him to make sure he and his brother got through the night and off to school the next day. Maybe Celeste wouldn't stay very long. Maybe she was just passing through. He didn't know the answer to that question any more than he knew when their mother would return or if, and when, he should stop keeping their secret.

"I know, Mari! I know," Carlos said. Marisol had called him on his cell phone while he was waiting for his father in the car. And once again, the topic of conversation turned to their plans for school.

"But you're going to tell them today, though, right?" she asked.

"I don't know."

"Carlos!"

"I'll try! Things are weird here with my cousin showing up. Everyone is freaking out over her, even my mom."

"Well, you need to tell them about our plans, but more importantly, you need to find out if they will help you with the tuition, since you're not going to Michigan. If they're not going to help you, we need to figure out what to do," Marisol said.

"I know, I know! I'm going to tell them. I promise. But the time has to be right."

Marisol was irritated, and Carlos didn't blame her. They had been talking about their plans to go to culinary school together for a year, and he'd just mustered up the courage to tell his father what he wanted to do when Celeste fell into their lives.

"Did you change your mind? Do you not want to go? Is that it?" Marisol asked, fearing the worst.

"No! That's not it at all! It's just that—man, I think I need a flowchart to explain what's been going on around here," Carlos sighed. "And you know how my dad is. You know how he's been about me going to his old stomping grounds. It's all he's talked about since I was a kid. He's not going to like this news. He might even disown me."

Marisol knew that this was ridiculous, but she also knew that this was Carlos's greatest fear.

"Honestly, I don't see that happening. I just don't," she said. "I know you don't want to disappoint him, but you can't go to school up there and try and become something you're not just to make him happy. It's your life, or it should be."

Carlos had a miserable thought. "Maybe you should go without me," he said.

There was a long pause on the other end of the phone. "Is that what you—"

"No!" Carlos said before Marisol even finished asking the question. The idea of Marisol leaving him made every part of him ache.

"Well then, you need to step up, baby cakes."

"Okay, okay. I'll come over later. I got to go. He's coming back." Carlos ended his call and tried to gauge his father's mood by the speed of his walk and the expression on his face.

Larry climbed back into the SUV, started the engine, and headed home. Carlos could see his father was distracted but didn't know when he'd have another private moment with him.

"So...Marisol...," Carlos said after they drove a few blocks in silence. "She really brought it yesterday, huh?"

"Who?"

"Marisol, Dad. My girlfriend? The one who made the cake?"

"Oh, yeah. Sure. What about her?"

"She made the Eiffel Tower cake, just like you wanted it."

"Actually, it was better than I expected," Larry said glibly. "Did someone help her?"

"No. That was all her!" Carlos said. "She assembled it and did the spun sugar netting at the house."

"That's pretty fancy stuff for a girl who makes pan dulce and those little brown pigs—what are they called?" Larry asked.

"Marranitos."

"Yeah, those. I love those."

"She's the one that makes them at the bakery," Carlos said, thinking that somehow this information would make his father like Marisol more.

"Well, good for her," Larry said. "So, you think she's going to take over her family's bakery someday?"

"No, I don't think so." *This is my in,* Carlos thought. *This is it!* But Larry had more to say.

"You know, going away to college is a big change, son. You're going to meet a whole new group of people, and things will look a lot different when you come back here to visit. It might be a good idea not to, well—you know—not to settle for a girl here. You're going to meet a whole new class of girls at school. You understand?"

Carlos understood, but he didn't like what he thought his father was saying. "Don't you and 'Amá both come from here?"

"Well, yeah, but we didn't meet here. We met at school. It was just a crazy coincidence that we were both from here. Sort of. I mean, I lived on one side of the river and she lived on the other."

"But you're both from here," Carlos repeated.

"Yeah. What's your point?"

"What's *your* point?" Carlos said. He could tell he was getting defensive.

"Look, son. I know you like this girl, but I think anyone who wants to make cookies for a living is probably not, well, someone that will keep your interest for too long. I mean, don't get me wrong. Marisa is a lovely girl and all, but—I just think you should keep your options open."

"Her name is Marisol, and I don't think that's going to happen," Carlos said.

"Oh, you say that now, but trust me," Larry chuckled. "You'll go off to Michigan and the world will seem like a whole different place."

"That's not going to happen, either," Carlos said. "I'm not going to Ann Arbor. I'm going to become a professional chef, and Marisol wants to be a professional pastry chef. We're going to culinary school in Vermont. Both of us. Together."

Larry pulled his SUV to the curb. "You're what?"

"We're going to culinary school, out East. Marisol and I."

"Let me get this straight," Larry began. "Instead of being an engineer or an educator—you could be an educator, or an administrator like your mom, there's nothing wrong with that—you want to be a cook for the rest of your life?"

"No, Dad. I want to be a chef. You want me to be an engineer. You want me to go to Michigan. But that's not what I want. I want to be with Marisol."

Larry turned off the car. The longer he was quiet, the more anxious Carlos got. After a moment, Larry started the car again and began driving.

"We'll talk about this with your mother when we get home."

At least the subject was now out in the open, Carlos thought. He was relieved but disappointed. How could his father not see what he saw in Marisol?

When they pulled up to the house, Erasmo and Norma were getting into their truck and Tony was helping Elaine waddle down the drive toward their car.

"I just got the beer! You're leaving already?" Larry asked with mock disappointment. He was happy to see them leave, even as he was unsure of what was waiting for him inside his house.

"We'll be back!" Norma sang. "You can count on it. I'm not giving up that easy. This isn't over yet." Larry had no idea what she was talking about but smiled back at her.

"Ya, mujer," Erasmo growled, slamming her door closed after she barely pulled her leg into the cab.

"Oye," Erasmo called to Larry. The two men staked themselves on the curb. "Look," Erasmo began in a low voice. "Norma has her ideas about what should happen to Celeste, and Beatriz has hers. Can you get Beatriz to, you know, see it our way?"

"And what's that?" Larry asked.

"Norma wants the girl to stay with us."

Larry couldn't have asked for better news. Erasmo leaned in to speak to Larry conspiratorially.

"She's lonely, and to tell you the truth, she's driving me crazy. We have the room."

"That's what I thought," Larry said with relief. "You know, I think that's a great idea. But what about them?" he said, looking over at Tony and Elaine, who were watching Erasmo and Larry with curiosity. "What do they have to do with this?"

"Pobrecita," Erasmo said, flashing a toothy smile and an upturn of his chin at Elaine. "She's no match for our women, and Tony will do whatever we tell him. It's up to us to get Beatriz and Norma on the same page, entiendes?"

Larry understood so well he almost danced a merry little jig.

"I got your back, so make Beatriz see it's the best for everyone involved for Celeste to come live with us," he said. The blare from Erasmo's truck horn shook them from their deal making, and when they turned to look, Norma was leaning over from the passenger seat, ready to give it another blast.

"Ya, mujer! I'm coming!"

The two men shook hands and Larry stood on his lawn, watching Erasmo and Tony drive off with their wives, satisfied that things were going to work out just the way he wanted.

ELEVEN

As Larry walked back into the house, he inhaled the quiet. He was still worried about what was going on with his sister and his nephews, and he was definitely not thrilled about what Carlos just told him, but somehow, with Erasmo's unexpected blessing, he felt as if he were all powerful, like all he had to do was flex his muscles, wave his hand, and stand extra tall, and things would work out the way he wanted, the way they were supposed to.

Beatriz was in the kitchen, wrapping up the leftover food while Carlos was putting the beer into the refrigerator. Larry took one of the beers from his son and opened it.

"I'll take one," Beatriz said. Carlos opened a bottle and poured it into a glass for her. "Thank you, son. Do you mind?" she said sweetly, nodding toward the door.

"But," he began, "shouldn't I stay?"

"No, no. I need to have a talk with your father."

Carlos was out of the kitchen before the foam shrank in his mother's beer glass. He was glad to be out of the line of fire. Marisol wouldn't be happy that he scuttled out like a startled rabbit, but he knew that when his parents were going to have one of their talks, it was best to keep a distance until it was all over. It wasn't the shouting that got to him or his brother. In fact, they rarely raised their voices. Instead, it was a peculiar tension that rang on a frequency that he was sure only they and dogs could hear. It made him and his brother squirm.

"Where's Raúl?" Larry asked. Beatriz nodded out the patio door. When he looked out into the yard, he saw his son and Celeste lounging on a sleeping bag laid out on the riser, staring into his portable DVD player. "I told him not to take that thing outside. It can get water damaged."

"It's not raining, Larry."

"But it's not made for outdoor use. That's how things get ruined."

Beatriz grinned. Her husband could be chocante to a fault sometimes. His prudence was one of the traits she admired most of the time. She found it amusing when he got tied up in knots and felt driven to play fire marshal, but when he crossed the line and climbed up on his high horse, he needed to be helped back down to the ground. Because she loved him, she tried to ease him down gently, but it wasn't beyond her ability to knock him down flat.

"Oh, Larry. Leave it alone." She sat at the kitchen table so she could see the kids in the yard then turned toward her husband. "So, let's talk."

Larry was going to join her at the table but decided he would stand—a power position, standing over her. *The man of the house*, he thought. And because he was so full of himself, and the beer was so refreshing after a long day, and he had just gotten a hand up from his brother-in-law, he was feeling—how did his wife say it?—*Todo chocante*. Even when she was annoyed, she said it with such affection it sounded like pillow talk to him.

"What's your concern with Celeste?" Beatriz began as if

she were soliciting official testimony. "Do you think her papers aren't real? You don't think she's who she says she is?"

"No, I already told you, the documents she came with look legit, but I'm kind of worried about some of the other papers she brought."

"What papers?"

"A bunch of notes and photocopies about a bunch of women I never heard of and I doubt you've heard of, either." Larry began to quickly edit in his head. He didn't want Beatriz to know the grisly images he saw. He didn't think she needed to know. "And a couple of those mini-drives— you know, the ones you plug into the computer?"

"Flash drives?"

"Yeah, those. I haven't had a chance to see what's on them. Have you?

Beatriz shook her head.

"It's all very—makes me nervous. There's something creepy about it. Why does she have this stuff? I mean, what does it have to do with her?" Larry said, looking outside at Celeste.

"That's it?" Beatriz said. "Some papers and flash drives?"

"No. It's more than that."

What Larry refused to say was that he was afraid, plain and simple. He didn't know what the connection was between Celeste and the Women of Juarez—or if there even was one. All he knew was that what he saw among Celeste's papers disturbed him. She disturbed him, small and dark and quiet. Larry prided himself on being a good Texas liberal. Hadn't he given money to all the right causes? Wasn't he a lifetime subscriber to the *Texas*

Observer? Hadn't he publicly declared that if one of his sons admitted he was gay, he would love him just the same—while being enormously relieved that Carlos liked girls? (He wasn't sure about Raúl, but he refused to think about that until he needed to.)

He didn't want to admit it, but when it came to Celeste, her unexpected appearance, the daughter of the black sheep of the family, who, like his own sister, Lucy, was a source of embarrassment and anxiety, Larry couldn't help himself. There was just something dangerous and, well, too foreign about Celeste that he couldn't shake. He could never admit that out loud, even if he had the words. In Larry's mind, he was being protective of his family, nothing more, nothing less. He loved Beatriz with all his heart. Wasn't it time he had her all to himself? Like it was in the beginning, when they were young?

"So, what is it, then?" Beatriz pressed.

"She can't stay here, Beatriz." He wanted his wife to burst into tears, to throw a tantrum. That wasn't her style, but this was a new situation for them. He was hoping for a new response, one that he could deride for its rashness, its raw hysteria, so he could stake a claim for being the rational one, the one in control.

But Beatriz was as still and serene as glass.

"And why do you think that, sweetie?" She slowly took a sip of her beer, daintily placed the glass on the table, and turned to look at him squarely in the face. Larry was thrown. So this is what they mean, he realized, when her colleagues talked about his beautiful wife having nerves of steel.

"Because she can't," Larry declared. "We have a full house, and Norma and Erasmo have room. And they want to take her."

"And I want her here," Beatriz said plainly.

It rattled Larry that Beatriz was this calm, but he was not going to give in.

"This isn't the way it's supposed to be!" he finally blurted. He didn't want to be the first to lose his cool, but it was too late. "We're supposed to be getting used to each other again, getting used to our kids growing up and having their own lives, and then—and then, that's not even working out right, either! Did you know that Carlos wants to go to culinary school?" He said it as if his son—his firstborn!—wanted to run off and join the circus or take up pole dancing.

"He and that girl have it all worked out, he says. He says he doesn't want to go to college, to a good university where he can get a real education and make something of himself. He wants to be a cook! A cook! And then your niece comes out of the blue with her packet of papers and all her drama, and my sister is...and my nephews are..." Larry could hear himself faltering. "It's not the way it's supposed to be!"

Beatriz took another sip of her beer and looked at her husband.

"Are you done?"

"I guess," he stammered.

"Are you done?" Beatriz asked more forcefully.

"Yes. For now."

"Good." She rested her elbows on the table and laced

her fingers together. "No. I did not know about Carlos and Marisol, but I can't say I'm surprised, and I can't say I'm unhappy. He wants to do what he loves, Larry. Why not? He's good at it. And they obviously love each other. What more can you ask for? And I bet he doesn't want to 'just be a cook.' You know our son will do more than that.

"I love you, but you know what your problem is? You think there's a script. You think it's all supposed to go a certain way, and when it doesn't, you try to make the pieces fit. You pound and pound and pound to make those pieces fit no matter how much they splinter."

Larry swallowed hard, because he knew Beatriz was just getting warmed up.

"I love you, Larry. But if you make me choose between you or my kids, you'll lose every time."

"What did you say?"

"You heard me. You will lose."

"How can you say that?"

"Because it's true, Larry. You know it's true! If you had to choose between me and the boys, you would choose them, wouldn't you?"

"But she's not ours, Beatriz!"

"She is now. She was sent to me. Not to Erasmo, or to Tony, or to the others, but to me."

Larry looked into his beer and decided it was time for something stronger. He went to the cabinet over the refrigerator and pulled out a bottle of whisky and two glasses and poured shots for each of them. If their kids were in the room, they would have found this gesture strange. It was a ritual only Beatriz and Larry understood. It marked the point where they had reached the crossroads in their low-intensity battle that required something to keep the centrifugal force from careening out of control, destroying everything in its way. It was a ritual created over time, without much talk, but deeply understood. They drank their shots together and Larry coughed. The liquor only seemed to make Beatriz's backbone stronger.

"You don't remember, do you?" Beatriz asked. "You don't remember what happened when Perla came to me, when we lived in Ann Arbor? We had just finished our first year of grad school—how she came to me looking for help. She took a bus part of the way and hitchhiked the rest. She was in trouble, and desperate, and I should have helped her, but I didn't. You know why? Because I chose you, I chose you over my own sister and sent her away."

"I—I didn't tell you to do that," Larry said.

"I know. But you didn't question it, either. Even when I gave her our last hundred dollars to put her on a bus back home. You didn't argue. But if I told you I wanted to take in my sister, with all her problems, and all her drama, and all her bad choices, you would have left me."

"That's not true!" Larry said.

"It *is* true!" Beatriz said.

Larry didn't respond. He knew, deep down, she was absolutely right.

"I chose you," Beatriz said. "I sent Perla back home. But she didn't come back here and instead ended up—God knows where! Who knows what kind of life she had, what kind of life Celeste had? But if I can fix it now, that's what I'm going to do. You don't have to be happy with this. I don't even care if you like her. But what I want you to do now is to choose me. Choose me like I chose you. Support me. Let me do what I have to do. And if you can't do that, then maybe..." Beatriz's voice began to break. "I crazy-love you, but that girl you met in Ann Arbor, the one who turned her back on her sister? She's not here anymore. I can't do it again. I won't."

Beatriz couldn't believe what she had said, but it felt right, it felt like the truth. But it burned. It burned both of them. And the look on Larry's face—he looked as lost and panic-stricken and alone as Celeste did the night she arrived. He set his empty glass on the counter.

"Maybe I should go, then," he said.

That was not the response Beatriz expected. "What? Go where?"

"I don't know," he said. "I've got to get out of here. I've got to think. I'll find a hotel," he said. He knew he was acting like a kid who had lost the game and was going to take his toys and go home, but he couldn't help himself.

"A hotel? Why?"

"I need to think about all this. I need to figure out where I belong in this new world of yours." Larry was feeling small and petty and he hated it. Beatriz bit her lip and inhaled deeply.

"Do what you need to do," she said. She didn't want Larry to leave. She was dying for him to take her in his arms and hold her and tell her how sorry he was. That he didn't understand before, but now he did and it would all be okay. How he should have said something back then—how she should have said something back then. She was waiting for him to hear how he sounded to her. But then a frightening thought came to her: *How do I sound to him?*

The idea that they were, after all these years, not operating on the same frequency, the one that had always drawn them together like homing pigeons meant for one another, made the ground shift. Beatriz accepted that life is full of the unexpected, but her connection with Larry—solid, comforting, and familiar—suddenly turned into a sinkhole beneath her.

"You don't have to leave, Larry. I don't want you to go."

"Yeah, I know. But I think I better."

"Larry..."

"Can we not argue about this one thing?" he snapped.

They both stayed where they were, unblinking, staring at one another.

"Fine. If you think you want to stay in a hotel, go stay in a hotel," Beatriz said. She meant it, but it tore her apart.

Josie had already pulled into the downtown hotel where she knew she could get a good deal, but she still needed some smokes and couldn't get "King William's Columns" or "Milligan" out of her head. *What the hell?* she thought. The King William neighborhood was only a few blocks away from the hotel where she was going to stay. She drove out of the lot and headed south.

After a half hour of aimless driving, Josie's resolve turned into skepticism. *I'm not going to find King*

William's Columns. I'd have better luck finding freaking Jimmy Hoffa, she thought.

She found herself driving up and down Flores Street, making note of landmarks, until the lack of nicotine poked at her nerves and she saw that her gas tank was near empty. The small gas station and convenience store she passed as she drove stood out among the Victorian-style houses but was a welcome sight. She pulled in, gassed up the car, and went inside.

"Do you have a phone book I could use?" she asked the man at the counter. The battery on her laptop was running low, and besides, Josie had stared at the screen for so long, running every Internet search she could think of, her drive was fading. Still, she couldn't give up. He handed her the massive book and she began to leaf through the curled pages. She found a whole chunk of Milligans in the phone book—a list considerably shorter than the pages and pages of Sánchezes. She flipped to the business pages and looked up "King William's Columns," and when she couldn't find that, she decided she had enough. She slapped the book closed and slid it back to the man behind the counter.

"Thanks," she said, patting her pockets for the lighter she was always misplacing.

"Didn't find what you were looking for?" he asked.

"No. I thought there was a place called King William's Columns, but I couldn't find it in the book. I've driven all around here, but I don't see it," she said, still thinking she was looking for a stone-carving shop.

"You mean the Columns?" the man asked.

"The Columns?" Josie repeated. "What's that?"

"It's one of those poofy bed-and-breakfasts. Is that what you want?"

Josie didn't know what she wanted, but a big poofy bed, with breakfast, no matter where it was, sounded good to her.

"Yeah, sure. Is it near here?" she asked.

"Down the street. It's kind of set back from the road. Easy to miss if you're driving and don't know what you're looking for," the man said. "Two blocks that way, on the left." He pointed with his chin as he slid a fresh book of matches toward Josie. "I don't think they allow smoking, though."

"Well, of course they don't," she sighed, accepting the matches. "Thanks."

The Columns bed-and-breakfast was right where the convenience store clerk said it would be. Josie pulled in, trying to remember how she had heard about this place, storing its name in the recesses of her memory, like that one bit of arcane knowledge game show winners cite as their saving grace. It would be too coincidental for them to have a vacancy, Josie thought, and probably no Wi-Fi. She was ready for an apology when she stepped up to the check-in desk, feeling especially dingy after a long night in her car. But sure enough, a cancellation had just come in an hour before, and the desk clerk was so happy to fill the empty room that she cut Josie a deal. When she mentioned in passing that a new wireless router had just been installed last week, Josie knew she had to stay. She would have called it fate or kismet, if she believed in that sort of thing. But of course, the only drawback, and just like the convenience store clerk had said, was that no smoking was allowed in the rooms.

"Outside," the receptionist pointed, peering at Josie over her glasses. "All the way in the back, close to the adobe fence near the jacaranda tree, we set up a place for smokers. You'll see."

Instead of heading straight for a smoke, Josie decided to head straight up to the room. She would try to sleep before finding dinner and making another shot in the dark to find Celeste. She turned on the TV and set it to her favorite cable news network as she began sorting through her things when her cell phone chirped. It was her mother.

"Bueno!" Josie said.

"Are you there?" Rita asked.

"I just got here."

"Why didn't you call me?"

"I just got here, I said." *Damn!* Josie thought. *How does she do that?* Josie flopped onto the bed, staring up at the ceiling fan. She could feel her body unfurling and relaxing as she sunk into the plush comforter. The frills and the lace and the overabundance of ruffles were not her style, but the bed was luscious. She thought she could die in the bed and never regret it.

"So, did you take care of your business?" Rita asked. Josie could feel her lids getting heavy.

"Not yet," Josie said lazily. She rolled onto her side, the faint smell of lavender falling over her like a gentle cloud.

"What's the matter with you?" Rita asked. "You sound drunk. And who's that talking?"

"I'm not drunk, 'Amá. I'm tired," Josie slurred. She turned down the sound on the TV. "I haven't been sleeping very well lately."

"Then you better pull off the road and take a nap," Rita said. She was worried.

"I am off the road," Josie said, rousting herself awake. "I'm in a hotel." Josie didn't notice the icy silence on the other end of the phone.

"You're in a hotel?" Rita finally said. "What do you mean you're in a hotel? I thought you had a delivery and then you were coming home."

Josie forgot that she hadn't quite told her mother the whole story—that she did have some business to take care of, but that she didn't know where to start, that she was starting from ground zero.

"Oh, my gato, Josefina! It's a sin to lie to your mother! And on a Sunday!" Rita said, sounding as deeply wounded as she possibly could.

"I didn't lie," Josie stammered. "And besides, isn't it a sin to work on Sunday, too?"

"We're not talking about me, we're talking about you!" Rita said.

Josie didn't want to argue with her mother. "'Amá, please. I'm too tired for this. I will try to do what I need to do and get back there tomorrow, but right now, I just want to lie here and talk to my kid. Can you please put her on the phone?"

"She's not here," Rita said stonily. "And besides, if she were, I'm not sure it's a good idea for you to talk to her."

This jarred Josie, and her eyes popped wide open.

"You're like her own personal Santa Claus. I tell her to wait, and wait, and wait, and then the day you're supposed to be here, you don't show. Do you know what it's like to deal with a disappointed kid?"

Josie felt as if she'd been slapped in the face, as if her mother were punishing her for a choice she'd helped her make.

"When she was little, it was easier, but she's growing up now. She's a person. She knows what it means to miss someone, Josefina, and it's..." Rita shook her head. Maybe she was to blame, she thought. Maybe she shouldn't have offered to help her daughter in the way she did. Maybe it would have been better if Josie stayed home, raised her child, and took whatever work she could scrounge up. Maybe, maybe, maybe...

"I want to talk to my daughter," Josie said more forcefully.

"I told you, she's not here. She's with your aunt Chata," Rita said.

"Well, can I have her cell phone?"

"She doesn't have one," Rita said. "You know how she is."

There were worse things than her little girl being with Chata, Josie thought. The thing was, Chata was already old when Josie was a girl, and Chata had only gotten kookier as she aged. Her aunt Chata was always good for a little chisme, but her specialty was wild myths from the ancient past. Her favorite story was of Mictecacihuatl, the queen of Mictlan, the underworld.

"Who?" Josie had asked when she was a girl, frustrated

with all the syllables and not really believing the stories were as authentic as Chata claimed. She'd never seen them in a library book, and she couldn't pronounce the names well enough to ask the librarian. The name sounded like hacking when Chata said it, and Josie thought her nutty aunt was trying to fool her with her own version of pig Latin.

"Mictecacihuatl!" the old woman had repeated when Josie interrupted. "Mictecacihuatl! Okay, let's just call her La Mikke. Now, let me get on with the story…"

It wasn't until much later, when Josie fell into a Mexican mythology class in college, that she realized that her aunt Chata's stories really were part of an ancient tradition.

"Hey, Tía! You didn't tell me La Mikke was like the Mexican Persephone."

"What makes you think Persephone was not like her?" the old woman scoffed. At the time, Josie didn't understand why her aunt was so annoyed.

Well, if nothing else, Josie thought, Paz will be entertained.

"Oye, Josefina? Are you there?"

"I'm here," she said.

"Hang up the phone, Josefina." Rita sighed. "We'll talk later."

"Okay," Josie said, as the phone gently slid down the side of her face onto the thick bedspread.

Maybe it was all the driving, all the worry, but Josie was finally drifting off into a deep sleep. Her limbs went limp, the furrow in her brow softened, and the tightness in her jaw came loose. She reached for the remote to turn off the set and when she couldn't find it, she couldn't bear to open her eyes to look for it. She had gone without sleep for so long, she clung to it ravenously. She could hear a voice on the TV intoning about some recent tragedy, with screams and gunfire in the background, and she pulled the fluttery bedspread over her head to block out the world. She was almost fully asleep when there was a slump on her bed, as if someone sat down next to her. Josie threw off the covers and sat up with a start, her cell phone and the TV remote, hidden in the folds of the bedcover, flying to the floor. Josie looked around the room, but there was no one. The only thing stirring besides her galloping heart was the image on the TV, now an annoyingly cheery commercial selling a time-share in the Bahamas. Josie gave up. She sat up and rubbed her eyes with the heels of her hands, realizing she was smearing whatever mascara was left but not caring. She decided she needed a smoke.

She weaved her way through the long backyard, through the carefully manicured garden, stepping on flat, granite stones that led to the back. Large, flowering hedges blocked her view of the adobe fence and the small settee that was placed there, out of sight, for the smokers. She lit up and inhaled deeply, watching the cigarette smoke rise above her and disappear into the sky. A gust of wind rattled the jacaranda over her, sending down a snow of florets, covering her hair and shoulders. She stood to shake them off and walked away from the flowering tree when she heard something eerie—strange music, like from an old-time horror movie. She thought she was imagining it and tried to ignore the sound until she heard a young voice intone with an overly studied British accent:

"'Even a man who is pure at heart and says his prayers at night may become a wolf when the wolfbane blooms, and the Autumn moon is bright.'"

The words were followed by a girlish giggle.

"You know all the words?" the girl said.

"Yup!"

"Are you going to say them through the whole thing?"

"I can!" the boy said brightly, then more shyly, "But I don't have to."

Josie stood and wandered to one of the openings in the fence to take a peek. Through the foliage, she saw a young boy and a girl laying on their stomachs on an unfurled sleeping bag, facing a small DVD player before them. The boy adjusted the screen, and the light from the player splashed on their faces. Josie couldn't believe what she was seeing. She reared away from the opening as if she'd been caught spying. She took a deep breath and turned back to the opening to take another look. Her head was spinning. She sat down to calm her nerves and finish her cigarette.

It can't be, Josie thought. She was elated, but suspicious. It would be a miracle if she saw what she thought she saw. She needed to tell someone, get another perspective. She called her mother again, thinking that when she told her the good news, her mother would congratulate her, tell her not to question it, just go with it, be happy—and get herself home. But the phone rang, and rang, and rang. Josie finally snapped her phone closed and sat there trying to make sense of everything. Maybe the conscious part of her sleep-deprived mind had helped her remember this place. Maybe Perla had told her about the bed-and-breakfast behind her sister's house. Josie was puzzled and amazed at once. Had she really seen what she thought she'd seen? She got up to go take another peek. The kids were still there, fully absorbed in the movie now that it got to the part where Lon Chaney turns into the wolf man for the first time. Josie finished her cigarette and decided to go back to her room and try and get some rest. She didn't trust that she was seeing what she saw. If she could summon a little sleep, things would make more sense in the morning. As she walked back to the house, another cool breeze tickled the jacaranda tree, loosening mauve florets that happily danced like ballerinas to the ground.

TWELVE

Beatriz stayed at the kitchen table when Larry went upstairs. She heard him knocking around in their bedroom above her. When it got quiet again, she went to the front of the house and saw him make his way down the stairs, carrying a small overnight bag.

She wanted to call his name as he reached the front door, but she was too stunned. When she opened her mouth, nothing came out.

"I'll call you from wherever I land," he said over his shoulder. Beatriz could only nod.

"Did you hear me?" he asked. When he turned toward Beatriz, their eyes didn't meet. He stared past her to the photos of their family on the mantle. She was looking at his bag, thinking it was the one with the broken zipper that he used only for emergencies. Was he really in that much of a hurry to get away from her?

Larry was hoping she would run over and throw her arms around him and beg him to stay. Beatriz was hoping he would drop the bag and take her in his arms. Their silence was thick with want but neither of them would bend.

Larry finally opened the door and stood there, fumbling with his keys, untangling the straps of his overnight bag so they would lie flat, before he finally left and closed the door behind him. Beatriz stood in the foyer, thinking that the door might swing back open and there he would be, standing on the porch, unable to leave after all. When that didn't happen, she went to the door and peeked out the narrow window alongside it. She watched him fling his bag into the backseat of his SUV and climb in. He sat there for a long time, staring into his lap, before he finally started the engine and took off. Carlos came downstairs as soon as his father pulled out of the drive.

"So, what did he say?" Carlos asked.

Beatriz was still in a daze. "Say what about what, mi'jo?"

"You all didn't talk about me?"

"I'm sorry, son. We didn't quite get to that," Beatriz said. "Don't worry. We'll sort it all out." She was trying to convince herself as much as her son.

"Okay, well, I'm going over to Marisol's."

"Sure, son. Don't stay out too late." After Carlos left, Beatriz returned to the kitchen and watched the kids through the patio door. She was pleased that Celeste was enjoying Raúl's old movies and tried to guess which ones they were watching. She slid open the door and called out to them.

"Hey! You all want some soda or something?" She was working hard to sound bright and nonchalant. From the distance, and because they were wrapped up in their movie, the kids didn't notice how shaken she was.

"I'm good!" Raúl answered back. He looked at Celeste, and she said something to him, after which he called out to his mother, "We're good!" Celeste pulled on his sleeve and spoke to him again. "Maybe some cake later!" he reported.

"Not too late," Beatriz said. Well, if Celeste wasn't talking to her, at least she was getting to know her son.

Beatriz wandered back to the living room, sat in the middle of the couch—the same couch that less than twenty-four hours before she and her husband were lazing on, happy and content. She could feel the full impact of what had happened hit her. She had to hold it together until the kids went to bed. And just when she thought she would lose it, she called Ana. "What are you doing?"

"Ironing, making some caldo for Diego. He seems to have come down with a bug." Ana paused. "Why?"

"Oh, I'm sorry. I didn't mean to bother you. I'll call back tomorrow," Beatriz said.

"No, no. He's asleep." Ana could hear the tension in her friend's voice. "What's wrong?"

"I—I—I don't know, but I think I might have just set the groundwork for my divorce," Beatriz said.

"What?"

"I told Larry I wanted us to keep Celeste, and he said he didn't want to. Then I told him he really had no choice, and then...he left."

"You had a fight? Ay, mujer! I'm sure he's just driving around to cool off," Ana said.

"No, he said he would check into a hotel."

"What?" There was a laugh in Ana's voice, but Beatriz was not smiling. "No! I don't believe it! I mean, he's just upset. Let him cool down. He'll be back."

"I don't know," Beatriz said, wiping the tears that were flooding her eyes. "I told him he had to choose."

"Between you and Celeste?"

"No—yes—I don't know! I don't even know what I said, but I told him that Celeste was here to stay. I owe it to Perla. I want to do it right this time. I can't turn her away like I did my sister. I was very direct about that." Beatriz leaned into the couch and pulled her legs up under her.

"Oh," Ana began carefully. She was beginning to put the pieces together of what happened between Beatriz and Perla those many years ago. "You put her out. Is that what happened?"

"Yes," Beatriz said in a small voice. "Larry and I had just moved in together. We were in grad school, and we were, you know, crazy in love, and things couldn't have been more perfect—well, except for the not having any money part. I never thought I would find anyone. Never thought someone like him would be the one."

"Why would you think that? There were boys around you all the time."

"Because—I don't know. I wasn't traditional enough, or girly enough, or whatever enough. Remember what my mother used to tell me? She always told me to stop reading and working already and go out and find a nice boy to marry and bring her some grandkids."

"Your mom was old school," Ana said. "So...you and Larry were doing great over there in Ann Arbor. I still don't understand where Perla comes in."

"She was messing up. Messing up bad. I guess she got

mixed up with some boy, and when she showed up pregnant, the tía she was living with sent her home."

"Perla was pregnant?"

"We never found out for sure. She was too scared to go to a doctor and too scared to go home, so she came to me in Ann Arbor. She was a mess. She begged me to help her, but I told her she couldn't stay. I told her I couldn't help her and that she needed to go back home."

"And that's when she went to El Paso?"

"Quién sabe?" Beatriz said. "It was like she disappeared! She didn't come back here and she didn't go back to Corpus. We looked for her, but it was like she vanished. I think that's what really made my mother finally let go, near the end. The grief, you know? And it was all my fault! It was all my fault that she disappeared. All because I wanted to protect my life, all because I wanted to make sure Larry would never leave me, and now—look! He's going to leave me anyway!"

"No, no, no," Ana consoled. "I mean, I'm sure he's upset, just like you. This is a big thing, a big change. And you know how he is—he likes things just so. You guys are a funny pair in that way."

"Why?" Beatriz sniffed.

Ana thought a moment. "Because you're like your hair—all crazy and wild—and he's more like a crew cut. He likes order and routine. I mean, that trip to Paris he arranged? I couldn't believe that!"

"That's not so surprising," Beatriz said. "He may not seem it, but Larry is really very romantic at heart. Of course, I'll have to work on him to throw out the itinerary

I know he's probably already written and rewritten and convince him to go off the beaten path. That is, if he still wants to go with me."

"Ay, mujer..."

"Maybe that's why we used to work so well. I loosened him up, and coming from my crazy family and their wacky ways, he was safe and dependable."

"Stop saying 'used to,'" Ana said. "He just needs to think, to get his head straight."

"Maybe."

Ana pondered what Beatriz had told her. She always remembered Beatriz as being as strong and decisive as she was now. No-nonsense, fearless. She never thought of her as a girl who made decisions based on her desperation to keep a man—any man. Then again, Larry was not just any man to her.

"Look," Ana said. "I know if you had to do it over again, maybe you would have told Perla to stay. And maybe she would have left anyway. I know you think that's what you should have done, but sending her back home like you did—that wasn't the wrong thing to do, either."

Ana let the idea hang in the air awhile before she added, "I know what *you* want to happen with Celeste. What does Larry want?"

"He wants me to let Celeste go with Erasmo and Norma."

"Well, would that be so bad?"

"You were the one who reminded me that Perla sent her to me, not to Erasmo or anyone else!"

"I know, but really—let's try and think about this dispassionately. Would it be the end of the world?"

But when it came to Beatriz and Perla, there was no such thing as dispassionate. When they were girls, it was all about the novelty. Perla was the new, shiny jewel of the family, and Beatriz was the older, amazing sister who would do anything for her baby sister. Anything. There was a mutual sense of awe they had for one another that quickly faded when Beatriz became a teenager and Perla was a girl. They forgot, the way children do, how much they meant to each other when childish squabbles and imagined slights began to grow like toadstools over their feelings for one another—large and ugly but ultimately rootless. Beatriz's wonder over those tiny fingers and toes, smiling to the music of baby Perla's coos, got lost over time in the frustration of a teenager who wanted to be free. And to Perla, Beatriz was the older, luckier sister. She got to leave the house when she wanted, had lots of friends, and could make the family listen to her, while Perla pulled at pant legs, trying so hard to be heard above their laughter.

Most of the time when Beatriz left the house, it was to go to work—nothing glamorous or mysterious about that. She had friends and boyfriends, but not as many as the little girl counted. And when Beatriz went off to work while her friends were hanging out, the sight of Perla play-ing in the yard was a reminder that her little sister was freer than she ever had been as the oldest girl among a family of boys. The grass is always greener.

"Really?" Ana asked again, trying to be helpful. "If Celeste lived with Erasmo and Norma, that would be the end of the world?"

"She was sent to me," Beatriz said. "Ay, qué no! Can

you imagine? Norma would turn the poor girl into a mini-Guadalupana in no time!"

"There is no such thing."

"Oh! You know she'd find a way. She'd have the poor girl in metallic chanclas and capri pants in no time," Beatriz said.

"You're worried about her fashion sense?"

"No, but living out in the country, alone, with Norma?"

"I don't know how Erasmo does it," Ana let slip. She wanted to bite her tongue, but Beatriz burst out laughing and Ana was happy to hear her friend return to her old self.

"So, have you checked out what Celeste brought in that envelope?" Ana asked.

"Not really. Larry said he looked inside and didn't like what he saw, and now—I guess I should take a look for myself."

"I can help you, if you want to bring it over here," Ana offered. "I don't want to leave mi'jo in case he gets worse. He never gets sick, so—"

"No, no, no. You stay with Diego. I can do it. I need to do it."

"Bueno, call me back if you need to," Ana said. "Any time, no matter how late."

Beatriz hung up with Ana and decided to look at the papers while the kids were distracted with their movie. She had to think back to where she'd last seen Celeste's envelope. When she remembered that Larry had been looking through it, she knew just where it was: wedged in the seat in the armchair in their bedroom. She gave Celeste and

Raúl one last check and then headed up to her bedroom, silently closing the door behind her. There it was, just where he'd left it. She took a deep breath, retrieved the envelope, and moved to the bed, where she dumped the contents before her. The first things that stood out were Celeste's birth certificate, which Beatriz had already seen, and then Perla's death certificate. She still couldn't bear to read that yet and turned it facedown. Inside a smaller envelope were two passports, one for Celeste, the other for Perla, which Beatriz looked at for a long time, studying the adult face of her little sister. The eyes and the shape of her face were the same, but the weight of twenty-some years that had passed between them was evident. There was a dullness to her complexion. A roughness, Beatriz suspected, that came from working outside, or in the heat, or from standing on your feet all day. There were no traces of the little girl she grew up with, the image Beatriz held on to, the one that came to her in her dreams, and that made another sinkhole in her heart.

The other papers were unremarkable but useful—Celeste's last report card, a name tag from a factory where Perla worked, the immunization report Beatriz had wondered about earlier...the odds and ends of a life that seem like clutter until it's all that is left for those who follow to try and extract some kind of meaning. Another envelope had three photos. One was of Celeste as a baby, and one was of Celeste and Perla, taken a year or so earlier. The last one was an older shot that Beatriz had almost forgotten: her school picture from her senior year at Our Lady of the Lake High School. Beatriz turned it over and saw handwriting from a younger version of herself: "Tomi tormenta." Beatriz shook her head, remembering how this was her last senior photo and how Perla had begged and whined and threw a fit asking for it, till her mother ordered her to give it to the girl. Beatriz hated that she was made to give it to Perla instead of the cute new boy at school. What was his name? She didn't even remember. The photo had obviously been carried for many years. A hard crease ran like a scar across Beatriz's younger face, but it had been flattened smooth over time. The ink on the back of the photo had obviously survived a run through the wash or an accidental spill, or the humidity of a pants pocket. Beatriz was touched. After all these years and all that had passed between them, Beatriz couldn't believe her sister had kept her photo among her most important things.

She turned back to Perla's passport photo, wishing it could speak when the other papers on the bed caught her eye. Most of them were photocopies of police reports about women and how they died. *Who are these women?* Beatriz thought.

The notes along the edges of the photocopies were in another person's handwriting. None of this made sense to her. She had gathered the papers and began to stuff them back into the envelope when she felt something in the bottom. She turned it upside down, but whatever it was, it was stuck inside. She looked in and saw the two flash drives Larry had mentioned taped to the bottom of the envelope. She reached in and pried them loose and held them in her hand.

What do you suppose…? she wondered. *There's only one way to find out.*

*   *   *

Raúl and Celeste had finished watching *The Wolf Man* and rolled onto their backs to look into the branches of the jacaranda tree.

"So, you liked that?" Raúl asked.

Celeste nodded. "I like those old scary movies."

"Really?" Raúl was amazed. "That's so weird!"

"Why? You like them."

"No! I mean, it's just that I never meet anybody who likes them as much as I do, especially girls."

Celeste shrugged. "My mom liked them, too. We used to watch them on TV when I was little."

"They didn't scare you?" Raúl asked.

"No."

Raúl was used to good monsters, monsters with souls, monsters who were misunderstood or who didn't understand themselves and wanted to belong. Movie monsters were nothing to Celeste. The kind of monsters Celeste truly feared were faceless, shameless, and without, it seemed, the capacity for mercy. The monsters Celeste feared were not anything Raúl could have imagined in his worst nightmare.

Raúl sat up to face his cousin.

"It's sure going to be different having a girl around here," he said. "All this time, it's just been us guys, except for 'Amá."

"Different how?" Celeste asked. She still wasn't convinced that staying was a good idea, but she was interested in hearing what Raúl thought it might be like.

"Well, like, what was it they were talking about in the

kitchen? You know, when Tía Norma got excited about you turning fifteen?"

"The quinceañera?"

"Yeah, that. What's that all about?"

Celeste shrugged. She didn't really want to talk about it. The whole thing seemed out of the question, now that her mother was gone.

"Well, is it fun?" Raúl pressed. "What do you have to do?"

"Well, if I did have one," Celeste began. Although it was a sore subject, she liked Raúl and appreciated his curiosity. She could see he had el corazón en la frente; he was all heart. "First we would go to church, and then later there would be food and a cake. Some girls have really fancy ones with a band and limos and stuff," she said. "But I don't think mine would be like that."

"That's it?" Raúl asked. "It sounds like a big birthday party at church."

"Sort of. The party isn't at the church, though. That's later."

"But why? How come girls do it but not boys?"

"Because you don't look as good in the dresses as we do," Celeste said with a straight face. It was the first time Raúl had heard her crack a joke, and it made him laugh.

"No, really—what's the big deal? What's so special about fifteen?"

Celeste sat and thought a moment. For her, the year she turned fifteen would always be associated with her mother being killed, of seeing her in a box and then taken away. She would associate turning fifteen with being alone in a strange city, meeting unfamiliar people she was told were her family, and wondering when the novelty would wear off and they would send her back home—her real home—where she belonged.

"Well, for me, nothing," Celeste said dryly. "But for mi 'amá, she thought it was important. I was going to do it for her. I thought maybe if I did it, I would figure out what it was about. So I guess now I won't ever know."

"I don't know," Raúl said. "It sounded like Tía Norma had it all figured out for you."

"But all that stuff doesn't mean anything if you don't have people around that mean something to you," she said.

"Oh," Raúl said awkwardly. "You don't like us?" He suddenly felt self-conscious, wondering if Celeste was just being nice, watching *The Wolf Man* with him when she was really bored the way his cousin Seamus always was when he watched Raúl's old movies with him.

"No, it's not like that," she assured him. "Everyone here is nice. But my home is in El Paso. I know mi 'amá wants me to be here, but I don't think I should be."

"Why? Because of Seamus?"

Celeste was still unsure of who was who.

"The two boys who were here earlier—Seamus and Wally. Seamus is the grumpy one. Don't let him bother you. And I already told you about Carlos. You're not going to tell anybody, right? What I said about him going to culinary school?"

"I told you I wasn't," Celeste said. She liked Raúl, and even though she could tell her aunt Beatriz meant well, her intense desire to get close to Celeste was having the opposite effect. No, Celeste didn't believe she belonged here, and she wasn't sure that she ever would.

THIRTEEN

Beatriz made her way downstairs and into Larry's office, turned on the computer, and stuck in one of the flash drives. It uploaded several electronic folders, each labeled with initials and a date.

Well, here goes, she thought and gave a short, silent prayer. She clicked on one of the folders, selected one of the files inside, and opened it. What she saw looked like scanned documents: police reports, newspaper clippings, and more death certificates. She could see that another folder was filled with JPEGs. She clicked on one to open it, and as soon as she did instantly wished she hadn't. She found herself looking at the most gruesome photos she'd ever seen: a mutilated body, so distorted and swollen it didn't look human. It took a moment to register what she was looking at, but when it came to her, she nearly shrieked.

"Oh, Jesus!" she said out loud. She ripped the flash drive from the computer. A warning on the screen indicated that the device she'd just removed hadn't been done so correctly and that she might have damaged the files. Beatriz didn't know if she'd damaged the files, and she didn't care; she just knew that whatever she'd seen was so horrendous, it would take a long time to wash the image from her memory. Whatever it was, whoever it was, she didn't want to imagine it or think about it ever again. She sat in the chair a moment and closed her eyes to calm herself. She could feel her heart pounding in her chest and her stomach churning. She might have let the full rush of nausea overtake her, except she was interrupted by a small voice.

"'Amá?"

Beatriz opened her eyes and saw Celeste and Raúl standing in the door. They could both see by the expression on her face that Beatriz was deeply disturbed by something, but neither of them knew what to say or how to react.

"Hi," Beatriz said, trying to sound cheery.

"She says she's tired and wants to lay down. Should I take her upstairs?" Raúl asked, motioning to Celeste.

"Sure, but let me go upstairs and change the bed for you," Beatriz said.

"No," Celeste said. She looked anxiously at Raúl, then down to the floor. Beatriz was happy Celeste was bonding with her son, but she could see she had a lot of work to do to make her way in with her, as well.

"Qué pasó, mi'ja?" Beatriz asked gently.

"Nothing. My stuff is down here. I just want to lay down," Celeste said.

"Okay," Beatriz said. "It's okay. If you want to sleep down here, you can sleep down here." She didn't understand why Celeste would turn down the comfort of a full-sized bed for a couch, but she stopped her impulse to convince her otherwise. She was still rattled from what she had seen, and she needed to gather herself to begin to ask all the necessary questions about what had happened to Celeste and Perla in El Paso. She wasn't sure she wanted to know, or if she would ever really know the truth, but she knew that she would have to be stronger and more patient than she had ever imagined.

Long after the kids were asleep, Beatriz sat in the living room, waiting for Larry.

Maybe Ana is right. she thought. *He just needs some time to think. Of course, he'll come home.*

Her heart leapt when the front door opened, but it wasn't Larry. It was Carlos, back from his evening with Marisol. Carlos didn't see his mother when he first walked in.

"Hola," Beatriz said lightly, trying not to startle her son.

"Crap! 'Amá! Why are you sitting in the dark?" Carlos turned on a lamp. "You should go to sleep, young lady," he joked. "Don't you have work tomorrow?"

"No, I took the week off," she said.

"Well, lucky you," Carlos said. He had to go to work early the next morning and was wiped out, spending the evening explaining to Marisol why he still hadn't settled things with his parents about going to culinary school. "When's Dad coming back?" He yawned.

"What do you mean?" Beatriz said, trying to sound casual. Carlos wasn't buying it.

"What's going on?"

"Nothing, mi'jo. Everyone is asleep, so try not to make too much noise up there, por fa'."

"Okay." But Carlos didn't move. He knew something wasn't right. "Where's Dad?"

"What do you mean, 'Where's Dad'?"

"'Amá, really? His car isn't outside."

"Oh. Well, he left, son. He'll be back. He'll be back."

Carlos's heart sank. "Did you all have a fight about me?"

"Why would you think that?"

"Because your eye makeup is still messed up, and Dad's not here, and you're acting all weird."

Beatriz thought about fibbing to her son, but as she looked into his face she could see he would not buy it. She motioned for him to follow her into the kitchen.

"Was it about me? Did he tell you about me and Marisol?"

"Oh, no, sweetheart! I mean, yes, he told me about your plans, but our little disagreement had nothing to do with you. Trust me," Beatriz said gently. "Don't worry, mi'jo. Pero, the kids don't know, so keep it to yourself, por fa'. Trust me. It will be over before you know it."

Beatriz placed her hands on either side of Carlos's concerned face. She looked into his deep brown eyes and saw that he was no longer a boy but a young man. The reality of her oldest child being grown enough to leave home amazed her. Was this the kid who got messy from head to toe making mud pies as a kid, selling them for a nickel—a dime if they were covered with stone "nuts"?

"I really pissed him off, huh?"

"You surprised him, that's all. You know how he is with surprises."

"But you weren't surprised?"

"Honestly, I didn't know what was going on, but I knew you weren't interested in going to school in Michigan the way he wanted. And I thought maybe you and Marisol were getting serious. That was about it." She leaned against the counter. "So, culinary school, huh?"

"I didn't mean to keep it a secret, but he's so hardheaded," Carlos scoffed. "He always thinks he knows the way to run everything, and when things don't go his way, he flips out!"

"I know, mi'jo. I know. In his heart, he thinks he's doing what is best." Beatriz thought it would do her good to remember that, too. "But look—he'll come around. Don't worry. "You should go to bed. It's late, and I know you have to get up early, no?"

"Yeah." Carlos kissed his mother good night and turned to leave when he stopped suddenly. "I'm sorry if I disappointed you."

"No, mi'jo. You could never disappoint me. Go on to bed. I'm going to stay up and wait for your dad. Trust me. Everything will be better in the morning," she said. But even Beatriz wasn't sure if that was true.

It was well past midnight when Beatriz had the sinking realization that Larry wasn't coming back. She reluctantly dragged herself upstairs, weary with exhaustion, and ran a shower. After she finished pinning up her hair, she stepped into the shower, sat on the spa chair placed inside, and cried. Her fingers were pruned and her hair flattened by the time she had finished letting loose all the tears she'd been storing up. As she dried herself off, she stood in the door of the bathroom staring at the bed she shared with her husband. She couldn't remember the last time she went to bed without Larry. Each of them occasionally traveled for work, but this time the bed looked different. When she crawled in, she noticed how cold it felt without him. She sank her feet deep into the covers and pulled the sheets over her head, but she couldn't relax. After an hour of frustrating restlessness, she finally took her pillow and the throw at the foot of the bed and went back downstairs.

When she reached the foyer, she peeked out the window. The glow from the street lamp above the pavement where Larry's SUV was usually parked made the empty space look large and barren. She wrapped herself in the blanket and went into the living room, where she curled up in a chair. She didn't think she'd fall asleep. She wanted to be there when Larry returned. She wanted to talk to him, to help him understand, to try and understand what his reservations were about having Celeste stay with them. But before she knew it she was asleep.

She felt the slump before she heard the scream. It was deep and heavy, as if someone or something had fallen into the chair next to her, and it woke her instantly. She thought it was Larry and blinked against the darkness, looking for his familiar outline, but there was no one. She could hear the sound of a car passing down the street and jumped up to see if it was him pulling into their drive, but when she got to the window she could see it wasn't. She stood there thinking she would go back upstairs again when she heard the bloodcurdling scream. It was a sound so ragged, so full of anguish, it made the hair on every part of her body rise. She immediately ran toward it.

When Beatriz turned on the overhead light, Celeste was standing on the couch, the sheets balled up and clutched against her chest, her face drenched with terror and confusion.

"'Amá! 'Amá! Don't let them get me!" she screamed.

Beatriz did the only thing she knew to do. She went to the girl and pulled her down from the couch.

"It's okay! It's okay! You're safe, mi'ja! Shh, shh, shh. No one is going to hurt you. I've got you! I've got you!"

The two of them collapsed onto the couch. Celeste was fighting Beatriz's embrace, unsure of who Beatriz was, of where she was. The girl was shaking so violently, Beatriz thought she was having a seizure. Beatriz had never seen a child so frightened in her life, and it broke her heart. She wanted to make it better—she *had* to make it better. Instinctively, she began to sing a song about doves that she hadn't thought of in years. The airy notes of the song were a stark contrast to Celeste's violent thrashing and her distorted expression. But Beatriz would not give up. She continued singing to the girl even as her voice quivered. She was almost as scared as Celeste by now, remembering what it was like when her boys got sick or spiked a fever and there was nothing to do but worry and wait. After what seemed like an hour, Celeste realized where she was and who was holding her. She finally understood she was safe and let herself fall limply into Beatriz's arms.

"Wh-wh-why did they do that to her?" Celeste hiccupped into Beatriz's chest. "Why did they take her from me? Why can't I..." But Celeste couldn't finish her thought. She began to sob as if her insides were slowly being pulled out of her.

Beatriz stayed with Celeste through the night, stroking her hair, whispering in her ear, and singing tender songs until she finally fell silent. By sunrise, Celeste was sleeping with her head in Beatriz's lap, her face quiet and her breathing serene. Beatriz had slept most of the night sitting up. She had kinks in her neck and back, but she was determined to stay there as long as necessary. She stroked the girl's face lightly and watched her sleep. She had no idea what Celeste had seen or heard before she came to her, had no idea how to take away the pain she had and was obviously reliving, but she felt rabidly protective of the girl. She knew she would do everything in her power to keep Celeste from being frightened or surrounded by danger ever again.

"Where's 'Amá?" Beatriz heard Raúl ask in the foyer down the hall. She could hear who she thought was Carlos answering him, on his way out of the house for work.

"'Amá!" Raúl called. Beatriz carefully moved Celeste from her lap and onto the couch and quickly made her way out of the office and down the hall to the foyer, where her son was standing in his pajamas.

"Shh, shh, shh!" she said, her finger to her mouth. She motioned for him to follow her upstairs.

"What's going on?" he whispered.

"Celeste had a little trouble last night," she explained.

"What's wrong? Was she sick? Did she throw up? Man, I hate that!"

Beatriz could see Raúl was deeply concerned, and it made her proud. She put her hand on his cheek and caressed it.

"Ay, no, mi'jo. She had trouble sleeping. She's okay now, and she's finally asleep. Everything is okay, mi'jo. Don't worry. But look at the time! You need to get ready for school. And your lunch—I'll give you some lunch money, okay?"

"Dad already said he would give me some money," Raúl said.

"He did?"

"Yeah," Raúl said. "He woke me up and said he would take me to school like always."

"Okay, honey." Beatriz was confused. "Go finish getting dressed." When she peered into her and Larry's bedroom, it was as she had left it the night before. She stepped inside the room and looked in the bathroom. The shower had recently been used. She was wondering who had used it when she heard the bedroom door close behind her. When she turned around, there was Larry, his hair still damp, holding his coffee mug with steam rising from it, dressed in his robe.

"Hi," he said timidly.

"Hi."

"I forgot a few things in my office that I need for work, and I...I didn't want to disturb you. I saw you asleep with Celeste in the office. Is she okay?"

"For now," Beatriz said. "She had a nightmare. It took a while, but I settled her down."

"Poor kid."

"Yeah, poor kid."

The awkwardness between them was screamingly loud and unsettling.

"So, I'm going to take Raúl to school, like always,"

Larry said. "I—I would appreciate it if we could keep the kids out of this. I don't want them to get wrapped up in our...thing."

"I agree," Beatriz said.

Larry began to move to the closet, then felt suddenly ill at ease. "I need to get some clothes for work," he announced.

"I know. Where did you sleep last night?"

Larry scoffed. "I didn't sleep. I went to a bar, then drove around. I came home around four o'clock, and when I didn't see you in bed, I went to look for you and I saw you with her. I figured something happened, but I didn't know what. Poor kid."

Beatriz was exhausted and exasperated. "Larry... what's happening here?"

"What do you mean?" he asked. "I'm trying to get ready for work and get my kid to school, just like always."

"You think just because you come back in the middle of the night that everything is better, just like that?"

"No. We still have some big things to discuss, but I don't want my kids' lives to be turned inside out. I thought we could just act normal and—"

"I don't believe this. I really don't believe this. You think we can just go back to the way we were, just like that?"

"Why not?" Larry asked sheepishly. "This doesn't need to be bigger than it is."

"You left me!" Beatriz hissed. "You left me!"

"Not so loud!" Larry hissed back. "I was only gone for a few hours!"

"You said you were going to stay in a hotel! You walked out! You wanted to hurt me!"

"And you didn't want to hurt me with all that talk

about how I would lose if you had to choose between me and the kids?"

"You know what I meant!"

"Come on, Beatriz!" Larry said, holding his coffee with one hand and shoving the other into the pocket of his robe. "I mean, I know what you were trying to say, okay. And I admit leaving last night was not cool. I needed to clear my head, but I didn't want to worry the boys. That's why I came back. So, yes, we still have things to discuss but...can't we try and get past last night so we can work things out, for the kids?"

"All the kids?"

Larry didn't answer.

"That's what I thought."

Larry sat on the arm of the chair across from his wife. He was as exhausted and frustrated as she was.

"Look. All I'm asking for is a little bit of time," he said sincerely. "This is a whole new ball game for me. I feel like I have a catcher's mitt when I should have a golf club. And I feel like you chose the game and made up all the rules by yourself. You didn't ask me what I thought. You just moved forward, just like that."

"I never had to ask you before," Beatriz said softly. She could see that Larry was trying to meet her halfway. "We were always on the same playing field."

"Well. We still are. Or at least I think we can be. This time—I'm not—I just need more time to figure out how I feel about all this and where I fit in."

"How can you not know?" Beatriz asked incredulously. As much as she tried to understand, Larry's reluctance to open their home to Celeste confounded her.

"I just don't!" he snapped. "Look, I'm sorry. I didn't come back here to argue." Larry was dying to take his wife in his arms but was so confused about what was happening between them, he was afraid she would rebuff him. He couldn't take that.

"I'm sorry you feel upended," Beatriz offered. "I feel upended, too, but I don't think we have the luxury to keep wishing for the way things were. We have to go with the way things are, no matter how crazy it feels."

Larry stood there looking at his wife, unsure of what to do.

"I really don't want to do this alone," Beatriz said. "I really, really don't. But...it's kind of up to you. Look, I'm with you about figuring this out and I agree we don't need to get the kids involved. I'm with you on that."

Beatriz wanted to take Larry's hand and pull him close to her, but she wasn't sure if he would take it or bat it away, and she was too afraid to find out. "You can finish in here. I'll go check on Raúl," she said before leaving their bedroom.

Larry sighed and placed his coffee on the nightstand and then slid into the armchair. He sat there for a long time, staring at their empty bed. He could feel his throat tighten and his mouth tremble. He pulled himself together, sat up, and went to the closet to decide what he should wear to work. That, he felt confident, was something he could control.

Breakfast at the Columns bed-and-breakfast was made to order. While the other guests requested omelets and lattes, Josie helped herself to coffee and a muffin set out early for the impatient. She'd managed three hours of fitful sleep and was even groggier than usual, but at least her hands had stopped quaking. When she finished her coffee, she slipped out of the house to smoke and to gather her thoughts. She walked around the block three times. The first time to figure out which house was the one where she thought she saw Celeste and the boy in the backyard. Had she dreamed that? Had she *wanted* to see Celeste so much that she had imagined her? In her sleep-deprived state, she wasn't so sure.

The second walk around the block was to work up the nerve to go up to the house and knock on the door. What could she say that didn't sound too crazy? Contemplating that took another walk around the block and a second cigarette. Josie slowed as she reached the house and paused. She still wasn't sure what she was going to say, but she made her way up onto the porch. She pulled at the hem of her sleeves and ran her hand through her hair—had she even remembered to brush her hair? she suddenly wondered. Too late now. She was about to knock on the door when she heard someone come up behind her.

"May I help you?"

It was Larry, dressed for work in pressed khakis, a white dress shirt, and a tie. He'd just returned from driving Raúl to school.

"Oh, hello," Josie said. She studied Larry's face, looking for something familiar. When it looked like she wasn't going to state her business, Larry tried to guess.

"Are you...lost?" he asked.

"No, I..." Josie reached into her breast pocket for a business card that she usually carried there but came up empty-handed. "I'm Josie Mendoza. I'm a writer, a journalist. I know you don't know me from Adam, but..."

Larry took in Josie's disheveled appearance. Her outfit was plainly professional, but her blouse looked as if she had slept in it. "I'm sorry—what's this about?" he asked.

"Look, I know this is going to sound crazy, but I was, I'm...I'm looking for Celeste Sánchez. I need to make sure she's okay."

Larry instinctively moved to block Josie from the door to his house.

"I'm sorry. I'm a little—I really can't believe this," she said. But when Josie spent too much time trying to find the right words, Larry lost his patience.

"You have one minute to get off my porch," he warned. "And if you're not gone by the time I pass through this door—"

"I knew Perla Sánchez!" she blurted.

Larry stopped and looked at Josie carefully, trying to

decide whether he should let her speak, or call the police. He thought about the articles in Celeste's envelope. Knowing Perla didn't set Larry at ease. Then again, maybe she could explain why Celeste had such things. And if he turned her away and Beatriz learned she had information about her sister...

"You say you're a writer?"

"Yes. I know I sound crazy, and I probably look worse," Josie said, realizing that she indeed hadn't bothered to run a brush through her hair or rinse yesterday's mascara from her face. "I don't want any trouble. I just need to find Celeste. I have something that belongs to her, that's all. I thought I was looking for Perla's sister, Beatriz—"

"Beatriz is my wife," Larry said. "I'm her husband."

"You're Milligan?"

"I'm Larry Milligan."

"Oh, my gato," Josie exclaimed. She couldn't believe her dumb luck. "You're not a stonemason, are you?"

"What?"

"Never mind," Josie said.

Once Larry was convinced Josie wasn't a serial killer, he brought Beatriz out to the porch and closed the door behind them, standing sentry with his arms crossed and his legs slightly spread while the two women talked.

"So, how do you—how did you know my sister?" Beatriz asked. She was suspicious, too, but also hoping that if Josie was telling the truth, she could give her some insight about Perla, something that Celeste might not be able to tell her.

"I am a writer. You can look me up online. My stuff should come up."

Larry and Beatriz looked at one another. Josie looked more like a meth addict than the stereotypical image of a sweater-wearing, pipe-smoking writer that popped into their minds.

"Our computer is in the office, and my niece is still asleep in there. I don't want to disturb her," Beatriz said.

"So, she *is* here?" Josie asked incredulously. "That was her I saw in your backyard?"

Larry's demeanor went from mildly frosty to stone cold. "When was this?"

"Yesterday evening. I'm staying at the B and B behind your house," Josie explained. "You share an adobe fence with them, right? I saw—or, at least I *think* I saw—her through one of the openings. Look, I know I sound like a stalker, and I wouldn't believe me if I were you, either, but I have something that belongs to Celeste. I don't want any trouble. I'm just thrilled to hear she arrived safely, that's all. And I owe it to Perla..." Josie could sense she was getting aggressive, the way she did when she interviewed politicians who said a lot but never answered her question or petty bureaucrats who gave her the runaround. When Larry pulled his cell phone out of his pants pocket and began feverishly punching buttons with his thumbs, Josie lost her nerve.

She held up her hands in defeat. "You don't need to call the police," Josie stammered. "I'm sorry, really. Look, I'll just go."

"Why do you think *you* owe Perla?" Beatriz asked. The way she emphasized the *you* told Josie that Beatriz had understood her. Or at least that she hadn't written her off just yet. Josie cast a quick glance at Larry, who stopped what he was doing and looked up at the women.

"I'm texting the office that I'm coming late," he said.

Josie turned back to Beatriz. "I owe Perla because she helped me and I..." She could feel her voice begin to shake. "She was the one who helped me see I had to write my book about the Women of Juarez. I was gathering their story—her story. But I stopped working on the project when Perla was killed."

"Killed?" Beatriz may have feared the worst for her sister, but hearing it spoken out loud was still a shock. She could feel Larry staring at her, and was thankful for his nearness.

"Oh, you didn't know." Josie was heartsick, realizing she was going to be the one to break this part of the story to Beatriz. She inhaled deeply and tried to calm the quiver in her voice. "Yes. She was killed. I'm so, so sorry. I shouldn't be the one to tell you this."

"No, you're the only one who can tell me, it seems."

Beatriz exchanged looks with Larry, who moved aside. They let Josie into their house and led her to the kitchen, where Beatriz offered her a seat. Through the window, Josie could see the adobe fence, orange on this side, and the riser before it where she had seen Celeste and the boy, relieved she hadn't hallucinated the whole thing.

"So," Beatriz said. "Tell me everything."

Josie wanted Beatriz to know how brave Perla was. She told her about Perla working at the grassroots level to provide relief for the victimized families. She told her about how Perla the organizer was not liked among factory owners, but the workers who knew her respected her and, above all, adored her. She told Beatriz how her sister Perla was fierce and stubborn and articulate and brave.

"Stop," Larry said when he saw the grief creeping into his wife's eyes. "Please stop."

"I'm fine," Beatriz said, squeezing her husband's hand. "Please, go on."

"She was much braver than I could ever hope to be," Josie continued. "She was very private about her personal life, but the most important thing I know is that Celeste was the most precious thing in her world. In the end, all she wanted was for her to be here, with you."

As the words sank in, Josie could see a mosaic of emotions pass over Beatriz's face. It was hard enough for Josie to share the news; she couldn't imagine being the recipient of it. She tried not to stare as Larry reached over and put his large palm alongside his wife's face, peering into her eyes for some indication of what to do next.

"I'm okay. I'm okay," she whispered.

Beatriz finally excused herself and left Josie alone with Larry. He began punching keys on his phone again, and Josie watched him, unsure.

"So," he said, reading his phone screen. "You're the Josefina Mendoza who was published in the *Dallas Morning News*?"

"That's me."

He scrolled through the other listings he brought up on his phone.

"And the *Atlantic*? Impressive."

"Yeah, I just look like a nutcase," Josie tried to joke.

Larry didn't smile. "I've been having some trouble sleeping lately," she explained.

Beatriz returned with the large envelope that Celeste brought with her the night she arrived and placed it on the table.

"What can you tell me about this?"

Josie gasped when she saw what was inside. "Where did you get this?"

"Celeste brought it."

"These—these are my notes! Some of my notes, but I thought I'd lost..." Josie bit her lip as she rifled through the material. "There was a point when I wanted to quit, and Perla told me I couldn't." Josie's mind raced, trying to figure out when Perla could have gotten hold of these notes. She remembered how she'd thrown them in a paper sack and said she was going to burn them. Was Perla there? Suddenly she felt sick. "Did you—did Celeste look at this?"

"I don't know what she saw," Beatriz said. "I didn't look at all of it, but I did look at this." She pulled out one of the flash drives and held it up in front of Josie's face. "Is this how my sister died?"

Josie took the small piece of plastic from Beatriz and held it in her hand. She was overwhelmed with how such a small thing could carry so much misery and placed the drive on the table.

"I'm so sorry," Josie said. The three of them stared at the small flash drive, and Larry, who had no idea of the horrors that it held, knew to cover it with his large palm and pulled it off the table, as if he were closing the eyes of a corpse.

"I can only hope to God Celeste didn't see any of this," Beatriz said.

She began to shudder, and Larry threw the flash drive into the envelope. He was livid. He felt as if someone had infected his house and that there was nothing he could do about it.

"Celeste knows you?" Beatriz asked.

"We met once." Josie didn't want to tell Beatriz when and where they had met. "But I wouldn't be surprised if she didn't remember me."

"I don't know if she's awake yet," Beatriz said. "It's been a long, very strange weekend. If you wait here, I'll get her up and bring her out."

Larry put his arm out to stop Beatriz.

"Where is this thing you said you need to give to her?" Larry asked Josie, remembering the original purpose of her visit.

"Oh!" Josie stammered. "Of course! I'm so not with it. Let me go get it."

"Wait!" Larry said, as Josie rose to leave. "Would you please take all this stuff with you? I can't have this in my house." He began to stuff the notes back into the envelope.

"All we need are the official documents," Beatriz added. "The rest you can take."

"Sure," Josie said. "I'd be happy to." She gathered the notes and ran back to the bed-and-breakfast, where her car was parked. When she opened the trunk, she threw the envelope into an already heaping box of paper and dug for Celeste's quinceañera book, carefully wrapped once in tissue paper, then again in plain brown paper, then again in plastic bubble wrap.

"Thank you," Josie said to the sky. She wasn't sure who or what she was thanking. All she knew was she was grateful to have found Celeste, to have met the family she was to live with now. She looked down at the quince-añera book and felt an enormous weight leave her. It was a small gesture, bringing the book to Celeste, but Josie could already feel a balance brought to her mind, and a warm embrace of her heart. She knew that, at last, her restless mind would let her sleep.

When Josie returned to Beatriz and Larry's house, Beatriz was seated with Celeste on the couch in the living room. Larry escorted Josie into the house, but Josie could tell he was still uneasy with her presence. He hovered in the back of the room, occasionally pacing back and forth, peering at his phone or glancing at his watch, carefully watching everything from a distance.

"Mi'ja, do you remember la señora?" Beatriz asked Celeste, who sat as close to her aunt as possible without sitting on her lap. Celeste looked at Josie and thought she looked familiar but couldn't quite place her.

"I thought you said you met?" Larry snapped, when he saw Celeste didn't recognize Josie.

"She said they met *once*," Beatriz corrected her husband over her shoulder. Then, keeping her voice even, her tone neutral, she spoke again to Celeste. "This is Josefina Mendoza. She says she knew your mother and that she has something for you."

Josie handed the wrapped package to Celeste, who held it awkwardly, unsure what to make of it.

"I only wrapped it up like that to keep it from getting dirty," Josie explained. "Go ahead. It's yours." As Celeste opened the package, Josie caught the harsh expression on Larry's face. She wanted to witness Celeste being reunited with the quinceañera book but got the distinct impression from Larry that her welcome had long been worn out.

"You know what? I should probably be on my way," Josie offered.

"Have a seat," Beatriz said.

Larry clearly didn't like that Beatriz had invited her to stay but remained silent.

When Celeste finished unwrapping the package and realized what was in her lap she leapt to her feet. "Oh! How did you...? Where did you...?"

"What is that, mi'ja?" Beatriz asked.

"It's the book. My book! The book 'Amá and I..." The girl could scarcely talk. She was so excited and so happy, she was speaking in fits and starts.

Beatriz was ecstatic. The child, who had been terrified just hours earlier, was suddenly buoyant and alive.

"Thank you, Tía! Thank you!" Without thinking, Celeste threw her arms around her aunt's neck and held her tightly. Beatriz was as elated as she was the first time her own babies smiled their first smile at her, called her "Mama," or put their small hands on her cheeks and said, "I love you!"

"You should thank Ms. Mendoza," Beatriz said. "She's the one who brought this to you."

Celeste turned her attention to Josie and politely extended her hand to Josie. "Thank you, señora. You don't know what this means."

"I think I know a little," Josie explained, patting the

girl's hand. "You're mother shared it with me once. That's how I got to know about you."

"Can I see the book, mi'ja?" Beatriz asked from the couch.

Celeste went back to her aunt and plopped onto the couch next to her. Josie smiled forlornly, recognizing Perla's smile on her daughter's face. She was struck by how such a small thing could open such a deep well of sadness, mixed with gleeful recognition.

"I bet your aunt would love to know about your book," Josie said, pushing past the catch in her throat. "But you know what? I probably should be going." She was beginning to feel self-conscious, the way her emotions were rising to the surface. And Larry was still boring holes into her when he wasn't looking over the back of the couch to see what Beatriz and Celeste were so excited about.

As if suddenly remembering Josie was still in the room—and that she was a guest and not a danger—Beatriz slipped into the role of the good hostess. "Please, stay. Let me get you some coffee," she offered. "We can have breakfast, and you can tell us how you came to have this book. I'd like to know. I bet Celeste would like to know, too, wouldn't you, mi'ja?"

Celeste nodded her head, but Josie couldn't be sure if she was agreeing with Beatriz, or reacting to a memory sparked by one of the pages in her book. What Josie was sure of was that Larry was not thrilled with the idea. Not one bit. This was a private matter. Josie had done what she had to do. Besides, she had her own little girl waiting on her.

"Thank you, but no. I really need to hit the road."

Josie stood up, reaching into her pocket. She felt something pressing against her leg and when she pulled out her hand she found a crumpled business card. "I knew I had a card!" She smoothed it on her leg and handed it to Beatriz. "Call me anytime. My number is right there."

"Let me walk you out," Larry said. Josie said her final good-byes and followed Larry to the door. Beatriz and Celeste were soon immersed in the quinceañera book, talking and reveling in an unexpected happiness as they pored over the pages, with Beatriz asking questions and Celeste suddenly come to life, explaining what they were looking at.

"Enjoy!" Josie called to them from the door.

"Thank you!" Celeste sang, smiling appreciatively at Josie before turning back to her book.

As soon as Josie stepped off the porch, she reached into her pocket for her cigarettes and lit up. Larry was right behind her, standing above her on the last step.

"You'll understand if you never hear from us again, won't you?" he said to her back.

Josie took a long, hard draw on her cigarette and inhaled deeply before she turned around. She knew her appearance was a shock, but Celeste and Beatriz seemed happy enough. Why was Larry still treating her like a criminal?

"What exactly is your problem with me?" she asked.

"My family doesn't need to be involved in this thing you're writing about. Let's be clear about that. Whatever you're writing, it doesn't involve us, okay?"

"Well, Perla Sánchez is your wife's sister, isn't she? She could help me fill in the blanks."

"But she doesn't *need* to. You don't need her. You don't need us," he said.

Josie didn't like how Larry was looking down at her, his chin at his chest, taking on a paternal air. But she could also sense that there was something else: a pleading look in his eyes that he couldn't hide, no matter how tough he was trying to act. She blew an angry cloud of smoke out of the corner of her mouth and started to respond, but Larry cut her off.

"My wife has been through enough." His voice was quivering. "I just want to protect my family. I don't want them involved. Whatever happened to Perla over there is done. Please, please keep my family out of it."

Larry wasn't angry, he was frightened. As soon as she realized that, Josie's anger dampened. Her thoughts turned to her own family, her own daughter, how she was long overdue at home, and how she wanted to share a quiet, tender moment with her Paz, like Beatriz and Celeste were having inside. She decided to put Larry's mind at ease.

"I don't need to talk to your wife. I just had some unfinished business to take care of, that's all. We're through." She paused to look into Larry's face. His anxiety subsided and he began to return to his old self.

"Well, you have a safe trip back," he said. As he turned to go back into the house, Josie spoke.

"I'm sorry for your loss." The words froze him. "Perla was a good person. I'm sorry you didn't know her the way I did."

Larry thought for a long time before he finally said over his shoulder, "Thank you."

Larry went inside the house, and Josie could hear the final, hard click of the deadbolt bidding her good-bye.

When Larry stepped back inside the house, Celeste and Beatriz were still huddled over the book splayed open on Celeste's lap. He stood in the archway that separated the foyer from the living room and tried to appear small and unobtrusive while listening to every word that was spoken.

Celeste was showing Beatriz the notes and pictures and drawings she and her mother had collected over the years to prepare for Celeste's quinceañera. They looked at each page, and Celeste carefully explained what she or her mother had been thinking—the ideas that seemed great one year but silly the next. She showed Beatriz the pages from the year Celeste thought it might be perfect to be dressed as a fairy, followed by the year she wanted to be dressed in bright checks.

"I'm glad you let that idea go," Beatriz laughed. "You would have looked like you were dressed in Chiclets!"

The two of them laughed. Celeste pointed out her crayon drawings, explaining when she made them and why, when she could remember, and was as amused as Beatriz was by some of the things she herself had placed in the notebook—bubble gum wrappers and the game from a cereal box.

As Celeste shared the book, she was astonished by the younger version of herself. "This is kind of stupid, huh?"

"Oh, no!" Beatriz said. "Are you kidding? I love this! It's like looking at a map of your life."

As they examined the pages, Beatriz read her sister's handwritten notes, looking both familiar and strange. Here and there, Perla's random thoughts about dresses, flowers, and cake flavors were interspersed with single lines about her daughter: "She moves like a dancer" or "Celeste's poem—third grade. She can say it out loud by heart."

Celeste watched Beatriz linger over the notes written by her mother—like she was trying to pull information from between and behind the handwriting.

"So, you don't think this is dumb?" Celeste asked.

"I think this is beautiful. I know this is something you and your mother did together, but this is a great gift for me. Thank you for showing me," Beatriz said.

"You have lots of stories about my mother, huh?" Celeste asked. "From when she was a girl, like me?"

"Of course," Beatriz said. "I knew her when she was just a button. And maybe you can tell me your stories from when you knew her. When you want. I want to hear them all."

Celeste looked at Josie's card and then handed it to Beatriz, who placed it into the pages of the book. The two of them sank into the delicate happiness that they shared with the arrival of this one, small book.

Beatriz turned her thoughts to fresh orange juice and pan dulce. She was about to ask Celeste what she'd like for breakfast, when Larry's cell phone bleated loudly. Beatriz and Celeste jumped. They had forgotten he was still there.

"Cripes!" he said, fumbling with his phone. He had set his phone alarm to go off for a meeting he had at work in thirty minutes. "Damn it!"

"Larry!"

"Sorry. I forgot about this meeting, and I need to get a few things from my office. Do you mind?" He was looking at Beatriz, and she looked at Celeste.

"He needs to go into the office for a bit, okay?"

Celeste shook her head and held the book close to her chest. She smiled tentatively at Larry. He nodded to her and Beatriz and finally left his perch to get his things.

"All right, young lady," Beatriz began with the enthusiasm of someone who has been given a second chance, "I think we should eat, and then we'll get dressed. Then I think we should discuss how we are going to make your quinceañera happen. Now we have a guide and no excuses!" She nodded toward the quinceañera book. "We'll get a calendar and some markers and work backwards from there. How's that sound?"

As Larry made his way down the hall, he could hear his wife and Celeste chattering softly. The girl seemed to be feeling more at ease, and Beatriz sounded elated. He wanted to go along with the obvious happiness that had finally brought Beatriz and Celeste together, but something inside him just couldn't let go of the idea that he was losing something he would never recover.

Larry got to his meeting just in time. He took notes, asked questions, spoke when spoken to, and gave the appearance that he was listening attentively. But in reality he was distracted. He figured in time he could get used to having a new person in the house, but it was the other thing—the trauma behind Perla's death—that he wasn't sure he could handle. It filled him with the same dread he felt when the police came to his house when he was a boy, looking for trouble and knowing they would find it there. Larry believed that if you let bad things into your life, they only attracted more bad things. Celeste seemed like a good kid, but the drama of her mother's death made him writhe with worry about what this girl was capable of drawing to his calm and peaceful world. *She's just a girl!* he'd screamed to himself last night as he drove around, no destination in mind but feeling like he couldn't be at home. She was just a girl. He knew this. He knew she was not to blame for the circumstances of her life. But what if this Mendoza person, this chain-smoking writer who seemed to know all about the violence that was part of Perla's world, wasn't the only stranger who had followed Celeste? As hard as he tried to shake his worry, the more it gnawed at him. And the more it gnawed at him, the guiltier he felt. He was the adult, after all. Celeste was just a kid. A kid who needed all the help she could get. But why did it have to come from them? Why did she have to come into their lives now?

By the time he left the office to pick up Raúl from school, he was sullen and out of sorts. But Raúl was full of chatter and could hardly wait for his father to pull into the school driveway to pick him up.

"Hi, Dad!" Raúl chirped.

Larry smiled. His kid's spirit was infectious. "Hi, son. Did you have a good day at school?"

"Yeah! And the countdown begins!"

"Countdown to what?"

"Summer!" Raúl said. "There's only ten days of school left."

Larry had forgotten. He had put all his attention on planning the anniversary party and the honeymoon trip to Paris, and he'd somehow lost track of this very important detail. The reality of summer vacation and the need to keep three boys active—Raúl and his nephews—began to sink in as he watched a woman in a minivan ahead of him. She was more intent on speaking on her cell phone than in maneuvering through the after-school traffic, and Larry was getting annoyed.

"So, Dad, is Celeste going to come to my school?"

"What do you mean?" Larry said, thinking that if he hugged the woman's bumper, maybe she would get the message and move.

"Well, she has to go to school, doesn't she? But school's almost out, so what's the point?"

"Right," Larry said. "What's the point? I'm sure she goes to school in El Paso."

"But...isn't she going to stay with us?" Raúl asked. He thought Celeste moving in with them was a done deal. In fact, he was planning on it. "Isn't she, Dad?"

Larry was losing his patience with the woman in the minivan. He tapped his horn to get her attention.

"Isn't she, Dad?"

The woman creeped farther in front of Larry, then stopped, still chattering on her phone, talked demonstratively with her free hand, completely oblivious to Larry.

"Come on! What the..." He tapped his horn a few more times.

"Dad!"

"What!" Larry snarled. The high spirits Raúl had were sucked out of him, and he slumped in the passenger seat, realizing his dad was in a piss-poor, sour mood. Larry knew he was the cause of this, but he was having trouble controlling his temper. The woman finally looked in her rearview mirror and waved at Larry apologetically before she pulled her vehicle out of his way. Larry surged forward and screeched to a stop next to the woman and rolled down the passenger-side window next to Raúl so he could talk to her.

"I'm sorry! I got distracted," the woman explained, pulling the phone away from her face.

"What the hell is wrong with you?" Larry demanded.

Raúl's head sunk into his torso.

"You think you own the road here? You think no one else is as important as you and your precious phone call?

You think I don't have better things to do than to wait for you to take care of your very important business?"

The woman stared at Larry a moment, but instead of answering back, her gaze turned vacant as her window glided up, activated by the push of an unseen button. She went back to her phone conversation and turned to face the opposite direction. Larry almost shot through the roof.

"Hey! Hey! I'm talking to you! I'm talking to you, damn it!" Larry leaned on his horn, his arm stiff and his face turning red. Everyone in front of the school stopped what they were doing to look at Larry with exasperated expressions. Adults on the sidewalk near the drive gathered their children to their sides and watched him carefully. When an opening in the bumper-to-bumper traffic finally yawned open, Larry lurched into it and sped away, cursing under his breath.

Raúl desperately wished he could slide off his seat and hide beneath the floor mat.

By the time they got home, Larry had calmed down, but his mood was still sour. Raúl went to his room, while Larry went straight to his office. He thought he might get some work done, until he saw Beatriz and Celeste sitting together at the desk.

"Oh!" Beatriz said. "I didn't realize the time."

"Is Raúl home now?" Celeste asked her aunt. "Can I go say hi?"

"Sure, sweetheart. He's probably in the kitchen."

"No, he went upstairs," Larry reported, looking through some file folders on the corner of the desk that he realized would have been useful for his meeting earlier in the day.

"I'm sure he'll be back down for a snack. Why don't you go find him?" Beatriz said.

Celeste could tell right away that Larry was not happy and quickly moved past him to avoid getting splashed by his foul mood.

"What's the matter?" Beatriz asked when she was sure Celeste was out of earshot. Larry took in the large calendar Beatriz and Celeste had been working on and the colored markers, in lavender, hot pink, red, and turquoise splayed across the desk. He could see they were using them to fill in the calendar with color-coded notes that had meaning only to them.

"For the quinceañera," Beatriz offered before Larry could ask. "If you need to use the computer, I'll get out of your way." She began collecting the materials that she and Celeste had spread on the desk.

"We need to talk," Larry said. He paced in front of the sofa where Celeste slept. Her bedding was neatly folded and sat on the end of the couch. The pile was small and unobtrusive, and yet it annoyed him. "I need my office back!" he finally blurted. The room had long gone from being his office to an all-activity room, but everyone knew he liked to call it his office. Beatriz didn't want to argue with him.

"Okay, I already said I'd get out of your way," she repeated, the quinceañera planning supplies in her arms. As she briskly made her way to the door, Larry's attitude softened. He didn't want to argue, either.

"No, wait, I mean—I thought she was going to sleep upstairs."

"She doesn't want to," Beatriz said, closing the office door quietly. "For some reason, she feels better sleeping down here."

"Well, then where am I going to sleep?"

"What do you mean?" Beatriz asked.

"Well, because of the way things are, I thought—"

"I didn't kick you out of our room. If you sleep down here, they're going to figure out something is wrong and start to worry."

This pleased Larry. He didn't imagine there would be any lovemaking anytime soon, but sleeping with his wife was more than he hoped for.

"Is there anything else?" Beatriz asked.

"Well, I was wondering...can we—are we still going on our trip?"

Beatriz hadn't given it any thought. She didn't want to stir up any more tension between them but realized that since the trip was scheduled soon, it was a subject that had to be discussed.

"Well," she began carefully, "I think it would be best if we postponed it."

Larry fell onto the couch.

"Why would we do that?" he asked, although he already knew the response.

"Because Celeste just got here, and I think leaving might be disconcerting for her. She really needs some stability and routine," Beatriz said. The whole idea of going on a romantic trip with Larry seemed as bizarre as having a girls' night out with her sister-in-law Norma.

"So, you don't want to go?" Larry said. He tried not to sound as wounded as he felt. Beatriz knew to choose her words carefully.

"I don't think the timing is right, Larry. Do you?"

Larry bit his tongue. "I need the computer," he said after a moment.

"You're mad."

"It doesn't matter what I am, does it?"

"Larry—"

"Look. I'm beat. I'm behind at work, and I forgot about school being out. I need to get the boys lined up with things to do over the summer to keep them out of trouble."

"Yeah, well," Beatriz began, trying to be diplomatic, "I was looking into getting Celeste signed up with Camp Fire Girls or something like that. And I found some karate classes that the boys had asked about last year," she offered. "I wrote the information down on the pad over there. And there's some swim classes, and baseball camp again, and Raúl is already signed up for his comic book thing. And we really should talk about Carlos—"

But Larry had reached his limit. He covered his face with his hands.

"I can't—I can't think about that right now," he said. He was working hard to make sense of things.

"Okay, well," Beatriz said, turning to leave the room. "I'm going to heat something up from yesterday and make a salad. I'll call you when it's ready." She hovered in the doorway a moment, and Larry looked at her expectantly.

"A lot has happened in a short amount of time. I know this is hard for you. This is hard for me, too. It's so weird how joy and horror can share the same space," she said, thinking of how elated she was that Celeste had finally accepted her, while learning of the circumstances that brought her niece to her.

"Yeah," Larry muttered. He wanted to say more, but his mind was muddled with guilt and want. "I'm exhausted. You must be, too."

"We just need some time. Can you—can we—give that to each other?"

How much time? Larry wanted to ask. But even he, even-keeled, by-the-book Larry Milligan, knew there was no real answer to that question.

When Carlos came home, he saw the strange mood his mother and father were in and decided that approaching his mother was the safest.

"So, did you and Dad talk about me?"

"No. Not yet, Carlos. Now's not a good time. Don't worry. We'll get to it. Sit down. It's time to eat."

The only person who spoke at dinner was Raúl, who made it his responsibility to fill Celeste in on everything that happened at school, the teachers he liked, the classes he was doing well in, the best day to eat lunch at school, and the fastest way to make it out of the building should there be an alien invasion or an attack by zombies. Celeste listened intently, amused by her cousin and his quirkiness. Beatriz picked at her food and tried to pay attention to her son, as did Larry, but as the meal wore on, he became more withdrawn. He finally set his elbows on the table and ran his hands through his hair.

"I'm beat. I didn't sleep much last night. I've got to lie down."

"Sure. I can hold down the fort. Go ahead," Beatriz said.

Carlos was perplexed. He looked to his mother, but when she closed her eyes and sat back in her chair, he knew, once again, that this was not the time.

By the time Beatriz made it up to their bedroom, it was nearly ten o'clock. Larry was sound asleep in the armchair, a file folder he brought home from work open on his lap, the contents fallen to the floor when he finally surrendered to sleep.

"Larry…Larry…" Beatriz was gently nudging him. When he opened his eyes, he saw her standing over him, a pillow and a sheet under her arm.

"Why don't you go to bed?" she said. He thought she'd brought the bed things for him so he could sleep in the chair and reached for them.

"Thanks."

"No, no. This is for me. Go sleep in the bed."

"Where are you going?"

"I'm going downstairs to be with Celeste."

This brought Larry to full consciousness. "What? Why?"

"I promised her I would stay with her until she fell asleep," she said. After a moment she added, "I'll be back up."

Larry hauled himself sluggishly to their bed and sat on it, out of sorts and unsure of what time it was. He felt like he did when their boys were babies—sleep deprived and surly, at the beck and call of a baby who demanded all their attention. But hadn't they already been through all of that? Wasn't it time to enter the next phase of their life as a mature married couple? Was that so much to ask?

Beatriz made her way to the door and turned back to Larry.

"Thanks for understanding," she said. "I really appreciate how understanding you're being." She smiled slightly at her husband, believing that his exhaustion and his silence were signs that he was coming to terms with Celeste. "It will get better," she added. "I promise."

She closed the bedroom door, and as soon as it clicked shut Larry fell back onto the bed and let out a long groan. He was glad his wife had no idea about all the thoughts that had passed through his mind.

Celeste and Raúl were watching the last of an animated TV show Raúl liked. They were dressed for bed, sitting on the floor near each other with their knees drawn to their chests, chuckling like amused chipmunks. Beatriz made up Celeste's bed on the couch, and as soon as the show ended Beatriz launched into mommy mode.

"Ok, mi'jitos. That's it. It's time to hit the hay."

"Ah!" Raúl whined. "There's another show on after this. Are you guys going to watch it without me?"

"No, everyone is going to bed," Beatriz assured Raúl.

"Why? She doesn't have school tomorrow."

"No, but you do. In the meantime, we are all keeping our schedule, just like always."

"Yeah, but—"

"Ya, ya, ya," Beatriz said. "Go brush your teeth, and I'll come up later."

"There's a mad scientist movie marathon on the Syfy Channel," Raúl said to his cousin.

"Really?" Celeste said. He was thrilled that this interested her, too.

"This is what we're going to do," Beatriz said. She picked up the remote control and used it to find the channel, and with a few quick clicks, her work was done.

"There. It will all be recorded and you two can watch it over the weekend. How's that?"

"Well, taught you, mother have I," Raúl said, the tips of his fingers pressed together lightly as he nodded sagely. Celeste laughed. The sound of her laughter was like tinkling pennies, and it made Raúl laugh, too. He decided he was going to make it his business to make her laugh as much as he could, whenever he could.

"Okay, Yoda. Off to bed." Beatriz kissed her son on the cheek, and he kissed her back. Raúl faced Celeste, unsure of what to do. She helped him out by raising her palm toward him and making a V shape between her ring finger and her tallest finger. Raúl chuckled in recognition.

"Ah, yes. 'Live long and prosper,' my cousin," he said. "Moi yami."

"Buenas noches, primo," Celeste said.

Beatriz helped Celeste get comfortable and turned off all the lights in the office except for a small lamp near the window. As she made her way around the room, she began to hum to herself.

"My mom knows that song, too," Celeste said. "I mean—she knew it."

Beatriz sat on the opposite end of the couch and wrapped her arms around her pillow.

"Are you going to stay here all night?" Celeste asked.

"I'll stay here as long as you like."

"I'm not a baby, but—"

"But what?" Beatriz asked.

"Can I...can you come over here?"

Beatriz got up and moved to the other end of the couch where Celeste was lying. The girl sat up and Beatriz settled in, as Celeste eased herself onto Beatriz's lap. Beatriz began to sing the song lightly, a love song in Spanish about two doves. When Beatriz forgot the words, Celeste filled them in until they were singing together, their voices mingling like chimes. After a moment, Beatriz realized Celeste was singing to stay awake.

"Nothing is going to hurt you." She began to stroke Celeste's hair. "I'll be right here."

Celeste fell silent and Beatriz thought she'd fallen asleep. She adjusted herself slightly, wishing she'd brought the pillow she'd left on the far end of the couch before she moved to Celeste's side.

"My dream is always the same," Celeste began. "I'm in the house, and these men come in. I run and hide upstairs—only in real life, we never had an upstairs."

Beatriz was about to interrupt Celeste but stopped herself, making herself listen with all her heart and all her senses. Part of her didn't want to hear, but the other part knew she needed to be a witness for Celeste. She let the girl continue.

"The men say they want to hurt me and yell at me to come out. They know they're going to find me, but I make myself small, the way 'Amá used to make me when I was little." She trembled, and Beatriz stroked her arm.

"But I make myself so small. I feel myself shrink. Then the men come into the room where I am, but they don't see me and I know I'm safe. They leave, but I stay small for a long, long time until I'm sure they're gone. And just when I think it's safe, I hear the sounds. They're hurting her. I try to go back downstairs, but the stairs aren't where they were before. I can't save her. She screams and screams and screams until they finish with her. And then they come for me. That's usually when I wake up," Celeste said.

Beatriz worked hard to keep her voice steady and calm.

"Is that how it happened? Did you see how your mother was…" Beatriz hated to say the word.

"Killed?" Celeste said plainly. "No. They took her away from the house and did it in the desert like all the others. I don't know why they left me behind. I was at home asleep. I didn't even know she was gone until the next day, when it was too late."

Beatriz was relieved. At least Celeste was spared this one indelible experience.

"I know it's just a dream and it can't hurt me, but it seems so real," Celeste explained. "So real, I can feel their breath on my face."

"But no one—this is important, okay?" Beatriz asked. "No one ever touched you or hurt you? It's okay, you can tell me. Okay?" She had to be sure that Celeste didn't need much more than some new clothes and a new place to live.

"No," Celeste said. "I know about the others, but that never happened to me."

"Gracia a Dios," Beatriz said. "Thank God."

Celeste fell quiet and Beatriz began to sing to her again. When she finished the song, she lay her head back onto the couch and closed her eyes. She wanted to cry out for her sister but would save that wailing for another time, when she was alone. Celeste needed her now, and she wanted to be there for her.

"What if I forget her?" Celeste whispered. "What if the only memories I have left of her are bad dreams?"

"I never forgot her," Beatriz began. "I've never forgotten her. She always has a piece of my heart. I think it will be the same for you. I know it will."

Celeste was quiet for a long time. "How come no one wants to say her name?" she finally asked.

Beatriz had to think before she remembered the gathering in the kitchen with all the aunts, and how Elaine was shushed before she revealed that she was going to name her baby Perla, if it were a girl. Beatriz had hoped that Celeste hadn't noticed that strange exchange, but the girl was much more perceptive than Beatriz realized.

"Sometimes, when something is painful or confusing, instead of talking about it, people think if they don't talk about it, the pain will go away. But that's not always how it works," Beatriz said.

"Why didn't you find her? Why didn't you find us?"

"Oh, mi'ja," Beatriz sighed. "Believe me, we tried! We tried really hard. I don't think your mother wanted to be found. She was always really good at hide-and-seek. And for whatever reason..." Beatriz didn't want to continue but decided she wanted to be as truthful with her niece as possible. "I think she was angry at me. Or she thought I was angry with her. Sometimes, when we were girls, we fought so much you would hardly know we were sisters."

"But you are sisters," Celeste said. She said it with such confidence it made Beatriz curious.

"Why do you say it like that?"

"Because of the way you are. Sometimes you hold your hands the way she does. When you think about something, you bite your lip in the same way. You talk the same. I mean, not exactly the same, but with the same way to make people listen." Celeste adjusted herself in Beatriz's lap. "She told me you would take me if anything ever happened. I didn't believe her, but..."

Her voice began to trail off, and Beatriz could tell that Celeste was falling asleep. And pillow or not, Beatriz closed her eyes, leaned into the couch, and tried to make herself comfortable for the night. As she was drifting off to sleep, the last thought she had was *There is nothing I won't do for this girl. Nothing.*

Beatriz was fast asleep when Celeste began thrashing in her sleep, fighting off the unknown demon that had cornered her in the night. She struck Beatriz in the lip with her elbow, and Beatriz could taste blood, but she kept her cool and soothed the girl, rocked her, and told her everything would be all right, until Celeste finally heard her, and slowly, slowly calmed down.

They carried on this nightly ritual for a week, and then another, and then another. Beatriz's back was wrenched and her neck was stiff, but she vowed to help Celeste tame her nightmares, for however long it took. She arranged to take a leave of absence from work; since it was nearing the summer, the timing was good. During the day, Celeste was fine. She and Beatriz got to know one another, poring over the quinceañera book and planning Celeste's party as they shared their stories about Perla. Celeste was coming out of her shell, and Beatriz was delighted with the girl, who was so much like her sister. In some ways she was like a small adult, but in others still very much a little girl, frightened by whatever was terrorizing her in her nightmares.

Celeste was glad when school was out, because then
she could spend more time with Raúl, and Raúl was
happy to have a willing companion to share in the whole
list of films he had decided they needed to watch. They
would start off the "Summer of Blood," as he called it,
by viewing the entire line of Bela Lugosi films. Beatriz
almost swallowed her tongue when Raúl brought the subject up, but when she saw that it did not unnerve Celeste,
and that, in fact, she was into it, she put her reservations
aside. She would let the kids have their fun, but she kept
a close watch on their activities in case the films triggered
any anxieties in Celeste. Instead, it was Larry who put
a dent in that idea when he enrolled his son, along with
Seamus and Wally, in baseball league, soccer camp, a
week of swimming, and karate—anything he could get
the boys into to keep them physically occupied for the
summer.

Celeste had her fun, too. When she and Beatriz were
not planning her quinceañera, she was going to her own
summer classes. At first, Beatriz worried that Celeste
would be too shy to participate and struggled to find just
the right activities for her—a pottery class at one of the
area museums, a filmmaking class for young Latinas at a

community center, a dance class, a paper-making class, a cooking class; but it was the last class that she enrolled Celeste in that revealed her untapped talent: softball. She and the boys all went to the same day camp, where they splintered off into their groups, came back together for lunch, then spent the afternoon playing in separate sessions before reuniting again to be picked up in the late afternoon by Larry, Beatriz, or occasionally Lucy. As the summer wore on, Celeste was immersed in so many activities, she was beginning to feel like part of the gang.

The kids didn't notice that organizing their activities was the only real time Beatriz and Larry communicated with each other. All their talk was centered on what was happening the next day: who was picking up whom, what uniforms needed to be washed, who needed a packed lunch, who needed lunch money, and who needed backpacks, shoes, sunblock, hats, and signed permission slips.

By the middle of summer, Celeste's bronze skin was a dark, nutty brown. In quiet moments, when she and the boys sat like weary sacks of bones as they were driven home, she would look out the window and think about returning to El Paso. Surely one of her mother's friends would care for her, if she asked. But the idea of leaving San Antonio and going back to El Paso didn't seem as urgent as it did when she had first arrived. She liked that she and Raúl looked out for each other, which was necessary more than ever, since they were spending so much more time with Seamus and Wally. Wally was cute, but Seamus—he was always in a bad mood. Why, she didn't know. But she knew to keep her distance, like she did from her uncle Larry, who always fell silent around her, exchanging only a few sullen pleasantries. He was never unkind; he just wasn't as present as her aunt.

Seamus, on the other hand, was a jerk. She was annoyed by his snide remarks and rude behavior. He never directed them to her, which was good. Instead he spoke past her and through her, as if she were wallpaper. When he had to acknowledge her presence, he did so with silent, simmering annoyance. He thought she didn't notice when he bored holes into the back of her head. But she knew. Celeste asked Raúl about their surly cousin, and he assured her he was like that with everyone. The best thing to do was ignore him. She took her cousin's advice, at first. And then Seamus went too far.

On the very last day of baseball camp, the kids were waiting for Lucy to pick them up. Tired, dusty, and sweaty, Raúl got his second wind, thinking about the "Fright Night Summer of Blood" movie marathon he had planned for the weekend. It was the first time since Celeste arrived that Seamus and Wally were staying over, and Raúl was looking forward to the party.

"Okay, so I have *The White Zombie* up first, and then we can watch—," Raúl began.

"Aw, man! How come you get to choose?" Seamus asked. He was testy. He'd been popped by a pitch on the shoulder and was still rubbing out the lingering sting.

"C'mon, Shay! We all want to watch the movie, don't we?" Raúl looked to Celeste and Wally for support. Wally nodded and Seamus shot his little brother an annoyed look. He didn't bother to consult Celeste.

"I don't think I've ever seen *The White Zombie*. Is it good?" she asked.

"You'll like it!" Raúl declared. "So, we'll get home, and I bet they'll make us take a shower, and then we'll order pizza and we'll watch it in Celeste's room. Curtain time is at eight o'clock, sharp."

Seamus began to throw a baseball into the air and catch it in his mitt.

"She has a TV?" Seamus couldn't believe it. *Why does Celeste get her own TV? That isn't fair*, he thought.

"I mean, in the office. You know, where the TV and DVD player are," Raúl explained. "She sleeps in the office." That shred of news diverted Seamus's attention, and the ball he tossed into the air hit the ground with a thump and a hop before it nested in the grass a short distance from him.

"Why is she sleeping in the office?" Seamus asked. It didn't make any sense. First, he and Wally got banished from the house to make room for Celeste, and then she wasn't even sleeping in the bedroom—*their* bedroom? He didn't like that. He didn't like that at all. Celeste put on her mitt and picked up the baseball, palming it into her glove, enjoying the warm smack of leather against leather. Seamus tried to pretend he didn't mind that Celeste was touching his baseball.

"So, why is she sleeping in the TV room?" he asked again.

"She's standing right there," Raúl said. But before Seamus could ask her himself, he quickly added, "She just does. It's not that big a deal."

"So, if it's not that big a deal, why don't you tell me?"

"Because it's none of your business," Raúl said protectively.

Celeste began to toss the ball back and forth with Wally. The little boy had a huge mitt, but no matter how gently Celeste tossed the ball, he was too uncoordinated to catch it.

"You throw like a girl," Seamus said.

"I do not!" Wally said.

"I wasn't talking to you," Seamus spat.

"I *am* a girl," Celeste said. "Besides, this is how they teach us to pitch."

"Yeah, like a girl," Seamus repeated.

"I've seen her pitch. She's got some heat," Raúl said.

"Oh, really?" Seamus said. This was his fourth summer going to baseball camp. He knew he was a good pitcher and figured whatever Celeste had, he could outdo ten times over. "So then, why don't we play Toss?"

Raúl and Wally groaned. Toss was a game Seamus made up, and one that he always won. He said he would go easy on his cousins, but when he had the opportunity, he would burn them with a stunning pitch that would either leave them with a stinging hand or running after a zooming ball that went far afield. The game started simply. The kids would stand shoulder to shoulder and toss the ball to each other, then move out in ever-increasing circles, until they were forced to throw the ball overhand. Whoever missed was out, and the last person standing won. Seamus always won because he had the strongest arm. Wally's hand-eye coordination was still developing, and Raúl usually chickened out by the time Seamus got his arm warmed up and started throwing fastballs.

"C'mon. I'll be gentle," he promised.

"Can I play?" Celeste asked.

Seamus thought a moment, and then made a counter-offer. "Okay, but if I win, you have to tell me why she sleeps in the office," he said, still not addressing Celeste directly.

"What if one of us wins?" Raúl asked.

"Yeah, right," Seamus snickered.

"Then why would we want to play with you?" Celeste asked. Seamus didn't expect Celeste to speak, and it caught him by surprise.

"Because if *you* win," Seamus said, finally looking Celeste square in the face, "I'll stop asking why you sleep in the office instead of upstairs."

"What if I win?" Wally asked. The older kids tried to conceal their pity. Wally was wearing a hand-me-down uniform that was still one size too large, and his new helmet sat on his head slightly askew. "If I win, I get a piece of your pizza, and we get to watch the movie, and you have to not talk through it," Wally proclaimed.

"That works for me," Raúl said.

"Me, too," Celeste said.

The kids started small, and slow, like always. Seamus kept his word to be gentle, but he didn't like it when Celeste held her own. Wally was out first, after Seamus lobbed a ball high into the air, thinking his little brother could not possibly miss it. But the ball hit the tip of his glove and went rolling away.

"The sun was in my eyes!" he protested over his shoulder as he went to retrieve the ball.

"Yeah, I feel your pain." Seamus smirked. He thought Celeste would be the next to go, but instead it was Raúl, when Seamus threw a blazing fastball to him.

"Hey!" Raúl protested. "You dork!" He retrieved the ball and dropped it at Seamus's feet.

"Oh, don't be a spoilsport, Miss Milligan." Seamus bent over to pick up the ball and then called over to Celeste.

"Don't worry," he said to Celeste. "I'll be gentle." He threw her a zinger that he was sure she would miss, but she caught the ball squarely in her glove, the smack of the ball hitting the leather sounding like a slap on the cheek.

"D'oh!" Raúl and Wally whooped.

"Shut up," Seamus muttered. Celeste took her stance, shifting her weight between her feet.

"Well, are you going to throw it or dance?" Seamus asked.

But Celeste refused to be rushed. She found her balance and then stood perfectly still before finally cranking up and throwing a ball with so much fire, even Seamus was surprised when he caught it. Raúl and Wally clapped and cheered, laughing at the expression on Seamus's astonished face and thrilled at their cousin Celeste's ability to keep up with him.

"Oh, hell no," Seamus muttered. He was through playing nice. He wound up his arm and made like he was going to fire another bullet but instead threw a high Hail Mary that sailed over Celeste's head. She followed the ball as it hung in the sky then finally began to fall as her cousins held their breath. The sun was in her eyes and she could feel the ground beneath her was uneven, but she caught the ball with a gentle plop in her glove. Raúl and Wally whooped and high-fived each other as she jogged back to her original starting position.

"I thought we were supposed to move out in rings?" she asked.

"He cheats!" Wally yelled.

"So, you know you're going to lose, right?" Seamus taunted.

"C'mon, Shay," Raúl said.

"Let me guess—maybe you sleep in the office because you peed the bed. Is that it?"

Celeste had had enough. She wound up her arm and shot Seamus the hardest, fastest, most furious pitch he'd ever received in his life. The ball screamed through the air, and before he knew it, it had flown past him and off into the field beyond him. Raúl and Wally roared in disbelief.

"Take that, sucker!" Wally cheered, doing his version of an end-zone dance, flapping his arms and legs wildly. Celeste was his new hero.

Seamus stood dumbfounded for a moment before he realized that a car was honking in the distance. It was Beatriz, trying to get their attention. Now, in addition to having lost at his own game, he had a deep, sinking feeling. Lucy was supposed to have picked them up, not Beatriz. *What excuse did my mother come up with this time?* he wondered.

"Well, don't just stand there. Go get my ball!" Seamus ordered Wally.

"You go get your ball," Celeste said, pulling Wally by the arm. "We'll be in the car."

Seamus would later complain that his arm still hurt, that the sun was in his eyes, and that the car horn had startled him, but no one believed him. He didn't like that he was shown up by a girl, and especially this girl. But when they got to the house and the evening was over, and he and his brother were allowed back into the bedroom— their room—while Celeste inexplicably bunked on the office couch, he tried to put the defeat behind him to concentrate on more pressing issues. Namely, what was his mother up to now, and how long did he want to continue going through another one of her disappearing acts?

SEVENTEEN

A beautiful Saturday morning, a brilliant blue sky, a choir of birds sweetly singing, a soft pillow, a comfy bed: the perfect day to sleep in—all broken by the sound of hammering, the clatter of tools, and an electric drill. Beatriz heard the racket first, still nestled on the office couch with Celeste.

"What is that?" Celeste whined in her sleep.

"I don't know. Go back to sleep, mi'ja." Beatriz unwound herself from her niece and struggled to stand up as Celeste pulled her pillow over her head and turned over to face the back of the couch. Beatriz had to massage the feeling back into her leg before she could walk, but she couldn't help but smile. It was the first time Celeste had slept through the night without a nightmare. She told Celeste she would stay with her every night, for as long as it took for the nightmares to go away. Had that time come? Could she finally get Celeste to move into the bedroom upstairs? For her neck and her back's sake, Beatriz was hoping the answer was yes.

Larry was padding down the stairs as Beatriz shuffled into the foyer. They sized each other up, recognizing that neither of them had slept well—Beatriz draped in an old terry robe, the stress of sleeping upright with Celeste on her lap for weeks taking its toll. Larry looked just as bad, his hair ruffled like overgrown grass, his eyes long and haggard. Sleeping without his wife made him restless and unhappy.

Beatriz went to the front door and peered out the window next to it. "Oh," she sighed. "My brother is here."

"Tony?" Larry growled. "I'm going to buy him a watch for his next birthday."

Larry and Beatriz trudged through the house into the kitchen and out to the backyard, where, sure enough, there was Tony tramping through their backyard, unfurling an orange extension cord from the outlet where he'd plugged it in on the side of their house, making his way to the power drill he left on the riser.

"Buenas!" he called to Beatriz and Larry, as they walked out to him.

"Buenas, yourself," Beatriz said miserably. "What the hell, Tony?"

"Mira!" he admonished. "And here I am, doing something nice for you." He motioned to the riser. "I'm finally taking it down." It had been weeks since their anniversary party, when Tony first built the riser. And after everything that had happened since then, Beatriz and Larry had forgotten all about his promise to take it down the Monday after the party. "I've got a deck job nearby later this morning, and I figured since I was in the neighborhood..." Tony wondered why his sister and brother-in-law looked like scarecrows. "Hey, girl, you got any coffee? I brought donuts!"

"I'm on it," Larry mumbled, as he turned back to the house.

"Where is everybody?" Tony asked, nodding toward the house.

"They're asleep, like most everyone else at this time on a Saturday morning," Beatriz said, massaging her neck.

"You know what they say about the early bird!" Tony began mindlessly revving the power drill he held in one hand, as his other hand fumbled in his pocket for the screw bits. The power tool sounded extra shrill in the new morning.

"Tony!" Beatriz implored. "Do you really need to do this now?"

"Norma's been bugging me to break it down and set it up over at her place," Tony said.

"What does she need with it?"

"I don't know," Tony said.

Beatriz could tell by how her brother was avoiding her eyes that he knew more than he was letting on. "She didn't tell you?" she asked.

"N'ombre! I'm just the contractor. You tell me where to build something, I build it. You want something taken down, I take it down. People always act like the contractor—"

"Ya, ya, ya," Beatriz said. "Why does she need the riser?"

"I don't know, I said."

Beatriz took her brother at his word for the moment, but she was suspicious.

"So, Elaine wants me to invite Celeste over for lunch today," Tony said. "She'd like to spend a little one-on-one time with her. Don't take this the wrong way, but you've kind of been hogging her since she's been here."

Beatriz twirled her head, only to discover that the kink she thought had disappeared had moved to the other side of her neck. "I know what Elaine has in mind. She wants a little mini-Mex to help take care of those babies you all keep popping out," she said.

"Very funny. And sure, we could use the help. What's wrong with that? It would be better than sending her to live with Norma."

"She's not going to live with Norma," Beatriz said. "She was sent to me and she's staying with me!"

"All right, all right! You don't have to be so chingona," he said. "What's going on with you, anyway? Why are you so punchy?"

"You mean besides you being here at the crack of dawn? My neck is messed up from sitting up all night."

"Why? Is one of the kids sick?"

"No," Beatriz said, hoping that would be the end of it.

"You look like hell, girl. Qué pasó?"

"Nothing. My neck hurts is all."

Tony could see Larry in the kitchen through the patio door, leaning on the counter, his head perched in his hand, his elbow resting on the counter, mesmerized by the stream of coffee from the coffeemaker filling the carafe. "So, what's his excuse?"

"Larry?" Beatriz said. "What about him?"

"He looks like he hasn't been sleeping too well, either."

"Hard week, I guess."

An alarm went off in Tony's head. "You guess?"

Beatriz ignored her brother. "Oye, Celeste and I are going to Connie and Sara's flower shop to decide if we want flowers for her quinceañera. If there's time, we'll stop by and say hi afterward, okay? It's too early for work. Come inside and have some coffee."

Once in the house, Tony obliquely observed Larry and his sister. He noticed how they barely spoke to each other, how they barely shared the same space. It may have been early, but Tony knew something wasn't right, so he put his hunch to the test. "Hey, man, your wife needs a visit from Dr. Feelgood!"

Larry liked Tony, but his playful attitude this early in the morning was like a poke in the ribs. "What?"

"Her neck, man. She's practically crippled."

Larry looked at Beatriz, who was pouring coffee into a mug for her brother.

"What's wrong?" Larry asked. He tried to sound as if he were merely gathering information, but he was concerned.

"It's nothing," Beatriz said, also trying to speak plainly.

Tony was waiting to see if Larry would go over and put his hand on his wife's shoulder, a small but intimate gesture that would indicate that he would tend to her later, in private. When that didn't happen, Tony was convinced something was up.

"I guess I'll get the boys up for karate," Larry said, pouring coffee into his "Go Blue!" mug.

"That starts today?" Beatriz asked.

Larry grunted. "If you're still here when me and the boys come back, we'll help you," he said to Tony. "I didn't know you were coming today."

"No worries, bro!" Tony said brightly. "It won't take

me long to break it down. It's the building up that takes time, especially if you want it to last."

Tony's offhand comment hung in the air like the scent of tar. On one level, his words were innocuous. He was talking about the riser he built, a simple structure made of wood and screws. But he could have been talking about their marriage.

Twenty-five years was a long time to be with someone. Spending those years without the other was unimaginable, yet the gulf between them, made visible by their sleeping arrangement, was becoming a frighteningly ordinary part of their lives. Beatriz and Larry had managed to fill their days with activities—going to work and tending to the kids while being careful to protect them from their rift. But in their exhaustion, in their sadness, in the early morning disturbance by their noisy visitor, Beatriz and Larry realized something important: Their life as they knew it might have been disrupted, but their love for one another was still there, still deep, still true. Somehow, they would have to make their way back to each other.

In the perfect world, that realization would have called for them to run into each other's arms and cover each other with wild kisses, violins swelling in the background. But this wasn't the perfect world. It was their world: messy, chaotic, strangely comforting, but never entirely predictable. Beatriz looked out the window at the riser, which just a few weeks ago served as the main stage for their wedding anniversary, where she danced with her husband and everyone toasted their ongoing happiness. Larry gazed at the translucent swirls rising from his coffee cup as he stood at the kitchen door, remembering how excited he was to surprise his wife with his present. He thought of how he recalled their marriage vows and repeated them at just the right moment, fresh and new as the day he first spoke them. Each of them would have been astonished to realize that these thoughts entered their minds at the exact same time, bringing them both to the one obvious conclusion: *We can't go on like this.*

"Sounds like the changos are up," Tony said, hearing the boys moving about above their heads. "Let me go get those donuts!" Tony left the house through the patio and walked along the side of the house toward the front, where he'd parked his truck. The thoughts going through his mind were very different from Beatriz's and Larry's, and he was anxious to share them with his wife. He stopped where he was and leaned against the house to call her.

"Elaine! Hey! Guess what? I think maybe there's a chance we could get Celeste over to our house after all.... Yeah, I'm for real!...I don't know. Something fishy is going on over here. I don't know for sure, but I think Larry and Beatriz are having problems. Big problems, from what I'm guessing. Quién sabe? Pero, oye, don't tell anyone but..."

Ah, the famous "don't tell anyone" command. Always said with the weight of gospel and agreed to with all sincerity—but ignored in an instant; and in Beatriz's family, the flint to set off a wildfire of wagging tongues. But, of course, Elaine couldn't keep the rumor her husband started about Beatriz and Larry to herself! And before anyone could say, "You didn't hear it from me," the Sánchez tsunami began to build and gather force. Elaine called her sister-in-law Connie, who called their sister-in-law Sara, who told her husband, Miguel, who called his brother Erasmo, who told his wife, Norma. In less than an hour, all of the Sánchez wives and brothers had discussed the details of Larry and Beatriz's pending divorce and what that would entail, and, more directly, what it would mean for Celeste.

By the time Larry got the boys up and ready to leave for their karate class, Tony was back in the yard disassembling the riser as Beatriz watched him sadly from inside the house. Tony worked with astonishing speed. Most of the time, the pieces came apart with a few strategic actions, but occasionally, a piece of wood would crack and splinter, or he would tap too hard with his mallet, and the newly damaged piece of wood would be set aside for scrap. Beatriz didn't understand why she felt as anxious as she did when the damaged woodpile was growing larger than the saved woodpile, and she hated it even more when her brother threw the good pieces of wood too roughly onto the salvage heap.

"Where is everybody?" Celeste asked, as she entered the kitchen.

"The boys are starting karate today," Beatriz said, turning to her niece. "You and I are going to go look at flowers, remember?"

"Oh, yeah," the girl said, looking at the open box of donuts.

"Go ahead, if you want one," Beatriz said. "Ana is coming with us. She should be here in an hour or so."

"Is Tía Norma coming, too?" Celeste asked, looking into the backyard. When Beatriz turned back, there was her sister-in-law Norma, dressed in blazing summer whites from her bucket hat down to her Roman sandals. She was talking to Tony, her huge silver bolsa flung over her shoulder, her chunky silver bracelets glinting as she spoke with her arms. Beatriz sighed.

"Did you already take a shower, mi'ja?" she asked Celeste.

"No. I was waiting for the boys to finish up there."

"Well, why don't you go ahead while I see what this is all about?" Beatriz cinched her robe tightly around her waist as the girl left the kitchen. "It looks like I've got a pest-control problem to deal with," she said to herself. When she stepped outside, Norma smiled brightly and waved.

"Hola!" she sang.

"Hola!" Beatriz sang back. She was also smiling but was far from happy. "What are you doing here?"

"Well, I knew Tony was taking down the riser today, and I wanted to make sure he knew to bring it to my house," Norma said.

"You don't have phone service out at the rancho anymore?" Beatriz asked.

"Oh, of course we do!" Norma laughed. "Erasmo has some business in town today, and I was out and, well, I heard about, you know."

Beatriz frowned. "You heard about what?"

"Ay, mujer. You're so brave," Norma said, her voice dripping with sarcasm.

Beatriz reared back. "No, really—what are you talking about?"

"Oye, don't act so sensitive. All I want to do is help."

Beatriz looked at her brother, who shrugged and kept working.

"You want to help with what? The quinceañera? We are just getting to the point where we are going to ask la familia to help," Beatriz explained.

"'Sta bien, 'sta bien!" Norma said, like she was talking to a half-wit. Then, with a serious, consoling face that exaggerated her jowls, "You don't have to explain! I understand. Things have changed. It happens! It's natural to be upset that things are not the way they used to be."

"I don't know where you'd get that idea," Beatriz said.

"Well, a man and wife don't sleep in separate beds when a marriage is happy," Norma said.

Beatriz shot Norma a sizzling mal ojo, but Norma was unfazed.

"What the hell are you talking about?" Beatriz asked.

"You know, if Celeste were out at the rancho with me and Erasmo, this probably wouldn't have happened! I know you like to be the woman who has it all, with the fancy career, and the kids, y todo, pero you should face facts. Children are a blessing, but they're also a lot of responsibility," Norma explained. "And you have your hands full, both of you so busy with work and always helping out with La Lucy's kids. And then, with Celeste on top of all that! And here I am, at home by myself all day, just ready to help!"

"Well, she probably would like the city better," Tony said, suddenly trying to wedge himself into the discussion. Beatriz was thoroughly perplexed.

"Who?" she asked.

"Celeste, hermana. Who else? And you know what? I was thinking of building an extra room onto the side of the house anyway. So we have room for her, too," Tony said.

Beatriz wanted to dropkick them, first Norma and then Tony.

"Look, I don't know where you chismosos get your information, but there's nothing wrong here."

"Okay, okay," Norma said, feeling very confident that she'd struck a nerve. "Pero, mira. I have an idea: Let's have the quinceañera at my house, and until then Celeste can come stay with me—just until the party—and maybe by that time you and Larry will have worked things out. And if not, then she'll still be where she needs to be anyway."

Beatriz had to give it to Norma—she had a lot of nerve. But she could not let Norma steamroll her way in, no matter what.

"Well, thank you for your concern, but there's nothing to worry about, and you know what? I think we're done here! Thanks for dropping by. Both of you."

"What?" Norma said, as if she'd been asked to leave her own house.

"I'm not finished yet," Tony said.

"Oh, yes. I think you are," Beatriz said pointedly.

"Who do you think you're talking to?" Norma scoffed.

"Oh, Norma! Please!" Beatriz bellowed.

For once, Norma was speechless.

"You think just because you exhaust everyone by being overbearing and pushy that you're going to get your way?"

"It seems to work for you," Norma spat.

Tony knew when a storm was about to erupt and began gathering up his tools quickly.

"Ay, no! This is my house! Not yours!" Beatriz said. "So, let me tell you how it's going to go."

Norma looked around, wondering if the neighbors were peeking out their windows to see what the commotion was about.

"Let me talk extra loud so everyone is sure to hear: Celeste is here, and she's staying here. She's not a pet you all can pass around. She's not your personal plaything, and she's not your live-in babysitter. I'm going to finish raising her. Perla sent her to *me!*"

Beatriz's saying Perla's name out loud made Norma and Tony gasp.

"Ay, por favor!" Beatriz groaned, enunciating every syllable. "Aren't you all tired of all that? Aren't you all tired protecting our precious family secret?" Her sarcasm made Norma blanch.

"N'ombre!" Norma said. "I don't care who you blab to! It's not my side of the family that has a black sheep to be ashamed of! If that's how you want to be, fine! Ya me voy. Don't ever say I didn't try to help you." She turned and left Beatriz in a huff, her chanclas smacking fiercely as she made her way out of the yard. Tony had already moved away from the sparring women, spooling his orange extension cord around his arm and hauling it and his tools out to his truck.

Beatriz went back into the house and crossed back into the living room to watch them from the window. She was pleased to see Tony and then Norma hoist themselves into their respective vehicles without saying a word to one another, driving off without so much as a wave good-bye.

Finally! Beatriz thought. *Maybe they will give it a rest!* She stood in the living room a moment to gather herself before she walked into the foyer.

"Celeste!" she called. It took a moment for the girl to answer, and Beatriz wondered if she was still in the shower.

"Yes," she finally answered from the office.

"Did you take your shower?"

When she didn't answer right away, Beatriz thought the girl hadn't heard her.

"Yes!" Celeste finally answered. "I'm done."

"Okay, I'm going to get ready, so listen for Ana. When she comes, let her in, okay?"

Beatriz realized that she didn't have much time. As she ran upstairs, she thought about how she talked to Norma, how she nor anyone else had ever been that blunt with her. She wondered if it had been the right thing to do, and how their exchange might come back to haunt her. She would not realize how immediate the result of their argument was until Ana was at her door, ringing the doorbell incessantly.

"There you are!" Ana said when Beatriz finally answered the door. "I was beginning to think I was confused. We're going to look at flowers today, right?"

"Yes, today is the day," Beatriz said, wondering why Celeste hadn't answered the door like she'd asked her to.

"You're alone?" Ana asked.

"No, Celeste is here."

But Celeste was already long gone by the time Ana arrived.

*   *   *

Larry could see that Seamus was in a strange mood when the boys piled into his SUV. He didn't know if it was because Raúl wouldn't stop talking about the movie he planned for day two of their Fright Night weekend or because they were awakened by Tony's early-morning activity in the yard.

"You guys have your karate gear, right?" Larry asked, as he pulled out of the drive.

"I do!" Wally said proudly. "He doesn't."

"Who doesn't?" Larry asked irritably, looking at the boys in his rearview mirror.

"Shay," Wally reported.

"You know they won't let you participate without your uniform, right?"

Seamus was mindlessly fingering the zipper on his backpack, looking out the window.

"Shay?"

"Yeah."

"I don't think we have enough time to stop back at your place to pick it up," Larry said.

"We're not supposed to be late," Wally said. "Especially on the first day."

"Well, I was going to run a couple of errands while you guys were in class. I guess you'll just have to come with me," Larry said. "How come you didn't bring your uniform? I told your mother."

"She packed our bags herself," Wally said. "She must have forgot."

Larry was annoyed. "Yeah, she must have forgot."

The karate class was only a twenty-minute drive, and Larry was pleased to find a parking spot right in front of the building. At least something had gone right that morning. Wally and Raúl had already climbed out of the vehicle and gone into the building, when Larry realized they had left their permission slips in the car.

"Oh, shoot!" he said, unbuckling himself and getting out of the SUV. "I'll be right back."

"I need to show you something," Seamus said.

"Okay," Larry said. But once he got a good look at his nephew through his window, he could see that the boy had something serious on his mind. "What's the matter?"

"I have to tell you something."

"Okay."

The boy was struggling to find the words. Larry stood in the open window of the vehicle and waited for his nephew to continue. "Did something happen?"

"Kinda."

Seamus finally opened his backpack and pulled out his karate uniform. He dug into the folds and pulled out an envelope and handed it to his uncle. Larry read the note that was inside. Seamus could tell his uncle got to the worst part when he saw his face fall.

"Did you read this?" Larry asked.

"Uh-huh."

"When?"

"This morning. I was checking my stuff, and that's when I found it," Seamus said. "Wally doesn't know."

"Jesus!" Larry said under his breath. He was so lost in his anger and disappointment he didn't realize Seamus was digging deep to the ends of his toes to ask the question he was dreading to ask.

"So, I was wondering," he began slowly. "I was wondering if you would please take care of Wally. He's little. I can go wherever."

Larry had no idea what Seamus was talking about.

"I—I don't think Wally would make a good Wednesday's Child," Seamus said, thinking his uncle would understand. "I can go to foster care. I won't be scared, but Wally—he needs someone to help him. I can take care of myself."

Larry couldn't believe what his nephew was saying. He climbed into the backseat with Seamus and sat silently for a long time before he reached over and ruffled his nephew's hair and then pulled him close and held him in a playful headlock.

"You're not going anywhere, you brat. Why do you think you can get rid of us that easy?"

"Because you don't have room for us with Celeste in the house, and because Aunt Beatriz wants her there because she's back from the dead and all that."

"We have room," Larry said. "We'll make room. Nobody is going to take care of my boys but me and your aunt Beatriz, you got that?"

Seamus looked at the note his mother had written, now crumpled in his uncle's hand, and wiped his nose on his arm. "For real?"

"Yes, for real! I'm sorry, but you're not going anywhere, buddy boy. So look, why don't you go inside and watch? Can you do that?" Seamus was still shocked and confused and angry, but moreover he was relieved that his uncle hadn't started the car and driven him to...wherever they drive kids abandoned by their mothers.

Larry entered the karate class with Seamus, and when he was sure his nephew was settled, he went back outside and walked around the parking lot, his hands clasped over his head to keep it from blowing apart. This was not the way it was supposed to be. This was big, even for Lucy. Larry felt sick to his stomach. He waited for the nausea to subside before he finally dug into his pocket for his cell phone and called his sister. Her cell phone immediately went to voice mail, and though he knew the response would be the same, he called the number again and again before finally giving up. He wondered how Beatriz was going to take this news. He knew there was only one way to find out, as he climbed back into his vehicle and called her.

"She did what?!"

"She left them," Larry said. "She scrawled a few stupid words on a note and she left them. Just like that."

"How are the boys?" she asked.

"Seamus is in shock. Wally doesn't know yet."

Beatriz's mind was racing on the other end of the phone.

"Hello?" Larry said.

"I'm here," Beatriz said. "I was just trying to remember if we had any more of their clothes here. You should stop by the apartment and pick up some of their things for the week and then bring them home."

Larry was relieved. But then, how else did he expect Beatriz to react? How else?

"But there's another problem," Beatriz said. "How soon can you come home?"

*   *   *

Celeste had gotten farther than anyone could imagine. Lithe and lean, she ran fast. As her aunt was talking to her from the foyer, she was feverishly packing everything she treasured into her backpack, changed into the clothes she wore that first night she showed up on her aunt and uncle's doorstep, and as soon as she was sure Beatriz was upstairs, she took off. She wasn't exactly sure where she was going, but once she got out of the neighborhood and onto a busier street, she searched the sky for the downtown skyline and headed toward it.

Celeste thought things were going okay. She was starting to get used to things in her aunt Beatriz's house, and she was starting to feel safe. The nightmares weren't so bad anymore, thanks to her aunt. In spite of her original doubt, Celeste was starting to feel something she never thought she would feel: that she *did* belong.

Now, after hearing everything she heard, she felt like an idiot.

Seamus teasing her was one thing. She could handle him. No problem. And it wasn't even when she overheard her uncle Tony, secretly talking to his wife—right under her window—that distressed her. But listening to her aunts Beatriz and Norma, arguing about her and the problem she was causing between her aunt and uncle, and especially her mother being someone to be ashamed of—now it seemed all wrong. How could she let herself believe she belonged here?

Celeste ran, her backpack pounding against her back. No, it wasn't good at first, she recalled, but it had gotten better when her aunt calmed down, and listened, and sang to her, and told her stories about her mother. She already felt affection for her cousin Raúl—how could anyone not adore him? Carlos seemed nice enough, not that he was around much since he spent so much time with his girlfriend. And she still wasn't sure what to make of her uncle Larry, but she assumed he was just quiet the way some people are. But now she knew the truth. She shriveled with embarrassment. Did he think of her as an intruder? Maybe that was why he was so quiet around her, the daughter of the black sheep of the family. What could there be to say?

Celeste kept on running, sweat gliding in pearls down her face and into her eyes. She ran into an intersection without looking, and a car screeched to a stop a few feet in front of her. Her heart leaped into her throat, but she kept on running. She knew that she had overheard conversations she wasn't meant to hear, but it was too late. Maybe she could run all the way back to El Paso. It wasn't right, Celeste thought, for her mother to be buried in the ground back there, so far away. So maybe hearing what she had heard was a good thing after all. Maybe it was meant to be. Maybe it was a sign.

She could feel a blister forming on her heel, but Celeste kept on running. Suddenly, the longing for her mother roared back, fresh and raw. She could feel a stitch forming in her side, so she pushed her fist into it and took bigger gulps of air, hoping to make it subside. But the stitch only got angrier and made her slow down, until she was limping and panting so fiercely, she was wheezing. She saw a bench under a tree ahead of her and sat there for a while to rest.

How could anyone be ashamed of her mother? Celeste had never given much thought about their life or her mother's work until she was gone. Her mother did honorable work, everyone said. And while everyone back home had only good things to say about Perla Sánchez, Celeste herself knew that her mother was the last person to say much about herself or her work. In fact, Celeste remembered how her mother avoided talking about the sad business she was involved in. She was always focused on the future, how things would be different when Celeste was grown. Celeste remembered how when another family's sister, mother, or daughter was found dead, Perla used that as her cue to talk about Celeste's quinceañera—how it would be a happy day, the threshold to her life, a happy life full of possibilities. Celeste didn't understand, at first. She didn't understand how another brutal death would launch her mother into dreamy talk about Celeste's quinceañera and life beyond it.

"Someday, you're going to have your own life. A good life," Perla had told her. Her voice had been full of such determination, Celeste wondered if Perla was trying to convince herself as much as her.

"But what will I do?" Celeste had asked.

"Anything, mi'ja! Anything!"

"Can I get a job in a factory, like you?"

Perla hesitated. "Maybe, but believe it or not, you might not want to do that. You might not even want to live here anymore. You might want to go away to school."

"I go to school now," Celeste argued.

"Sí, but I mean, you do so well in grade school, you will go to junior high, and then to high school, and then off to an even bigger school called college. Like my sister, your tía Beatriz. Remember, I told you about her? You're just like her."

Beatriz was the only person Perla had talked about when she finally talked about her past.

"She went to a big school up north and became a great woman. So smart, so..." Celeste could see that Perla always got sad when she talked about Beatriz in San Antonio. The one thing Celeste never understood was why, when talking about her made her so sad, she was the one person her mother talked about the most.

Celeste pulled her backpack off and rooted inside, making sure she had packed the most important things: her wallet with exactly twenty-three dollars inside, the bolsa Ana gave her, her mother's photo, her white hoodie, and her quinceañera book. She pulled the book out and began flipping through the pages, stopping to look at one of the last things her mother had entered. It was a picture of a basket of lavender daisies she had come across in a magazine. Her mother had carefully clipped and taped the image onto the page and wrote underneath, *I think I would like to wear this flower in my hair.*

The flowers, and her mother's handwriting, and the stitch in her side, and the overwhelming stupidity she felt made Celeste cry. She pulled the book up to her face, wishing she could inhale something of her mother from the last thing she wrote, and when there was nothing, she let out a sob that rattled her ribs and made her head throb.

The ring of a bell announced the arrival of the trolley, which stopped in front of her. Several babbling tourists climbed off, all looking like startled insects with their enormous sunglasses, trying to get their bearings. The trolley driver offered last-minute directions, as the tourists plotted their course and walked away.

"Are you coming, miss?" the driver asked Celeste. She sniffed and looked at the driver.

"Where are you going?" she asked.

"Downtown." The driver nodded down to Celeste's feet. "Did you drop that?" When she looked down, she saw Josie Mendoza's business card, from the day when she delivered the quinceañera book to her. This gave Celeste a new idea.

"Do you go by the Greyhound station?" she asked.

"I can get you close enough. But c'mon, if you're coming. I have a schedule to keep."

EIGHTEEN

By the time Larry got to the house, Beatriz was in over-drive. She sent Ana out into the neighborhood to look for Celeste while Beatriz tore through the house, thinking that maybe Celeste was hiding. She wanted to believe the girl was playing a simple game of hide-and-seek, like Perla used to. If Beatriz looked hard enough, she knew she would find her.

"Where are the boys?" she asked Larry when he walked in the house.

"They're still at karate. They're okay, for now."

As soon as Beatriz knew it was just the two of them in the house, she fell apart.

"I can't believe this! I can't... I can't lose her! She can't just disappear on me like that! Please, help me find her!"

Larry followed his wife as she tore down the hall to the office. He could tell immediately that Celeste was gone. Beatriz began to frantically pull the cushions off the couch and open cabinet doors and desk drawers, as if the answer to where Celeste had gone would be found there.

"She must have left a note or an explanation!" Beatriz said. "She must have left some information!"

"Beatriz... Beatriz, baby, she's not here," Larry said gently.

"Don't say that!"

"Her backpack is gone."

None of this made sense to Beatriz. "But...why? Why would she leave? Where would she go? What did I do?"

"Nothing. You've been great with her," Larry offered.

"But why would she leave me? I don't understand."

Larry began to feel small. He had been polite but kept Celeste as a distance. He could admit that. He had spent very little time getting to know her, keeping himself wrapped up in work and then in as many activities as he could with the boys. He could see that Beatriz was working prodigiously to make Celeste feel at home, to help her work through her grief while putting hers on hold—or had she? He had no idea how his wife was working through the loss of Perla, too wrapped up in his own percolating jealousy because the girl got to have Beatriz all to herself when he was most used to having her—at night. He could see that Beatriz was pained and confused and he would do anything to take it away for her.

The house phone ringing startled them and made Beatriz stop rifling through the office.

"Maybe it's Ana," she said. "Or maybe it's Celeste. Does she know the number to the house? Did I ever tell her that? I should have told her that."

When Larry answered the desk phone, he was surprised by who was on the other end.

"Hi there. This is Josie Mendoza. We met when—"

Larry grimaced. "Yes, I remember. This isn't a good time," he said.

"No! No! Don't hang up!" Josie interjected. "Do you realize that Celeste is not there?"

"Yes. How do you know that?" Larry said.

"She just called me."

"Celeste called you?" Larry repeated. Beatriz clasped her hands over her mouth.

"Yes, she asked me if she took the bus to Austin if I'd pick her up and take her back to El Paso," Josie explained. "I told her to wait there and that I would come get her, but I'm calling you instead. I think you might want to get to the Greyhound station as soon as possible. The thing is, I think she has just enough money to get to Austin, if she changes her mind and decides not to wait for me."

"Oh, thank you—thank you very much," Larry said. When he hung up the phone, he took his wife by the shoulders.

"I know where she is. Can you call Ana and have her pick up the boys? I'll go get her."

"I want to come with you," Beatriz said.

"I know. But I need to do this, and I need to go now! Please wait here. I'll bring her back. I promise."

Larry drove like a madman, breaking several traffic laws. When he arrived at the Greyhound station, he dashed inside when he heard the last call for the bus leaving for Austin, then rushed outside to the bay where the bus had just finished loading and ran around it, jumping up, looking into the windows for Celeste. When he didn't see her, he began to call her name. Everyone on the platform looked at Larry with irritation or amusement.

"Pobrecito," someone muttered.

The driver was about to close the door when Larry grabbed the edge and fought to pull it open.

"Sir! We're about to leave!" the driver shouted.

"I'm looking for someone."

"Sir, I have to go! If you don't have a ticket, you need to stand back."

"No, please, please. I need to check. Celeste! Celeste!" Larry called into the bus.

"Ya! She's over you, foo'!" someone on board yelled. "Give it up! She's into me now."

Larry called Celeste's name again as the driver slammed the door, nearly snipping off his fingertips. He dashed back inside the station and broke to the front of the line at the ticket counter.

"Hey! What the hell, man?"

"Sir, you need to wait your turn," the attendant snapped.

"Please, you have to help me. I'm looking for a little girl," Larry began. "She might be on that bus. Do you have a list of the passengers I can see?"

"Step aside, sir."

"No, please! You don't understand."

"Sir, I'll help you in a moment!"

"Yeah, man—wait your turn!" someone shouted from the back of the line.

Larry was unsure of what to do—jump into his car and follow the bus to Austin or make an effort to commandeer it. His decision was made for him when he saw Celeste come out of the ladies' room. He marched over to her, and Celeste hesitated a moment before she turned to reenter the restroom.

"Please, don't make me follow you in there," Larry said.

Celeste froze, hugging her backpack to her chest. When she finally decided to face Larry, he motioned to a nearby row of seats. She stood still for a long time before finally deciding to cross over and sit down, her arms strapped around her backback, her knees clenched together, and her head sunk between her hunched shoulders. Larry paced in front of her before finally taking a seat next to her. He had no idea what to say; all he knew was that he had to say the right thing.

"So, that lady called you, huh?" Celeste said.

"Yeah."

"And she's not going to come get me?"

"Nope. Sorry."

"Are you going to make me go back with you?"

"I don't want to *make* you do anything," Larry said. He looked at the vending machine that stood near them. "You want to share something?"

Celeste shrugged. This was the longest conversation she'd ever had with Larry. Part of her was curious, but a larger part was skeptical that there was anything he could say that could convince her to go back with him.

"I like the ones with peanuts," he said, fumbling in his pocket for some coins. "Can you eat peanuts? Your throat's not going to close up if you eat them, right?"

"No," she said.

Larry put the coins in the machine and shoved his hand into the bin where the packet of candy dropped, pulled it out, and tore it open.

"You're mother liked these, too," he sighed.

"You knew her?" Celeste asked. It had never occurred to her that Larry had known Perla. He offered her some candies and she slowly extended her open hand so he could pour some into her palm.

"Not as well as I should have," Larry said. "The last time I saw her was in a bus station like this. She was afraid and angry, kind of like you are now. We sat and ate candies while we waited for her bus. I thought, if I just made sure she got on the right bus, everything would be fine. I thought she thought the way your aunt Beatriz and I did: that going back home made sense. But now...now, I wish I would have said the right thing, instead of watching her get on the bus and disappear."

"What would have been the right thing?" Celeste asked.

"I don't know. Maybe if I would have invited her to stay, things would have been different," Larry said, popping one of the candies in his mouth and chewing it. He remembered how he and Beatriz were struggling back then, but their life was good. They were good. Maybe it wouldn't have made a difference if they had invited Perla to stay. He had no idea. All he knew was that Perla had made her choice without hearing that she was wanted. She believed she had no other place to go, no other choices. How many times had poor choices been made with a lack of information or faulty assumptions? How many times had a few consoling words been all that was needed to change a poor decision into a good one?

Larry began to wonder where his sister, Lucy, was. In her note to the boys, she promised to let them know where she landed, when she finally got to where she was going. Larry hoped she'd keep that promise. "Someday," he remembered reading in the note, "you will understand."

Larry turned to Celeste. "I don't understand how you feel or what you're thinking right now. But I would really like it if you came back with me so I could learn. Your aunt Beatriz would like you to come back, and I know your cousin Raúl would like it if you came back."

"I don't want to be the reason you and Tía Beatriz don't get along," Celeste said. "I don't want to be the reason she fights with everybody. I don't want to be the reason you all feel embarrassed."

"No one's embarrassed..." Larry suddenly thought of his mother, and her ritual "walk of shame" from the past. "No, no!" he said. The thought of Celeste feeling ashamed the way he did as a boy made his heart ache. He looked at her with new eyes and thought a moment. Celeste wondered why her uncle was looking at her so strangely, an expression that astonished her with its softness.

"Well, everyone has very strong feelings when it comes to you," Larry said. "I can't promise everyone will always get along, and I can't promise that we won't mess up. What I can promise is that I will do my best to make you feel welcome. Mi casa es su casa. Okay? And you already know your aunt Beatriz feels that way, right?"

Celeste held one of the candies in her mouth and cracked the hard shell with her teeth and began sucking the chocolate inside as she thought about Larry's words.

"But," he began, "and this is the important thing: If you want to be part of this family, and things go wrong, you can't..." Larry began to think of how angry he was at his sister for running out on her boys. He began to think about how Perla ran away all those years earlier and the repercussions of that decision. And then, worst of all, he began to think of how he left the house in a huff after he and Beatriz had their first hard discussion about Celeste, and how he had hurt the woman he loved most of all. He sighed a heavy sigh. "It's important," he said slowly, thick with recognition, "to stay and figure things out. You owe it to the people you care about, no matter how hard it is."

"Seamus hates me," Celeste said.

"Seamus hates everyone right now," Larry said. A young mother with three small children walked past them. One child was throwing a tantrum while the other two stared at their sibling, shell-shocked and bewildered, hauling bags twice their size as their harried mother tried to control her unhappy child. The two of them continued to eat the candies until they got to the bottom of the pouch. "Seamus and your cousin Wally are going to be going through a rough time right now. That's something I think you can understand," Larry said. "Seamus knows. Wally doesn't. Not yet." He waited for Celeste to ask what the trouble was and was relieved when she didn't. It was enough for her to be taken seriously. "Seamus and Wally are going to be staying with us for a while, and it might be uncomfortable at first, but I think Seamus might learn something from you."

"Like what?"

"Well, Seamus acts tough, but he's not. You're the one who can teach him about what it means to be strong."

Celeste looked at her uncle, wondering if he was trying to play her.

"I'm just a kid. I don't know anything."

"You're a kid, but you're not a baby anymore. And I think you know more than you think," Larry said.

"Your aunt and I could use your help when it comes to your cousin, but we want to help you, too. Okay?"

Celeste ate the last of her candies and looked at her uncle, trying to decide what she wanted to do.

"So, can I give you a ride home now, or should I buy another pack of candy?"

"Candy," Celeste said.

Larry dug into his pockets for some more change and bought another bag. The two of them sat in silence, watching the passengers walk past them, passing the packet back and forth, until it was empty.

When Larry and Celeste walked in the door, Beatriz was relieved. Celeste walked over to her aunt.

"I'm sorry," she said. "Am I in trouble?"

"Well," Beatriz said. "Not yet." She opened her arms to the girl, and Celeste fell into them. "We'll talk about this later, okay?"

Celeste nodded her head.

"Go ahead and put your things away. Everyone is in the kitchen. Carlos is cooking."

When Celeste went down the hall to the office, Beatriz turned to her husband.

"Thank you. Thank you so much."

Beatriz leaned her head into her husband's chest, and he embraced her lightly. It had been so long since they had touched one another, it was as if they were touching each other for the first time. The old, familiar closeness began to overwhelm them with nostalgia, like hearing an old song that brought back bittersweet memories.

"So...we're good?" Larry asked.

"We will be," Beatriz said. "We can talk more later, if you want."

"I want," Larry said. "I do."

When Beatriz, Larry, and Celeste entered the kitchen, Ana and the boys were seated around the counter so they could watch Carlos work. The boys were particularly fascinated as Carlos unrolled his collection of chef's knives and sharpened them, and began pulling ingredients out of the refrigerator.

"I didn't know that was in there," Beatriz said, as her son pulled out an enormous slab of salmon, a bag of mussels, and herbs and vegetables from the nooks and crannies of the refrigerator and throughout the kitchen.

"Are those the things that look like giant boogers?" Wally asked, pointing to the mussels. "I'm not eating that!"

"You'll like it the way I make them," Carlos said. "I cook them in wine!" he whispered to the little boy, whose face lit up as if he were going to be allowed to do something dangerous. Carlos began chopping garlic and mincing herbs, and soon the kitchen was infused with the anticipation of something exciting about to happen. Celeste managed to creep around the counter to peek over Carlos's arm, careful to stay out of his way but watching his every move.

"Mira, how this one is! He's going to make someone very happy one day," Ana joked.

"He makes someone very happy now!" Beatriz said.

She felt a sudden pang, realizing that her son was now a young man, ready to leave her and go out into the world.

"Oooh! Carlos has a girlfriend," Wally teased.

"That's old news," Raúl laughed.

"What? No one tells me anything!"

Seamus looked at his brother sadly, and then to the floor. His uncle Larry put his hand on the boy's shoulder and leaned down to whisper into the boy's ear, "We'll get through this. I promise."

Ana pulled herself away from the counter to speak to Beatriz. "I'm going to take off," she said.

"Oh! But it looks like there's going to be plenty. Are you sure you can't stay?"

"Do you need me to stay?" Ana asked, looking over to Celeste and Carlos in the kitchen with the boys and Larry all around, eagerly watching.

"I guess not. I think everything's going to be all right."

"We'll go look at flowers later this week. There's still time," Ana said. "Oh! I forgot to tell you, I got the music set up. So cross that off your list." She turned to call over to the group, "Oye, Carlos—rain check, okay, mi'jo?"

"You don't know what you're missing, Tía, but okay, adiós!"

After Beatriz said her good-byes to Ana, she came back into the kitchen. "Is there anything I can do to help?" she asked.

"No!" the boys said in unison.

"Oh, stop it! I made a perfectly good salad the other day!"

"I'll thank you to stay out of my kitchen," Carlos said, flipping his chef's knife into the air so it spun like a mad pinwheel and catching it by the handle. Everyone gasped.

"Do it again!" Wally squealed.

Beatriz looked at Larry, who was staring at their son in disbelief.

"I've got this, 'Amá," Carlos crowed. He continued cooking, keeping the kid's attention, explaining what he was doing, throwing in a little showmanship at every opportunity, while making small bites to eat as he prepared the main meal. Even Larry could see that Carlos loved what he was doing. He was in his element, at ease and in control.

"The only thing I don't have are tortillas," he said.

"I can run out," Larry offered.

"No, no! I'll come up with something else."

"I can make some," Celeste offered.

"Really?" Carlos said.

"Yeah, but only if you don't shish-kebab me if you don't like how they come out," she said, looking at the knife Carlos held in his hand.

"N'ombre!" Carlos laughed. "Besides, they can't be any worse than mine. Show me what you got, chula."

Carlos pulled out the ingredients for the girl and watched her work from the corner of his eye as he continued preparing the meal. Four simple ingredients— flour, water, shortening, and a little salt—that was all, but somehow, his never came out right. So he was beyond impressed when Celeste's tortillas came out powdery soft with just the right amount of chew.

"These are perfect!" Carlos said. "How come I can't make them like this?"

"Who taught you, mi'ja?" Beatriz asked.

"Mi 'amá," she said. "She said she learned from her 'amá. I guess that would be your mother, too."

Everyone happily slathered butter on the warm tortillas, eating them and moaning with delight. Celeste smiled, feeling the first glimmer that maybe she did have something to offer. Maybe she did belong to this family and brought something of value—something that came as naturally to her as breathing, something that was passed down to her from a memory, an experience that was meant to be shared.

"Ya! Save room for later!" Carlos said. "But you've got to show me how you make them later, mi prima. I mean it! I've got to learn before I leave for school…" His voice trailed off, self-conscious of the unfinished business about when and where he was going to school and his father's attitude about it.

"How about we talk about that after we eat?" Larry offered. Carlos felt unsure of what was in store for him—a huge lecture or something worse—and his face revealed it.

"Calm down, son," Larry offered. "We'll work it out."

And they did, after their huge lunch. Larry, Beatriz, and Carlos went into the office to talk while the kids went in the backyard to eat ice cream. Celeste stayed close to Raúl, wondering when the dark cloud around Seamus would burst, while being amused by Wally, who entertained them all by showing off the karate moves he'd learned in class earlier in the day and the ones he was going to learn. When he finally ran out of gas, he plopped onto the grass panting.

"Can we watch a movie or something?"

"Go ask Mom, and then maybe we can watch *The Wolf Man*," Raúl said.

"'Even a wolf who says his prayers may turn the wolf into the moon at night'—that one?" Wally asked, mangling the quote from his cousin's favorite movie.

"I have so much to teach you," Raúl said, shaking his head.

"Yay!" Wally ran into the house with Raúl following, leaving Celeste alone with Seamus.

"He's seen that movie a hundred times," Seamus said. He wasn't looking at Celeste, and she wasn't sure he was talking to her. She stood up to leave but changed her mind, remembering what her uncle told her at the bus station.

"What's wrong with you?" Celeste asked. She struck a nerve, but Seamus ignored her and kept eating his ice cream, loudly scraping the sides of his dish with his spoon.

"Never mind. You don't have to say," she said.

"What makes you think something's wrong with me?" His tough-boy mask slipped, and the tender layers of his wounded self were peeking out.

"I don't know. It's the way you look," she said plainly. "I've seen it before."

Seamus finished his ice cream and stood up to leave.

"My mom used to tell me that it's okay to be scared. I think it's okay for boys, too."

Seamus wanted to kick something, punch a hole in a wall, or kick a ball high into the sky until it made angry rings around the moon.

"Your mom? The dead one?"

"Yeah, the dead one," Celeste said without flinching.

Seamus was amazed. Annoyed and amazed. He had no idea that his stony silence did not hide the way his shoulders sloped, the way his face hung, the way his jaw rippled as he ground his teeth. Everything about him made his pain obvious to someone like Celeste, who had experienced so much of it herself. And if he didn't know it for sure when they were playing Toss, he knew it now. Celeste was tough, no matter how much he wanted to believe she was just a stupid girl. In spite of himself, Seamus felt a reluctant kinship toward her, though he would do his best not to show it. Not all at once, anyway.

"When are you going to tell him—whatever it is you don't want to tell him?" she asked.

"I don't know. I guess when he needs to know," Seamus conceded. He leaned against the house and looked at Celeste from the corner of his eye.

"So, your mom—what's that like? I mean, do you get used to her being gone?"

"I don't know. But I doubt it."

"Mine left," Seamus finally said.

"Where did she go?"

"I don't know."

"When is she coming back?"

"I don't know."

"Well," Celeste said. "At least she can still come back, if she wants to."

"That's the part that sucks," Seamus said. "I don't know if she wants to."

*   *   *

When Beatriz and Larry came into the backyard, Celeste and Seamus stood up and gave them their attention.

"Well, guess what? Carlos is going to take all you kids out to a movie," Beatriz announced. "They're looking at the listings now. But before you go cast your vote, we have a couple of things to say. You're going to take your things and put them in Carlos's room," Beatriz said to Seamus, and then to Celeste, "and you're moving into the bedroom upstairs. Carlos is going to stay in the office until he leaves for culinary school."

"Really?" Seamus asked.

"Really," Beatriz said. "Don't worry. It was his idea."

"What about Wally?" Not that he wanted to keep sharing a room with his little brother, but he wanted to know where he'd be.

"He's going to stay in Raúl's room. He said something about you snoring," Beatriz teased. "And besides, now that you two are the oldest kids in the house, we thought you might like your privacy. Okay?"

Seamus and Celeste looked at each other and silently agreed to this arrangement. As they began to go inside the house, Beatriz held Celeste back.

"I'll still stay with you at night, if you want," Beatriz said. "But I think you're ready to move upstairs. Do you?"

Celeste thought a moment and nodded. "I'll try," she said. "I think I can do it. You'll be nearby?"

"Always. We're here for you. No matter what," Larry said.

Beatriz watched from the front door as Carlos finished loading up the kids in the SUV. Carlos was happy. The conversation he had had with his parents wasn't so hard after all. Larry finally got it. Their son wanted to be a chef, and Carlos promised to be the best one he could possibly be. With a few keystrokes on the computer, Carlos's first term was paid in full, thanks to Beatriz and Larry's hard work and determination to send their son to college. It wasn't exactly how they thought it would turn out—definitely not what Larry had planned for his son—but Carlos was going to do what he loved, what he was good at, and that was the thing to be thankful for. Beatriz began to remember her boys playing like puppies in the backyard. And now, here was her oldest, behind the wheel of his father's SUV, ready to leave and start his own life in a few short weeks. Carlos waved as he pulled away, and Beatriz waved back, smiling through glassy eyes.

When she closed the door, the house was eerily quiet. She walked into the living room, looking at the photos of the kids and smiling wanly at their toothy grins from over the years. She paused when she reached the photos of her and Larry assembled for their anniversary party a few weeks earlier and picked up a wedding photo, taken back in Ann Arbor: Larry with a full beard and Beatriz with her wild tangle of curls. They were smiling like they didn't have a care in the world, like anything was possible. Everything was fresh and new then.

The clatter of pots rousted her from her thoughts and she went into the kitchen to investigate.

"I think Carlos used every pot and pan in the house," Larry said. He had just gathered and piled all the dirty dishes near the sink for washing. As soon as he finished, he went to the liquor cabinet above the refrigerator and poured himself a whiskey and returned to the sink, where he took a sip, then set down his glass on the counter, wondering where to dig in first.

"Can I help you?" Beatriz asked.

"Sure."

They could have loaded up the dishwasher and left it at that, but instinctively they knew they had to sort through their dispute like their messy kitchen, slowly and by hand.

"I wash, you dry?" she offered.

"Okay," he said.

They didn't speak for a long time. At first, they were clumsy, as if they had never washed dishes in that kitchen before. But as they continued, there was something about the rhythmic motion of their work, the running of the water, and the gentle clink of plates and glasses that calmed them. When everything was washed, dried, and put away, Larry finished off his whiskey and then poured some more and took a sip. Beatriz absentmindedly picked up Larry's glass to take a drink. But she suddenly felt self-conscious.

"Can I?" she asked.

"Sure."

She took a long sip of his whiskey and delicately put the glass down near the sink.

"Oh, do you want me to pour you one?" he asked politely.

"Can't we share?"

"Sure."

They were still unsettled; hurt feelings still needed to be soothed, and a balance of wills needed to be restored. Being surrounded by people and distractions made it easy to avoid each other. Now they had no excuses.

Larry poured some more whisky into the glass and handed it to her. As she took a sip, she looked up at her husband, and those huge, dark eyes of hers caught his and made him swoon. He took the glass from her and put it on the counter and then turned and took in every feature of his wife's face.

"I'm sorry," he said.

"I'm sorry, too."

"I shouldn't have—I didn't know you had all those feelings about when Perla disappeared, and of course you would want Celeste to be here. Of course! It's just—"

"I know. I never talked about it. I should have talked about it with you. And it's a big decision, taking in Celeste. If you would have done that to me—"

"But I did do that to you!" Larry said. "I brought the boys in and you didn't say a thing, you didn't flinch. I was so wrapped up in the trip-to-France thing, and our life after the kids are gone, and how I thought it was all going to work out..." Larry sighed. "I'm a boob."

"You're not a boob."

"I'm a boob."

"Well, then, you're my boob," Beatriz teased. Larry

put his hands on Beatriz's shoulders and pulled her close to him and inhaled her hair.

"I can't believe we inherited three kids. We send one on his way and get three in return. And the munchkin is how old? Seven? We're never going to get out of this house," Larry sighed.

"N'ombre!" Beatriz said. "Something will work out." She took another sip from the glass they were sharing and passed it to him. He drank, put the glass down, then wrapped his arms around Beatriz's shoulders.

"I'm kind of...scared," he said.

"Me, too."

Larry and Beatriz began to sway in rhythm to each other's breath, the effect of the whiskey settling over them like perfume.

"I don't even know where to start tomorrow," Larry said. "I mean, should we wait and see if Lucy reappears? Should I empty their apartment? Should I try to find her? Should I..." He picked up the glass to take another sip, but Beatriz took it from his hand and set it on the counter.

"You know what? Why don't we start right here?"

She leaned forward and kissed Larry on his chin. "And here," she said, as she kissed his cheek. Larry kissed Beatriz on her forehead, then slowly ran his hands alongside her face, stroking her temples with his thumbs, then leaned down to kiss her tenderly on the mouth. It was a kiss full of want and hope, forgiveness, and understanding; as sweet as a first kiss, but as familiar as the lingering scent of a loved one on bed pillows. The sultry flavor of the whiskey was still on her tongue, and Larry swallowed it and immediately wanted more. Beatriz pressed herself into her husband, wanting more of him. He lifted her up to sit on the counter and ran his hands over her hips and thighs. They began kissing with an urgency that said what was unspoken: *I want you. I won't leave you. I am yours.*

He moved his hands under her top, ran them up her torso and over her thick breasts. Beatriz could feel herself stir, that sudden, luscious ache deep inside. She untucked his shirt and reached beneath to caress his nipples with her thumbs. She knew he liked this. It made him catch in his breath, and he smiled that tranquil smile, full of pleasure. He began to kiss the arch of her neck, and she bit her lip to keep from gasping too loudly. He knew she liked that.

"I think we better get upstairs," she whispered.

Beatriz and Larry moved as fast as they could through the house and up to their bedroom. Larry closed the door as Beatriz pulled off his shirt and covered his chest with kisses, working her way down. Larry fumbled to lock the door and pulled Beatriz up and led her to their bed, where they finished undressing each other. They faced each other, kneeling on the bed, naked, panting, and frantic with desire. Her aroma made his body scream, and he thought he might explode. He pushed her onto the bed, and just as he was about to climb on top of her, she pushed him over onto his back. They giggled as Larry lifted his naked wife over him. She sat there a moment, gazing into her husband's face.

"I missed you," she said.

"I missed you, too," he said.

They exchanged a long, silent smile, and then Beatriz slowly rose and fell, rose and fell, as their hearts raced and their skin flushed. In that moment, there was no one else in the world but them.

No one could have picked a more perfect day for Celeste's quinceañera. It was unseasonably cool for July. The sun was bright, the sky was crystal clear, and all living things—plants, animals, humans, and spirits—were lively and lush. The typically oppressive Texas heat had miraculously disappeared, as if the sun had sent its boorish companion away for the weekend, off to the gulf, where the ocean dwellers welcomed an excuse to be near the water and slurp raspas lazily by the sea.

Beatriz was surprised by how easy it was for her and Celeste to plan the quinceañera. When Beatriz began to go overboard, Celeste would find a way to rein her in. When Celeste became too detached, Beatriz would find a way to remind her that celebrating her life, the fact that she mattered, that she was part of the family, was at the core of the celebration. Sometimes it was a touch. Sometimes it was a glance. But ultimately, they both came to understand that the event they were planning represented something larger than they could express. All the things attached to the ceremony were just small, tangible representations of a much deeper sentiment.

"What do you think your mother would think?" was the question Beatriz asked her niece when they came to a fork in the decision making. This often launched them into stories of Perla as a mother, a sister, a girl, a community leader—stories shared with laughter and tears, but always with great affection and curiosity.

Carlos had found his own special role in those few weeks before the quinceañera. He decided it was his mission to plump up Celeste with a series of "exploratory meals" he made to test out new techniques in preparation for culinary school. "Damn, girl. We need to get some meat on those bones!" he claimed. But he also wanted every opportunity to learn how to make the perfect batch of tortillas from Celeste. He was a diligent student, and she was an eager taste tester. Like Celeste, and her mother, and her mother before her, Carlos was soon able to take those few ingredients and turn them into something that would not only fill an empty stomach but would nourish a body the way only a meal made with real affection could. After a month mastering rouxs, clarified butters, cream sauces, and finely marbled meat dishes, Carlos considered it a personal accomplishment when some curves appeared on Celeste's slender frame, so that when she wore her quinceañera dress, it was clear she was not a little girl but a lovely young woman.

The lavender dress they found for Celeste's quinceañera wasn't a formal, but it was perfect. The linen halter dress buttoned behind her neck and the bodice hugged her, the skirt flaring from her hips and falling to her ankles. Celeste worried about having to walk around the yard in high heels, so when she and Beatriz found leather flip-flops that were the exact color of her dress, they marveled at their good luck.

"Can we wear flip-flops, too?" Wally asked. That was the one concession Beatriz made to the boys. She'd asked them to wear matching guayaberas for the occasion, and the response was mixed. Wally didn't give it a second thought, but the vivid shade of green made Seamus balk.

"I feel like a gecko," he said, looking at himself in the mirror.

"It's not so bad," Raúl said. "It's comfortable."

"Whatever," Seamus sighed.

Beatriz had kept close watch over Seamus since Lucy left. It had been several weeks, and still no word from her. Larry tried to contact her several times at all hours of the day and night, until one day her cell phone service was disconnected. Although Wally was finally told of his mother's departure, he held on to the hope that she would return, explain herself, and all would be forgiven. He was the one who slept with the note she left behind under his pillow. He was the one who always carried it, shoved deep in his pocket. The note survived at least one wash, but as long as it remained intact, no matter how grimy and tattered it became, it was the one thing that gave the little boy assurance of his mother's return.

Seamus was more difficult to gauge. Beatriz wasn't sure how he was taking the new changes in his life and worried that Celeste's quinceañera would make him feel neglected.

"So you're okay with all this?" she asked Seamus the morning of the event.

"The shirt? I said I would wear it."

"No, I mean the quinceañera."

"Why wouldn't I be?

"Well, I don't want you to feel—I don't know. Left out," she said.

Seamus thought a moment. Although his mother had still not bothered to send word about where she was and when—or if—she was coming back, compared to Celeste, he didn't have it so bad. Seeing his mother again might not be likely, but it was at least a possibility. Seeing her mom again was more than Celeste could hope for.

"Just remember, estas en tú casa," Beatriz said.

"What does that mean?"

"It means this is your home, no matter what."

That was enough for Seamus. "It's cool," he said.

Beatriz took him at his word.

It was a small ceremony, made special with simple, homey touches. The night before, Beatriz invited anyone who wanted to help to come by the house and make paper flowers from stacks of wide tissue paper drenched in oranges and reds, hot pinks, and soft yellows. Connie and Sara had offered roses from their shop, but Celeste said she liked the homemade look of the paper flowers. Raúl and Wally helped and—to Beatriz's surprise—even Larry offered to help. When Wally got upset because his flowers were crooked, Celeste assured him they were beautiful and wore one on her wrist for the rest of the night. Carlos boiled crawfish and corn on the cob for the flower makers, which they ate in the backyard under the loquat tree. Afterward, everyone hung the cheery flowers on the backs of chairs, around the food table, and around the perimeter of the riser Beatriz had her brother Tony reassemble for the day.

Late into the evening, people told stories about other family events, and everyone seemed to have a "the time Beatriz tried to cook" story. The tales always ended in a laughable disaster. Celeste learned a little something about her aunts and uncles, her cousins, and family friends, but when Beatriz got on the subject of her own quinceañera—a preposterous tale of a fallen cake, broken high heels, and lost trousers where everyone played their own wacky part—Celeste began to understand why her mother loved her big sister so much. Beatriz could hold her own among her bellowing, back-slapping brothers with firecracker responses that were as pointed as they were affectionate.

Everybody came to Celeste's quinceañera. Ana and her kids were there. Her gift was a guest book where she would later attach photographs, so Celeste could remember who was whom. Carlos made all the food, of course, and Marisol made a luscious pound cake with buttercream frosting that looked like a giant daisy with pale lavender petals around a sunny dot. Bumblebees were suspended above it, and Wally decided they represented him and his cousins because they were the ones who were always buzzing around Celeste.

"Sure, that works," Marisol grinned.

Carlos got keyed up when he noticed his father spending time talking to Marisol on the day of the quinceañera. He watched them through the patio door as he finished setting up the food table. She was in the kitchen, assembling the cake and frosting it, as Larry stood nearby asking questions and making comments. Carlos tried not to stare, but when he heard his father explode with laughter, it unnerved him so much that he had to go inside to find out what happened. Larry had already left the kitchen to take care of something elsewhere when Carlos entered. Marisol was chuckling to herself as she continued working.

"What happened? What was he laughing about?"

Marisol gave Carlos a quick peck on the cheek and shook her head. "Your dad is a cupcake. I don't know what you were worried about."

All the aunts and uncles and their kids showed up for Celeste's quinceañera, too. Norma was appalled that they didn't have a quinceañera mass, even after Elaine reminded her it was wedding season. The church Norma suggested was booked and everything else was taken. Beatriz prayed for patience as Norma pointed out all the ways it was not a "real quinceañera" like her Angie's until Celeste herself said it didn't matter. The cathedral of the trees arching over them in the backyard was enough for her.

Finally Erasmo urged his wife to hold her tongue. Norma promised to do her best, but still let slip a few choice comments about the quinceañera's many shortcomings. But in the end, even Norma did her part. Her gift was a Bible bound in white leather and a matching rosary that Celeste accepted graciously. Elaine gave Celeste a pair of pearl earrings and a matching teardrop necklace. Celeste didn't have a tiara—she would have felt silly wearing one. Instead, Connie and Sara made a garland for her hair from a huge basket of fresh daisies they brought from their shop.

"How about you all wear the extras as boutonnieres?" Beatriz suggested to Larry and the boys.

"Ah, man...," Seamus scoffed.

"C'mon, Seamus. Be a sport," Larry said. He was up for anything. Thanks to Ana, he and Beatriz were going to be able to make their trip to Paris after all.

"Not a problem," Ana had said. "All you guys had to do was ask." Larry and Beatriz were elated, confident they were leaving their family in good hands.

"I'll wear a flower!" Wally volunteered cheerfully.

"Me, too. It's dapper," Raúl said. Everyone looked at him. "Well, a rose would be dapper, but a daisy is okay. I'll do it." They all turned to Seamus.

"Whatever," he sighed. But when Beatriz went in search of some stickpins, Seamus conveniently made sure he was off somewhere else when she returned.

"So, I think we're ready!" Beatriz said to Celeste and Ana, as they decided what to do with Celeste's hair before the guests arrived.

"Well, there is one more thing," Ana said. "Who's going to present her?"

"You mean, walk her in?"

"Well that, but also present her," Ana said.

"Well, I guess Larry could do that," Beatriz said.

"Why not you?" Celeste asked.

"Oh! I would be honored, mi'ja, but wouldn't you rather have your uncle Larry or Erasmo do that?"

"No," Celeste said. "You should stand in for my mother. I think she would like that, and I would like it."

Beatriz was touched.

"You heard the young lady," Ana said. "And then what?"

"And then I say my speech," Celeste said. "And then ya! We eat!"

"Is this how you want it?" Larry asked. He and the boys had just set up chairs in rows in the backyard in front of the riser. Celeste looked unsure and turned to Beatriz for guidance.

"We'll do it however you want," he said.

"We want a circle, on the riser," Celeste said.

"Yes," Beatriz agreed.

Larry and the boys did as they were told. Seamus watched Celeste out of the corner of his eye as she and Beatriz took two of the chairs and draped them with white cotton and adorned them with some of the large paper flowers made the night before.

"What is that, like, your throne?" he asked when the adults were out of earshot.

"You'll see," she said.

When everyone had arrived, Larry led them all into the backyard, where Sonia, the guitarist Ana brought, played a gentle tune. It wasn't what you would call traditional, but it was what Celeste had asked for: a circle of chairs on the riser, with the two draped chairs sitting royally, side by side.

Norma frowned disapprovingly at the setup and

commented to no one in particular, "Mira. Like the musical chairs."

After everyone was seated, Beatriz and Celeste emerged from the house, walking arm in arm. They stepped inside the circle as the onlookers waited expectantly. When Sonia finished playing, Beatriz spoke.

"Hola. Thank you all for coming. We couldn't have asked for a more glorious day," she began. "I don't have much to say except that I am so grateful to see this day come, when I can present to you, mi sobrina, Celeste Josefa Sánchez, the daughter of our dear, departed sister..."

For a split second, Beatriz could sense the catch in her throat, as if all those years of imposed silence might cut off her breath and keep the words from coming out. But Beatriz was tired of being silent, tired of feeling guilty, tired of not saying the name of her sister.

"Perla Sánchez, en paz descanse," Beatriz said proudly. She waited for the response that should have immediately followed, but Perla's name hadn't been spoken in so long, Beatriz's brothers and their wives had to let her name echo inside their heads before they remembered what they were supposed to do.

"Perla Sánchez!" Beatriz repeated clearly, loudly, and without hesitation.

"Presente!" Celeste said. Erasmo and the other uncles looked at her, at their wives, then at each other.

"Perla Sánchez!" Beatriz called.

"Presente!" Celeste and Larry said.

"Perla Sánchez!" Beatriz shouted.

"Presente!" Erasmo responded with Celeste and Larry.

"Perla Sánchez!"

"Presente!" the group roared.

Maybe it was her imagination, but Beatriz felt as if the air had gotten lighter, as if a fresh rain had cleared the air and the guilt that had suffocated her all those years had been cleared like cobwebs and let loose to fly off and away. Everyone looked around, sensing the newness of the air around them.

Celeste walked to one of the chairs draped in white and placed a red rose onto it.

"This is my mother's place," she said. "And this," she said, motioning to the other chair she and her aunt had dressed earlier, "is for anyone else who should be here and isn't."

Her words stabbed Seamus in the heart, and he fought hard to swallow his tears.

"I would like to say some words my mother used to say to me. I don't know where she got them, but I think I still remember how they go," Celeste began.

Beatriz was amazed by how the girl seemed to bloom before her eyes. It wasn't just the dress, or the way she and Ana had pinned up her hair; it was something else, as if Celeste were no longer that timid little girl who first arrived at her door but a young woman, full of the confidence and the conviction of someone who knows what she needs and wants to do.

"I didn't really understand what she was saying when I was little, but now the words make sense to me," Celeste continued. She took a deep breath. "'Do not press me to leave you or to turn back from following you. Where you go, I go: where you live, I will live; your people are my people. Where you die, I will die. I will be there, even if death parts me from you."

Celeste opened a small purse Beatriz had given her and sprinkled the red rose petals in it over the chair she had dressed for her mother and then over the other chair. There was a moment of silence while Celeste walked to an open chair and sat down.

Beatriz nodded to Sonia, who began to play the delicate opening notes to "Piel Canela." Celeste burst into a smile. The lively, vintage bolero was one of her mother's favorite songs, and Celeste happily swayed to the music. Larry rose and offered his hand to Celeste. She accepted and joined him in the center of the circle, where they danced until Sonia finished the song with a delicate flourish. Larry gave Celeste a gentle twirl. She giggled when he bowed to kiss her hand.

"Eso!" Erasmo said, clapping his thick hands together. Everyone joined in the applause and the party was officially started. "Eso!" he repeated. Norma shot him a dour look and he waved her off. "It was *nice*, mujer. Let it rest," he murmured to her.

Norma positioned herself behind the guitarist in the buffet line.

"You know, I sing." Norma was talking to the person behind her but said it loud enough for Sonia to hear her.

"Really?" Sonia said, turning back to Norma. "I would love to play something for you."

"Oh, no. I couldn't," Norma demurred, but before anyone knew it, Norma was singing her heart out, belting

out "Como la Flor" like she was center stage at the Ala-
modome. She changed keys a few times, and Sonia had
to play some extra notes to bring Norma back in tune,
but overall, she made Norma sound good, and Norma
thought Sonia was the most talented musician she had
ever met.

"Oh, my!" Beatriz laughed. "I forgot she had it in
her."

"Encantando!" someone declared. "Otra, mujer, otra!"

Champagne was opened. Norma was encouraged to
sing another song and then another, until Erasmo pulled
himself up and over to Sonia.

"Oye, señorita, do you know 'Volver'?"

"Por supuesto, señor. What kind of Mexican doesn't
know 'Volver'?!"

Erasmo sang at the top of his lungs, while the uncles
threw gritos. Even Norma got a kick out of her husband
singing, and everyone clapped wildly and sang along to
that song and all the other songs that followed when they
knew the words—and even when they didn't, singing, and
swaying, and laughing, and enjoying the company of family and friends.

"Hey," Seamus said to Celeste, as she was happily
dancing with Wally. When Celeste turned around, she
saw her cousin standing there, holding one of the daisies.
"Will you pin this on me?"

Beatriz and Larry sat and watched it all from where they
were seated near the loquat tree; their hands were clasped,
and the couple was quiet and content as the voices and

laughter babbled all around them. Beatriz could not stop smiling.

"Ay, comadre, this is really so sweet," Ana said to Beatriz, as she sat down next to her. "Just *so* sweet."

"Yeah, but I wish...," Beatriz began.

Larry squeezed his wife's hand. He knew who she was missing. The three of them watched Elaine hand one of her little boys a piece of cake and direct him to sit at a nearby table. Instead, the little boy walked past where he was told to sit and kept on walking.

"That's a huge piece of cake for such a little bitty boy," Larry laughed. "I hope he makes it!"

When the little boy placed the cake on the chair prepared for Perla, then ran off to play, a bell of recognition rang inside Beatriz, and she believed with all her heart that Perla was with them after all.

READING GROUP GUIDE

1. Did you have a quinceañera, a Sweet Sixteen, or a bat mitzvah? What did it mean to you? To your loved ones?

2. Traditional quinceañeras have deep ties to Catholicism. How is religion treated in this novel? In your opinion, is it a good thing that traditionally religious celebrations (like the quinceañera) are becoming increasingly secular? Why?

3. Do you believe quinceañeras as a cultural tradition will continue or be lost over time?

4. Beatriz and her husband, Larry, could be said to have a "mixed marriage," since she is Mexican American and he is Irish American. What do you see as their common bonds? Their differences? What roles do culture, race, and class play in their relationship?

5. As working mothers, Beatriz, Josie Mendoza, and Lucy Milligan are starkly different. In what ways do you identify with each of these women?

6. In the beginning of the book, Beatriz has a number of startling "incidents" but is reluctant to talk about them, even to her best friend, Ana. To what do you attribute her experiences? Do you believe

it was her conscience, a dream, or the ghost of her sister, Perla, that was truly "haunting" her?

7. In the beginning, Beatriz has a hard time relating to her niece, and Celeste feels out of place in her aunt's world. Besides the sudden newness of their situation, what else do you think contributed to their difficulty in connecting?

8. Beatriz is adamant about taking in her niece, Celeste, even as it threatens her marriage. Did Beatriz put her marriage in too much danger? Does family come before everything in your life? Why or why not?

9. Besides celebrating her fifteenth birthday, what do you believe was the meaning behind Celeste's quinceañera?

10. Celeste and her cousin Raúl hit if off almost immediately, while her other cousin Seamus is severely threatened by her appearance. What do you imagine Celeste's relationship will be like with Seamus and her other cousins in the future? Between Celeste and Beatriz? Between Celeste and Larry?

1. ¿Tuvo usted una quinceañera, una Sweet Sixteen, o una bat mitzvah? ¿Qué significó a usted? ¿A su familia?

2. Los quinceañeras tradicionales tienen lazos profundos al catolicismo. ¿Cómo se trata la religión en esta novela? En su opinión, ¿es una buena cosa que las celebraciones tradicionalmente religiosas (como la quinceañera) están llegando a ser cada vez más seculares? ¿Por qué?

3. ¿Cree usted que quinceañeras como una tradición cultural continuará o se perderá con el tiempo?

4. Se puede decir que Beatriz y su esposo Larry tienen un matrimonio mixto debo que ella es Americana-mexicana y él es Americano-Irlandés. ¿Cuáles son sus enlaces comunes? ¿Y sus diferencias? ¿Qué papel desempeñan la cultura, la raza y el sentimiento de clases en su relación?

5. Como madres que trabajan fuera de la casa, Beatriz, Josie Mendoza, y Lucy Milligan son muy diferentes. ¿Cómo identifica usted con cada una de estas mujeres?

6. Al principio del libro, Beatriz tiene un número de incidentes estorninos, pero está maldispuesta de

hablar de ellos, ni con su mejor amiga, Ana. ¿A qué atribuye sus experiencias? ¿Cree usted que era su conciencia, un sueño o la fantasma de su hermana Perla quien la estaba persiguiendo?

7. Al principio del libro Beatriz encuentra dificultad en relacionar con su sobrina Celeste, y la niña se siente fuera de su lugar en el mundo de su tía. Además de lo nuevo de su situación, ¿qué más contribuye a la dificultad en conectar?

8. Beatriz está firme en tomar a su sobrina Celeste a su casa, aunque esto amenaza su matrimonio. ¿Cree usted que Beatriz puso su matrimonio en peligro? ¿Cree usted que la familia debe de venir primero que todo otro en su vida? ¿Por qué o por qué no?

9. Además de celebrar su cumpleaños de quince años, ¿qué mas cree usted fue la significación de la quinceañera de Celeste?

10. Celeste y su primo Raúl se llevan bien inmediatamente, mientras su otro primo, Seamus, está amenazado con ella. ¿Cómo imagina la relación de Celeste con Seamus y sus otros primos en el futuro? ¿Entre Celeste y Beatriz? ¿Entre Celeste y Larry?

ABOUT THE AUTHOR

BELINDA ACOSTA has written and published plays, short stories, and essays. As a journalist, her work has appeared in the *Austin American-Statesman*, the *Austin Chronicle*, the *San Antonio Express-News*, the *San Antonio Current*, *AlterNet*, *Poets & Writers*, and on National Public Radio's *Latino USA—The Radio Journal of News and Culture*.

Belinda received a master's of fine arts in writing from the University of Texas in 1997.

She lives in Austin, Texas, and is the TV and media columnist for the *Austin Chronicle*.

IF YOU ENJOYED
*SISTERS, STRANGERS, AND
STARTING OVER,*
THEN YOU'RE SURE TO LOVE THESE
EMOTIONAL FAMILY DRAMAS AS WELL—

Now available from Grand Central Publishing

"Lyrical, poignant, and smart, as compassionate and hopeful as it is heartbreaking…a novel you will never forget."

—*New York Times* best-

ACOST   HLOOW
Acosta, Belinda.
Sisters, strangers, and starting over
:a Quinceanǀâera Club novel /
LOOSCAN   nd
10/10   ar-

ing group of people in search of their own American dream…A delightful feast for the reader."

—*New York Times* bestselling
author Susan Wiggs

A secret journal threatens to destroy a young woman as she uncovers the truth about her deceased mother's past in this stunning debut novel.